# WINTER MAGIC ON RAILWAY LANE

ALISON SHERLOCK

Boldwod

A CIP catalogue record for this book is available from the British Library.

Paperback ISBN 978-1-80426-459-1

Large Print ISBN 978-1-80426-458-4

Hardback ISBN 978-1-80426-460-7

Ebook ISBN 978-1-80426-456-0

Kindle ISBN 978-1-80426-457-7

Audio CD ISBN 978-1-80426-465-2

MP3 CD ISBN 978-1-80426-464-5

Digital audio download ISBN 978-1-80426-462-1

Boldwood Books Ltd
23 Bowerdean Street
London SW6 3TN
www.boldwoodbooks.com

# 1

Libby Jacobs had always declared that the best part of being a flight attendant was the freedom and adventure that travelling the world brought her. The worst part was the occasional rude passenger.

But at least those passengers would never be rude to her ever again. Because she had just completed her last ever flight for the airline.

Libby angrily slammed the car into fourth gear as she headed out of Aldwych town and onto the narrow country lane towards her home village of Cranfield.

In the inky darkness before the dawn of an October morning, she could barely see any distance ahead, despite the car headlamps being on. Being in the middle of the English countryside, there were no streetlamps along the country lanes. Luckily, she knew this journey like the back of her hand. She had lived in Cranfield all of her life and knew every corner and crossing on the ten-mile journey ahead.

Which was a good thing, because she was barely concentrating on the road at all, such was her despair.

She groaned once more and shook her head, mainly at her lack of self-control. Ten years in the job and she still couldn't control the rebel that she had been throughout her teenage years.

It wasn't her fault that the budget airline she worked for had decided to branch out into long-haul travel. Nor was it her fault that the company's expansion had been a complete and utter disaster.

However, it *was* her fault that she had already received two written warnings for being rude to difficult customers in the first-class section of the cabin that she had looked after. That meant that when the airline had announced the previous day that they were stopping the long-haul route with immediate effect, as well as a wave of redundancies, Libby was first in line to be out of a job.

The panic on the loss of her job was huge. Her monthly wages really helped to keep paying the bills on the little cottage on Railway Lane where she lived with her dad.

But, despite that, a tiny part of her was actually glad to be finally stopping the exhausting cycle of jet lag and disturbed sleeping patterns. The fact was that she was tired. Tired of spending so long away from home in order to support her dad. Tired of enduring a job which she no longer enjoyed. Tired of the overnight stopovers in bland hotels which were barely distinguishable from one city to the next, desperate to be back in Cranfield instead.

This craving to go home would have astounded the much younger Libby, who had yearned for nothing else but to escape and run far away from her home village.

Growing up, she had had a turbulent relationship with her father. Philip Jacobs had been the headmaster of the local infants school and liked everything regimented and in order, both at work and at home. He had never hurt her and Libby knew that her father loved her, even though they never said such things to each other.

However, Libby had inherited both her mother's pale blonde hair as well as her nature. Her mother had been a free spirit who couldn't stay within the constraints of normal limits either and drifted from job to job without a care in the world, preferring to be at home in the kitchen or the garden.

Love had seemingly overcome her parents' different approaches to life. Her mother was the peacemaker, always soothing over yet another argument when Libby had been late home after playing too long in the fields or had ignored her father's request to tidy her messy bedroom.

To escape what felt like his constant disapproval, Libby had rebelled against him every step of the way. Despite being bright, she had never taken her studies seriously and had often not turned up at all to most classes. To her father's obvious disappointment, she had left school with hardly any qualifications and no ambition either, except to flee her stifling home life.

After a few years of trying out every job she could find in the area, the discovery that she could escape to the skies as a flight attendant had been too much of a lure to resist and Libby had signed up for training.

Of course, the reality was that there wasn't an awful lot of glamour to being a flight attendant. The hours were long and hard, with the majority of time spent on her feet, especially when covering the long-haul flights in the past couple of years. She had been paid to go to some of the most amazing destinations in the world, but it wasn't a holiday. Most of the time, she would arrive at the hotel booked for the flight crew, go to sleep and then head back on the next flight in the morning. It was a hard job and she had grown weary of it as the years had passed. Now in her early thirties, the despondency felt even worse.

She glanced at herself briefly in the mirror, despite the darkness inside the car. She could still make out her blue eyes lined with mascara and her make-up immaculate even many hours after she had applied it. Her long pale blonde hair was scraped back into a perfect bun.

*Libby Jacobs*, she silently told herself, *you're a long way from being a rebel now.*

But some things had survived from her turbulent childhood and acting on impulse was one of them. Her quick temper and sarcastic way had ensured that she had just completed her very last flight. And with two written warnings, any other airline was unlikely to take her on either.

Libby sighed heavily as she turned a sharp corner down the dark country lane.

She had felt so differently about the job at first. She had attended the interview with the airline and it had gone so well that she could still feel the broad smile on her face as she had driven home that day ten years ago. She would finally have enough money to move out of home for good. She would be free of her father's disappointed looks. She couldn't wait.

But it had swiftly turned into a bittersweet day after being offered her dream job. Her mother had been unwell for a couple of years and the test results her parents had received that day had been the worst news possible. Her mother's health had quickly deteriorated and she passed away only a couple of months later.

Libby and her dad had struggled on through their grief, trying to come to terms with the massive loss in their lives. Any arguments had been swiftly replaced with a stunned silence whenever Libby was home from her flight attendant training course.

They had managed to get through the funeral, to say their last goodbyes and Libby began to tentatively plan to pick up the pieces of her life and move out a short while later when she began to fly around the world with her new job.

However, the terrible series of events seemed set to continue when her father had a massive stroke one morning soon after the funeral. Whilst Philip had thankfully survived, the stroke had taken its toll on his physical and mental well-being. He had to give up work as he had lost some use in his right arm and right leg. Heartbroken from both the loss of his beloved wife and the abrupt halt from his life of teaching, he spiralled into a deep depression.

He effectively shut down to the outside world, rarely leaving the house. He became a self-imposed prisoner of his own home, cutting himself off from their friends and neighbours. A decade had passed and nothing had changed for the better for Philip. Apart from his daily walk to pick up the newspaper, it was a world mostly devoid of human contact too, apart from his daughter and church on a Sunday morning. She had gently encouraged him to try to find new hobbies outside of the house to no avail.

Libby had always blamed herself for her father's stroke. It was all her fault, of course. If only she had behaved better growing up and not put so much stress and strain on him. If only she had taken better care of him, as she had promised her mum during those last wretched weeks. Now he was trapped inside his own insular world and Libby was trapped there as well.

As the main breadwinner for the household, there was no way she could have left him. She had briefly contemplated giving up her new job to look after her dad but the money had been too good an opportunity to pass up. But whilst Philip had recovered enough to be able to take care of himself, she felt too guilty to move out and so, ten years later, she was still there, at the age of thirty-one. But without a job to support them both, what on earth was she going to do now?

Her friends all thought that she had this amazing life, dating pilots and travelling the world. But the truth was that most of the time she was away, she was lonely. Really lonely. Perhaps now she could find a job closer to home and be with the people she loved more often.

For a brief moment, she wondered about whether losing her job might just give her the push to turn her hobby into something more permanent.

Growing up, her favourite time of the week was when she and her mum had made different flavours of chocolate truffles in their tiny kitchen at home. The smell of cocoa still invoked the warmth and love that her mother had given her.

After her mother had passed away, Libby had stopped making chocolate for a long time. Then, on a stopover in Switzerland a couple of years ago, on a whim she had booked herself in for a chocolate making course. From there, her curiosity had grown into a full-blown obsession.

She didn't want to upset her dad as it had been his wife's favourite hobby. So when he was at church on a Sunday morning, for one morning of the week she would make all sorts of chocolates and truffles. For those couple of hours, she would forget about all of her worries and just focus on the fabulous flavours that she could concoct. However, she always ensured that everything was cleared away by the time her dad returned, with no trace of what had occurred for him to suspect. Only the alluring, sweet aroma of cocoa hung in the air afterwards.

Eventually, she had been brave enough to show her friends what she had been making. And after much positive feedback, Libby had even sold quite a few boxes of her handmade truffles from a small stand in Platform 1 – the coffee shop in the village owned by her friends Ryan and Katy.

But Libby had a dream. And that was to make chocolate from bean to bar so that she could control every step of the process and ensure it tasted just right. On a flight to Venezuela, she had taken time to source a local cocoa bean farmer. She had even bought a small bag of cocoa beans and had taken time to roast the beans herself when she had got home. It had been such a success that she had ordered a couple of larger bags for future use.

The trouble was that the kitchen in the tiny cottage in Railway Lane was miniscule and there was no way that she could up production to any degree without her dad finding out. She had even changed the name on the packets that she sold in Platform 1 on the off chance that he happened to come across them. She couldn't upset him any more. He had already been through so much.

But despite the secrecy, chocolate brought her joy. It felt as if it was the only thing that she did solely for her own pleasure. The only selfish thing she could call her own when nothing else made her feel whole, not even the endless stream of first dates she went on each month.

As if on cue, her phone lit up in the darkness. She could just read the beginning of a flirty message from one of the pilots she had met on her outbound journey. She would press delete as soon as she parked up the car, having already spotted his wedding ring whilst they had been chatting.

She rolled her eyes in the darkness. Men! She had dated many but none had compared to Ethan Connolly. Upon thinking of him, as usual she was instantly irritated at her lack of self-control. Surely she should be over him by now?

She had grown up with Ethan and his elder brother Ryan,

who both lived at Cranfield station with their family. But she had always been closest to Ethan, who had become her best friend throughout their childhood. Together they had rebelled, bunking off school when they should have been studying or messing about in the classroom whenever they did decide to attend.

But as her teenage years had progressed, Libby had become aware of something else, wanting something more from him. When Ethan had asked her to the prom, she had thought all her secret dreams were about to come true. But Ethan had been a completely different person that night, cold and uncaring towards her. She had totally misread the situation and had quickly realised that he didn't care for her at all. So the evening had ended in disaster with Libby not speaking to him.

Then her mother had grown ill and Libby didn't have the time or energy to question what had gone wrong in their friendship. So they had slowly drifted apart when she had never needed Ethan more. She remembered him giving her a hug at her mother's funeral. But, after that, he had left Cranfield to work abroad, rarely coming home to visit his family.

Whenever she did bump into him, eager to protect her still vulnerable heart, she treated him with cool indifference and sarcasm. And apart from one catastrophic lapse in judgement a couple of years later, they still barely conversed with each other.

Libby shook her head. She couldn't think about Ethan now. She had to concentrate on working out how she was going to pay the bills when her redundancy money ran out.

Annoyed at herself for giving in to the old familiar feelings he always seemed to invoke in her, she put her foot down and the Mini Cooper quickly accelerated. However, she took the next corner too fast and almost ended up in the ditch at the side of the road. With a squeal of tires, she slammed on the brakes and took a deep breath to steady herself.

As she sat there, a gust of wind blew some nearby fallen leaves across her windscreen. Autumn had arrived and the air was noticeably cooler.

With a shiver, she put the car into first gear and then drove more slowly as she neared Cranfield. Once more, she wondered how on earth she was going to tell her dad that she had lost her job. What was she going to say? How could she allay his fears and worries about money when her own were already almost overwhelming?

As she passed the sign for Cranfield, she saw that the tiny hamlet was still in darkness. But on the far horizon, beyond the green rolling hills, the first glimmer of daylight was beginning to appear as dawn began to break.

All the houses were in darkness. Except one, she realised, slowly drawing the car to a halt. The old infants school, long since closed, sat at the very end of Railway Lane where she lived in one of the cottages with her dad.

When her father had lost his job, the school had been shut down and the children moved to a bigger school in the next village. The schoolhouse had remained empty for the past decade until it had been bought and renovated a couple of years ago. Even then it had stayed empty. But as Libby looked through her windscreen once more, she knew that she wasn't mistaken. There was most definitely a light on inside. It looked like a torch flicking around, its beam showing through the glass windowpanes.

Suddenly, all her frustrations boiled over. The school, so beloved to her dad, was precious, with its memories of happier times, long since gone, when life was simple and complete, before the pressures of growing up had come upon her. How dare someone decide to break in, no doubt to steal whatever was left inside!

Ever impetuous, Libby grabbed the first thing she could think of from her carry-on bag as a weapon – a square marble pastry board she had bought from a cook shop in Washington DC on her stopover the day before. Although she had been intending to use it to practise tempering chocolate, it was certainly nice and heavy, she thought, weighing it in her hands.

And then, carrying the marble board and still in a fury, she got out of the car and raced up the short path to the front door of the schoolhouse.

Noticing it was ajar, she stepped into the entrance hall, fumbling for a light switch. But before she could adjust to the darkness, she found herself blinded by a light shining straight into her face!

Libby reacted instinctively, lifting her arm up high and bringing down the marble board onto the intruder's head with as much force and pent-up anger as she could muster.

In the darkness, she felt the person slump to the floor and heard him swear.

Then she heard a familiar voice drawl, 'Always a pleasure to see you too, Libby.'

The torch on the man's mobile suddenly lit up his face and Libby found that she was staring into the eyes of Ethan Connolly.

## 2

Ethan Connolly rubbed the sore spot on the top of his head and squinted up at Libby in the semi-darkness from his prone position on the floor.

'I know you hate me, Libby,' he said, wincing as his fingers touched the tender skin. 'But could you refrain from actual physical violence in the future?'

As he slowly stood back up again, he drew his phone back up to light up Libby, who was still scowling at him. Libby was not normally a person to apologise even when she was in the wrong and it looked like she wasn't going to start now.

'What are you doing in here?' she snapped at him instead. 'Why are you creeping around the old school in the middle of the night?'

'What I do in the privacy of my own home is entirely my business,' he replied, feeling around on the top of his head once more. Luckily, he could find no bump nor, as he brought his fingers out in front of him, could he see any blood.

'Your home?' repeated Libby in a shocked tone.

'As of two days ago,' he told her.

To be fair, he was almost as surprised as Libby at the thought of him buying a property in sleepy Cranfield. It had been his home village since he was born, but he had no love for it. Not anymore.

However, the apartment above the station where he had grown up was now a love nest for his older brother Ryan and his girlfriend Katy. Ethan loved them both, but three was most definitely a crowd, and with no spare bedrooms in the nearby cottage on Railway Lane where their dad and grandad lived, Ethan wanted his own accommodation when he came to visit.

Over the summer, he had found out that the old school was up for sale after the previous owner had run out of money for the renovations and so Ethan had proceeded with the purchase.

He had kept this quiet from his family in case the purchase didn't go through. He didn't want to get their hopes up. Nor their expectations that he would be living in Cranfield full time, because that was never ever going to happen, as far as he was concerned.

The school, thankfully, turned out to be in a relatively decent state. The previous owner had fitted a high quality kitchen and bathroom, as well as new oak floors. The only immediate problems had been the need for a new front door as the existing one wouldn't shut properly and the electrics, which had shorted out on him half an hour ago when he had got up, unable to sleep.

He had switched on the torch on his phone whilst he had repaired the fuse, when he had suddenly heard movement nearby. Fearing a break-in, before he had time to react, he had been whacked on the head and rather than finding a thief, he had come across Libby instead.

'So, are you carrying some sort of roof slate around with you now?' asked Ethan as he felt around for the overhead light switch to find out if his repair of the fuse had been successful. 'Hoping to diversify into the building trade or just trying out a new form of self-defence?'

He finally found the switch and flicked it on.

After the initial bright glare blinded him temporarily, his eyes quickly adjusted to the overhead light. Still standing in front of him was Libby in her glamorous flight attendant's uniform. That amazing long pale blonde hair was scraped back into a bun, although some silvery strands had escaped. She was just as beautiful as ever, even after presumably yet another long-haul flight.

'It was the first thing I could grab,' said Libby, looking downcast. 'It's a pastry slab. I only bought it yesterday.'

His eyes automatically moved down to look at what was lying broken on the floor before he once more rubbed the top of his head, which was still throbbing. So that was what she had hit him with!

'Well, it certainly packs a punch,' said Ethan, still wincing. 'What were you doing barging in here like that?'

'I told you. I thought you were a burglar.'

'What on earth would I be stealing?' he said, gesturing around with his arm.

Apart from a couple of suitcases that he had brought with him the previous afternoon and the camp bed that he had set up, the place was completely empty. Certainly nothing to induce him to think of it as a home yet. Would he ever think of it like that? Probably not. After the sale of his flat in Hong Kong, buying the school was an investment and it was highly likely that he would sell it on before too long. After all, he had never wanted to stay around in his home village since the age of sixteen.

A few yards away, the railway station in Cranfield had been the actual family home since his older brother Ryan had been born thirty-four years ago. But it had been in the Connolly family for many decades before then. His great-grandfather, his grandad and his dad all had the railways in their blood and had loved working on the trains and at the station. His grandad Eddie had been the stationmaster before passing on the rented apartment and the job to his son Bob.

Growing up in a close-knit community such as Cranfield, the brothers had enjoyed the freedom of the countryside and the excitement of the station bustling with people from the nearby villages using the short train line into the town of Aldwych ten miles away. But then the small branch line had been closed, along with many others around the country, due to government cuts. Their dad had reeled from the shock and had found himself lost without his beloved trains to look after. Cranfield, the village, had also closed down without the station in use.

However, things were finally beginning to turn around in the village's favour. After years of neglect, the previous winter, chef Ryan, with the help of newly arrived Katy, had turned the old station into a successful coffee shop by day and Italian restaurant by evening, as well as providing takeaway pizzas to local customers. The station had begun to be filled with people once more. Meanwhile, Ryan and Katy had made a happy home for themselves upstairs in the family apartment.

The brothers were only three years apart and yet worlds apart in their attitudes towards pretty much everything. Ethan deliberately didn't like to treat anything seriously, whereas Ryan had a more steady, methodical approach.

They were even different in looks. Ethan had blonde hair and was blue-eyed, like his mum, whereas Ryan was dark-haired, after their dad.

There was only one way in which the brothers were alike. And that had been both of their inclinations to run away as far as they could instead of watching the collapse of their parents' marriage year by year.

Ethan had known it was coming and yet his dad had been blissfully unaware that his wife's sniping and nagging was a consequence of her deep unhappiness in their marriage. Ethan had always presumed that their mum must have loved their dad once but any affection for him seemed to fade year on year.

But that wasn't the worst of it. The worst part was her affairs, which Ethan had become aware of early in his teens. Then, one wretched summer day when he was sixteen, Ryan had been driving them into Aldwych so that Ethan could pick up a rented tuxedo for the prom. However, on the way, they had seen a couple obviously making love in one of the many fields that surrounded the village and had realised, to their horror, that it was their mother and the local vet.

Having had a few years to get used to the betrayal, Ethan had only felt a dull ache as opposed to the deep shock that Ryan had displayed.

'I don't believe it,' Ryan had spluttered, obviously trying not to cry. 'I knew she was unhappy, but this? What do we do?'

'We don't do anything,' Ethan had told him after taking a deep breath. 'She always leaves them and goes back to him. So what does it matter?'

Ryan had looked heartbroken as he realised the truth. That their mother had had many affairs and Ethan had known all about it. Ethan had immediately blamed himself for revealing the full truth to his brother and causing him yet more pain.

So they had reluctantly agreed not to tell their dad about the real state of his marriage. He was a gentle, kind soul who adored his wife, never seeming to mind her endless criticisms about his love of the railway or even how he dressed and acted.

But the brothers had been badly affected by what they had seen. Until then, their childhood had been a happy one, but that had crashed to an abrupt halt on that day and they had both had to grow up fast.

Unable to view the sham of a marriage, Ryan had graduated from catering college and swiftly left home. Younger by three years, Ethan had kept out of the house as often as he could until he too had his electrical qualifications and could leave Cranfield to pursue his own career.

They both still had to return home for birthdays and holidays though. Ethan in particular found Christmas an especially miserable time, inwardly horrified at the fake festive atmosphere. He had often used his work as an excuse and sometimes didn't come home for a whole year at a time.

Thankfully, his work as a lighting specialist kept him busy. He helped project manage all the technical lighting required for large-scale events, such as concerts and theatre productions. In addition, sometimes his work led him to commercial projects as well, such as shopping malls and even airports.

Whenever he had any spare time, he would fill his diary with as many dates as he could manage, not wanting to spend any time alone. He always warned any woman that he had no intention of any relationship becoming serious. His mother's view on that had hit him deep. 'Don't fall in love,' she often told him. 'It'll bring you no joy.'

So Ethan had kept all women at arm's length and avoided coming back to Cranfield as much as he could until his parents' marriage had finally completely broken down a year ago, when their mum had walked out on their dad to start a new life in Spain with her most recent lover. Ethan wasn't entirely sure that she was happy with her decision, but he was glad for his father's sake that his broken heart had slowly mended and that he was happy at last.

Their newly single dad Bob had moved in with their grandfather, Eddie, and was now living in one of the small cottages on Railway Lane, only a short distance from the station. The first few months of being single had been tricky for Bob but his love of trains had helped him through the tougher times.

Ryan at least seemed to have finally made his peace with the past and, after moving back home to support his dad after the breakup, was now happily settled in Cranfield with Katy, who he adored.

However, Ethan still struggled with his role in keeping the secret of his mum's affairs. But he had tried to come home more often in the past year.

Ethan looked at the empty room once more before concentrating back on Libby, who was still frowning at him.

'So, what?' asked Libby. 'You're living here now?'

'Don't worry, Libs,' he replied, with a grin. 'I'll make sure I irritate you at every opportunity.'

'No change there then,' she replied, with a roll of her eyes. 'Well, now that I've ensured that the local crime rate is kept down, I'll get out of here. Some of us have actually been working all night.'

She abruptly spun on her heels and marched over to the front door, which she had left wide open when she had rushed inside a few minutes earlier.

She totally ignored Ethan as he followed her before leaning on the doorframe to watch her drive the short distance down Railway Lane to park up in front of her cottage.

When she got out of her car, he gave her a wave. He knew she had seen him as she turned her head away, deliberately ignoring him, and walked up the front path out of view.

Ethan stood there for a moment, smiling to himself at his favourite, cherished memories, which were always those with Libby.

In the early days, they had been close – as thick as thieves, his grandad had often said. He enjoyed the company of all his friends in the village, as well as his family, but his relationship with Libby was different. Special, maybe. Unique, definitely.

She had rebelled against her father for most of her childhood. Wild-spirited Libby had broken the mould and Ethan had always been drawn to her for as long as he could remember.

Ethan was the only one who understood why she acted that way. He was always rebelling too, taking rule-breaking to the max, trying not to think about his mother's affairs.

Once they had reached sixteen, he had invited Libby to go to the prom with him. He had been hoping that it would be the day to turn their friendship into something more. To finally stop joking around and tell her how he really felt. How she was his first love. Perhaps even his forever one too.

But that was before he and Ryan had spotted their mother in the field on the day of the prom. When the truth of their parents' marriage had come crashing down on his elder brother and Ethan could no longer protect him from the truth. They were both feeling heartbroken and nothing could cheer Ethan up, not even taking Libby to the prom. In the end, Ethan had got drunk and called his brother to take him home, abandoning Libby at the prom. She had been angry with him and rightfully so. But he couldn't tell her the truth. No one was to know, according to the pact he had made with Ryan.

His close friendship with Libby had abruptly halted at that moment. She obviously hated him. He'd ruined her prom and she could never forgive him. In truth, he couldn't even forgive himself.

But no woman had ever compared to her, despite the many years of dating, looking for an alternative to the bluest eyes that he knew, as well as that gorgeous long blonde hair, so pale it was almost silver.

His mother had told him true love didn't exist and having seen his parents' marriage at close quarters, he knew she was right, despite his friends in Cranfield and even his brother proving him wrong over the last year or so by falling in love.

There had only been one time when he had felt that love was real. One night when he had unexpectedly bumped into Libby in Las Vegas and been true to himself and the deep feelings he held for her. She was the only one to have ever got close enough to him to reveal his heart. But it had been too close for the both of them, as it turned out.

It had been a night to forget as far as Libby was concerned, but despite nearly eight years passing since, why couldn't he do the same?

So he joked and wound her up whenever he came back to Cranfield, all the while trying to ignore the Libby-shaped hole in his heart.

He glanced once more up Railway Lane, but she had long since disappeared from view. So he turned around and closed the front door behind him.

## 3

'So that was your last flight?' came the shocked chorus from around the table.

Libby gave her best friends, Harriet, Flora and Katy, a grimace as she sank down onto the chair in Platform 1, still in her flight attendant's uniform.

After quietly dumping her flight bag in the hallway, so as not to wake up her dad, she had texted her friends a short while ago that it was an emergency and Katy had opened up the coffee shop early just for them.

'Yup,' Libby told them. 'Those of us being made redundant received the email just before we boarded the flight, can you believe? I am one hundred per cent out of a job as of right now.' She tried and failed to smile. 'But, hey, on the plus side, no more jet lag, so that's something.'

Katy pushed a large mug of coffee towards her. 'Here,' she said. 'Drink this. It's our new special. Pumpkin spice latte.'

Katy and her boyfriend Ryan had opened Platform 1 in the old railway station to great success the previous winter. It was a cosy mix of old railway memorabilia, wood panelling and leather benches.

Libby thanked Katy for the drink and took a grateful sip. It was delicious and brought a much-needed warmth to her insides. She hugged the mug close to her chest.

'I don't understand,' said Harriet, as she unhooked the lead for her golden retriever Paddington to settle down underneath the table. 'You've been with them for how long now? Two years?'

'Three,' Libby told her. 'So I'll get a whole three weeks' extra pay for my efforts.'

'But surely there are other flight attendants that have less experience than you?' asked Flora, frowning. 'You've been doing the job for ten years.'

'Corporate business doesn't always work like that, unfortunately,' Katy told her, shaking her head.

Katy knew all about the cut-throat business world as she had been a high-flying executive before being made redundant a year ago. Thankfully, it had worked out for the best for Katy, who had fallen in love with both Cranfield and chef Ryan Connolly. She had also been warmly welcomed by Libby, Harriet and Flora – all of whom had been childhood friends – into their close-knit group.

'Can't you appeal?' asked Harriet, still looking upset. 'What about your union? They might be able to get your job back for you.'

Libby looked at soft-hearted Harriet with a suppressed smile. She had known Harriet since they had been children and she had never changed her positive outlook of everyone and everything. She was the complete opposite of cynical Libby, even down to the long red hair that swung wild and free around Harriet's pretty face.

'I don't think it's going to happen,' Libby told her. 'I've got those two written warnings, haven't I? Apparently I've got a reputation for being a little difficult, according to my ex-work colleagues.'

Her three best friends all exchanged a knowing look.

'Yeah, yeah,' said Libby, sitting back in her chair with a heavy sigh. 'Me and my big mouth.'

She gave a jump as she felt something under the table before she realised that Paddington had placed his head on her lap and was staring up at her with sorrowful dark eyes. She smiled at him and ruffled his fur.

'You just speak your mind,' said Flora, reaching out to give her other hand a squeeze. 'That's all.'

'Exactly,' said Katy, with a firm nod of her head. 'Nothing wrong with that.'

'You're always honest and that's refreshing,' added Harriet.

'Refreshing isn't going to pay the bills in the future,' said Libby, grateful for their support nevertheless. She had her redundancy money and then that would be it. What on earth was she going to do now?

'We'd offer you a job here,' said Katy, looking around the coffee shop. 'But it's a little slower now that the summer rush has gone.'

'Unfortunately, Nico and I spent yesterday packing up the tents for winter,' added Flora, who ran a glamping site from Strawberry Hill Farm with her Italian boyfriend. 'Now that the site's closed until next Easter, we've got the renovations to get sorted.' She shot Libby a grin. 'Unless you've got any secret plumbing skills that you haven't told us about.'

Ever practical and steady, Flora had surprised everyone the previous summer by changing the farm, which had been close to bankruptcy, into a glamping site to huge success. Equally surprising was when Flora had fallen in love with Nico, a glamorous ex-playboy. But Nico had turned out to have a heart of gold and so had been readily welcomed inside their circle of friends.

'Well, the lavender spa is still busy,' said Harriet before biting her lip. 'But with the fields now closed for winter, Joe's just doing a lot of online stuff instead, so he's able to help me out more.'

Harriet had inherited the lavender fields on the opposite side of the railway track, which had been opened to the public for two successful summers in a row, alongside her fiancé Joe. She had also turned the small post room at the far end of the station into a successful spa, using her talent as a beauty therapist to work wonders with the lavender products.

'It's fine,' said Libby quickly. 'I never meant for you all to offer me a job. Just keep the coffee and gin coming and I'll be okay.'

'That's one bit of good news then,' said Harriet, with a soft smile. 'It's gin night tomorrow night.'

It had long been a weekly tradition, where the four of them got together to discuss life and everything else over gin cocktails. Lately, though, their busy schedules had got in the way and they had missed the last couple of weeks.

Libby was the only single one now in the foursome and sometimes felt a little apart from her friends, who were happy and loved up. They often professed how much they envied the perceived glamour of her job, travelling the world and staying in amazing places. But the irony was that she envied them and their happy, steady lives here in Cranfield.

'How about my place for a change of venue?' said Katy. 'And before you object, Libby, it's an Ethan-free zone now. You won't believe it! Ethan has bought the old school at the end of the lane, so he won't stay with us any more!'

Libby kept quiet, having mistaken him for a burglar only an hour ago.

'Seriously?' said Flora in amazement. 'Wow. He bunked off so often from school I'd have thought it would be the last place for him to call home.'

'As I remember, he used to bunk off with Libby,' said Harriet, with a grin.

'He was a bad influence on me in those days,' remarked Libby in a prim tone.

'Oh yeah?' said Flora, raising her eyebrows. 'What's your excuse these days?'

Libby stuck her tongue out in reply to prove how much more mature she was now. Then, upon seeing Ethan walk through the coffee shop towards the kitchen, where his brother Ryan was working, she carried on sticking her tongue out at him instead.

As usual, he merely gave her one of his winning smiles and carried on walking away. He was tall and good-looking, with ruffled blonde hair that appeared to be permanently messed up. Was it the hair that drove women crazy? Or his laid-back charm that contributed to the busy dating life that Ryan was always speaking about. Thankfully, she knew that Ethan's handsome looks no longer had any effect on her.

At least that's what she had to keep reminding herself.

She turned back to look at Katy. 'Well, now that the upstairs apartment is most definitely an Ethan-free zone, then yes, I would love to come to your place tomorrow night,' she said.

'Excellent!' said Katy, standing up. 'I need to get ready for opening time. I want to be all set before the great steam engine excitement this morning.'

Due to everything else that had happened overnight, Libby had completely forgotten all about big event until that moment. Bob and Eddie had been working on the abandoned steam engine in the train workshop for many years and it was due to have its maiden run that morning.

'Look,' said Katy, in a serious tone as she looked at Libby, giving her a squeeze of her shoulder. 'We'll think of something to get you out of your financial hole.' She brightened up. 'And at least you've got time to make some more chocolate. Nearly all the boxes you gave me last week have sold out already. There's only one left.'

'They have?' Libby was pleased. She had never imagined that complete strangers would pay money for her own creations.

Katy nodded thoughtfully. 'I wonder...' she said, tapping her chin.

'What's going on in that busy brain of yours now?' asked Flora, raising her eyebrows.

Katy had a tendency to have huge ideas which turned out to be successful business plans but also extremely hard work for everyone involved.

'Just an idea,' said Katy, before breaking into a smile. 'But I won't share any details until I've got something concrete.'

'I suppose I'd better go and see Dad before all the train excitement begins,' said Libby, the dread hitting her stomach as she thought about the conversation she would need to have with him.

'It's all starting in an hour's time apparently,' said Harriet, her eyes lighting up. 'I can't wait to see the train actually move after all this time! I wonder if we might be able to get a photograph next to it on our wedding day,' she added with a misty smile. 'Wouldn't that be amazing? Oh and by the way, I'm going to bring all my bridal magazines with me tomorrow night!'

She and her fiancé Joe were getting married at the end of January and most of their conversations had been all about the big day ever since Joe had proposed at the end of the summer.

Libby groaned. 'Can't we have a romance-free evening for once?' she asked.

Harriet bit her lip, looking panicked. 'I can't. We've only got just over three months to go. I know I said I didn't want a big do and all that, but even so, there's so much to think about and nothing's been decided yet! I'm talking dresses! Theme! Hair and make-up!'

Katy held up her hand. 'Stop spiralling,' she said. 'You know how organised I am. I love a good checklist. Just think of me as your free wedding planner. We'll get it sorted. Now just breathe.'

'Thank you,' replied Harriet, with a sigh of relief, giving her a hug. 'Thank God I've got you three as my bridesmaids.'

Flora gave Libby a nudge with her elbow. 'And we'll all help with the wedding stuff, won't we?' she said in a pointed tone.

Libby hesitated. 'You know I love you and Joe,' Libby told Harriet. 'I'm just not a romantic, that's all.'

She wasn't anti-relationships. After all, she had encouraged each of her friends to follow their hearts and was pleased with how happy they were all now. It just wasn't for her, that was all.

'I think there's a little secret part of you that dreams of romance,' said Harriet in a wistful voice.

'Well, hand me a shovel so I can bury it in the back garden,' replied Libby.

Her friends all burst out laughing.

'Okay. We know you hate weddings,' Harriet told her. 'So seeing as you'll never have one of your own, just help me plan mine. Please?'

Libby felt a shiver down her spine.

'Of course I will,' she said, fixing on a wide smile before bending down to give Paddington a cuddle and hide the fake look on her face. 'I can't wait to celebrate you getting married to Joe.'

That at least was the truth.

But there was one secret that she had never admitted to

anyone, even her friends. She had been married once, a very long time ago, and it had been an utter disaster.

On a drunken whim eight years ago in Las Vegas, there had been one reckless moment when she had given into her heart at last and married Ethan Connolly. But she had woken up supremely embarrassed and had left before Ethan woke up.

Her long-held dream of being loved by Ethan had merely been a drunken mistake. As far as she knew, without having signed any annulment, they were still secretly married, but they had never discussed it since, nor had she ever told anyone. Perhaps given how drunk they both were, there was a chance that Ethan didn't even remember getting married and had dismissed it entirely from his mind.

Their friendship was now beyond repair. Perhaps that's how it was meant to be, she had decided. No matter how much her heart ached for him. No matter how much she missed having him in her life.

She glanced at him briefly as he chatted to his brother before abruptly turning away and walking out of the coffee shop, her high heels clicking on the wooden floorboards as she went.

# 4

Ethan had learnt three important things about women over his many years of dating.

One, women do not actually want an honest answer to the question, 'How do I look?'

Two, only women understand the need for guest towels and 'good' china.

Three, that if the word 'fine' is used swiftly followed by a soft sigh, then the woman is most definitely not fine.

Frowning, Ethan looked at his brother as he worked in the tiny kitchen at the back of the coffee shop.

'What's wrong with Katy?' asked Ethan.

Ryan looked up from the pizza dough that he was kneading with raised eyebrows. 'Nothing,' he said. 'Unless you've said something to upset her.'

'I haven't said anything,' replied Ethan, shaking his head. 'I just asked her how she was this morning.'

Now it was Ryan's turn to sigh. 'You know Katy,' he said, with a small shrug. 'She thinks of you like her own family. But after your announcement last night that you've bought the old school, she thinks it's her fault that you've moved out.'

'Of course it's not her fault,' said Ethan, quickly.

He thought the world of his elder brother's girlfriend. She was funny, kind and smart. He couldn't have wished for someone better for Ryan to make a life with.

'I know that,' said Ryan. 'It's your fault, as per usual.'

Ethan rolled his eyes. 'Yeah right. As if you really wanted me hanging around in your love nest upstairs.'

'Oh no,' said Ryan, with a grin. 'Three is most definitely a crowd. So I'm quite glad that you've now got your own place.'

'My point exactly,' said Ethan. 'But seeing as I've invited myself over for a Sunday roast, then you won't exactly have time to miss me.'

'So how long are you staying this time?' asked his elder brother in a pointed tone.

Whereas Ryan was now happy to be back in Cranfield full-time, Ethan still found the place unsettling and full of painful memories of his parents' disastrous marriage. Therefore he tended to stay only a couple of weeks at a time before moving on to the next work contract far away.

'Long enough to wind you up,' replied Ethan, with a grin before his smile slipped. 'Actually, because that shopping mall in Seattle isn't ready yet, I've got about a month until my next contract starts, so I thought I'd take some time out to get my new home in a decent state. Maybe I'll even have some furniture by then.'

Ryan looked surprised but pleased. 'Great,' he said. 'Dad and Grandad will be pleased. We'll all enjoy having you around for a bit longer. Well, maybe right up until the time when we can't stand the sight of you.'

'Feeling's mutual, bro,' said Ethan with a wink. 'And you've only got until the start of November.'

Despite their banter, Ethan was warmed by his brother's reaction. After so much time apart over the past decade, they had begun to grow closer once more over the past year and Ethan was actually looking forward to spending a bit of time with his family over the next few weeks.

He headed outside along the single track to the large train workshop a few yards away. In the old days when the railway had still run, the workshop had been used to service the modern trains. But when they had stopped running twenty years ago, his dad had had the incredible idea to renovate the full-sized steam engine that had been in the back of the workshop for as many years as Ethan could recall.

Bob's obsession with the steam engine had been one of the reasons that their mum had finally declared enough was enough and moved to Spain with her lover. They spoke occasionally, but she had pretty much drawn a line under her life in Cranfield and, it felt to Ethan, to her two sons as well.

With their grandad widowed, the two older men had hunkered down in their combined grief and worked on the steam engine each and every day. It had needed major renovations to even get the engine going once more, but part by part, day by day, year by year, slowly the train had been repaired until finally it was ready to go out on the tracks for its first journey in more than fifty years.

He found his dad and grandad already in the driver's cab and looking excited. Ethan knew how much this day meant to them both.

'Good morning,' said Ethan.

'It certainly is,' replied Eddie, with a grin. 'A great morning, in fact.'

'Morning,' replied Bob, also beaming from ear to ear.

'Everything looking okay?' asked Ethan.

'All set and ready for her first run,' Bob told him.

Ethan was feeling equally excited as he climbed up to join them in the driver's cab. But there had been one worry that he kept him awake the previous night.

'We've definitely contacted the right authorities about taking it out on the track, haven't we?' asked Ethan, a little worried about his dad's laid-back approach to rules and regulations. He'd always assumed that's where he had inherited it from.

His grandad nodded. 'Oh yes,' replied Eddie, smiling. 'You wouldn't believe the forms we've had to fill out and all the endless inspections to make sure that it's safe.'

'It's a fire-breathing dragon on giant wheels moving through the countryside,' said Ethan, glancing at the large steam engine. 'I'm not surprised that everyone wants it to be safe.'

'She'll be fine,' said Bob, reaching out of the open cab to pat the massive side panel.

'I thought you were going to repaint it?' remarked Ethan, glancing over the rusty red paint as he climbed up into the driver's cab to join them.

'No time,' replied Eddie. 'We wanted to get it going first.'

Ethan blew out a long breath. 'So what's the drill here? Who's in charge?' he asked.

'Not you, son,' said Bob, laughing. 'Your grandad and I will be the drivers, keeping an eye on the track as well as all the gauges.'

Thankfully, it was quite a simple set-up with the water and temperature gauges the main ones to watch.

'And what will I be doing?' asked Ethan, glancing down at the blue overalls that his father had given him to wear.

'Stoking the fire,' said Eddie, pointing at the large pile of coal next to them.

'Good job I had an extra coffee this morning,' said Ethan, with a grimace.

But despite his laid-back tone, in fact he was as excited as his dad and grandad. The steam trains had finished running a long time before he was born. He'd seen them in the movies, of course, but had never been on one, let alone up in the cab when it was moving.

He picked up his shovel and began to move the coal. Once that job was complete, he wiped his forehead. 'Glad we're not doing this at the height of summer,' he announced.

But Ethan couldn't deny that the engineering side interested him. After all, it had been his dad's love of trains that had first made him fascinated by engineering at an early age. He had always loved fixing things, creating circuits – something that he had carried on into his job. Although that love had paled slightly lately.

'So this is it,' said Ethan, with a slight hesitation. 'We're off? What if it doesn't work?'

'It'll work,' replied Eddie confidently.

'As long as we don't have a crowd,' said Ethan. 'Then nobody has to know even if we can't get it going.'

'Yeah,' said Bob, looking sheepish. 'About that...'

'We may have mentioned it to a few people,' added his grandad.

Ethan cocked his ear and realised that he could hear excited chatter in the distance. He peeked his head out of the train cab and looked along the short distance to the station. As opposed to the normal couple of dog walkers and customers heading into Platform 1 for an early coffee, there was a rather large crowd of people gathered expectantly, as if waiting for a show.

He sighed before turning to his dad and grandad.

'Well, if we're going to fail, at least it'll be in front of a large audience,' he told them, holding up two fingers tightly crossed.

## 5

Libby shivered in the cool autumnal breeze and decided to quickly change out of her flight attendant's uniform and into something warmer in order to watch the inaugural journey of Bob and Eddie's steam engine.

She glanced down, reminding herself that it would be the last time she wore the uniform. There was a mixture of sadness for her lost job but equally a sense of relief that perhaps the days of mixed up sleep patterns were finally behind her.

Her walk led her along the platform and past the end of the station where Harriet's lavender spa was situated. Then the platform backed onto the picket fences of the gardens of cottages on Railway Lane. A glance over to the lavender fields on the opposite side of the track showed the mist was hugging the cold ground. Autumn had definitely arrived.

It was one of Libby's favourite times of the year and yet the all-encompassing dread of having to tell her father what had happened was stressing her out. He would be worried and, no doubt, once more disappointed in her behaviour.

As she came upon the very last cottage along the short row,

she let herself in through the rickety white picket gate that led to the back garden. Expecting to find her father in his usual place at the kitchen table at that time, such was his rigid routine, she was surprised to see him standing behind the picket fence. He was wearing his smart overcoat, gloves and scarf in deference to the cool morning air.

'Good morning, Dad,' she said, going over to give him a kiss on the cheek.

'Good morning, Elizabeth,' replied Philip, the only person to have ever called her by her full name. 'I saw your suitcase in the hall. Glad to see you safely back from your travels once more,' he added, giving her a gentle pat on the back with his good hand.

His entire right-hand side of the body had been almost destroyed by the stroke that had so nearly killed him. It had been over ten years and most people would no longer be able to see the slight droop of his face on one side. Libby would always be able to tell, though, and when her father was overtired, he slurred his words ever so slightly.

He had slowly regained partial use of his right arm and leg, but it had been the depression afterwards that had devastated his career as a headmaster. Her father had always been highly intelligent, focusing all his time on educating both his pupils and himself. Libby knew that the embarrassment of having to give up his job had never left him.

He still took his daily walk to keep his muscles and body moving, but he always made sure that it was at first light when there was hardly anyone else around. He barely left the house for the remainder of the day, with only Radio 4 for company. He read the newspaper all morning and then a book in the afternoon. During the summer months, the garden would keep him occupied. But the winters were the longest time for them both.

This year, though, when winter arrived, she wouldn't even have her work to take her away.

'I was waiting to catch a view of the steam engine,' he replied. 'You've arrived home just in time.'

Libby looked out along the tracks to where the steam engine stood, proudly waiting for its big moment in the spotlight. The front of the engine was black, along with the short chimney from which steam was beginning to rise. The main barrel shape of the engine was red, along with the small square driver's cab at the back, where Bob, Eddie and Ethan could be seen moving about.

'I'll just go and get changed quickly,' Libby told him before rushing up the garden path and through the back door into the small kitchen.

Even now, despite having been away for one night, she could still make out the sweet smell of chocolate in the air. What had started as a hobby had grown into a passion, one which she could lose herself in. It wasn't bringing them in any money, except a small amount which Libby had made from selling her home-made truffles at Platform 1. People seemed to enjoy the different flavours she liked to experiment with, such as raspberry or praline, but most of all, she enjoyed the process. The alchemy that happened when she melted the chocolate and immersed herself in the creative process. She could forget all her worries. Forget everything, except the magic.

Libby headed through the front room. None of the cottages along Railway Lane were very large, but they all shared a certain charm, with the exposed brickwork and cosy fireplaces. There was just enough space for a modest sofa and an upright winged back chair that her father sat in each evening.

There was no hallway to speak of, merely a patch of worn carpet with a couple of hooks for coats. The stairwell was narrow and steep, but thankfully her father seemed able to manage.

At the top, there was a small landing, from which led the two bedrooms and a bathroom. Libby headed into her bedroom to get changed, carefully hanging up her uniform in the wardrobe and wondering whether it would have to be returned to the airline at some point.

She checked her emails and sank down onto the bed as she read the one from her supervisor. It was all very formal, very finite, she realised. It really had happened. She hadn't imagined it after all. She was out of a job. It was a mess and she had no idea how to make her life better.

After going back downstairs, Libby grabbed her coat from the hook before going outside to join her dad.

She cleared her throat as she went to stand next to him, knowing she couldn't put off the moment any longer.

'Dad, I've got something to tell you,' she began, giving him a tentative look. She felt all of ten years old again when she had to tell him that she had lost her bike in a ditch and it was in pieces.

He raised his eyebrows at her but didn't reply.

'So, er, they've announced a whole load of redundancies at work and I've been laid off,' she said, her words coming out in a rush. 'With immediate effect.'

'I see.' He looked a little alarmed as the silence stretched out between them.

'But don't worry,' said Libby, giving him one of her wide smiles. 'They're going to give me almost a month's pay due to my years of service and I've got lots of feelers out for the next job. I'll get one in no time.'

'Of course you will,' he replied, looking relieved.

Libby's smile grew rigid as she tried to maintain it. 'Just thought I'd better keep you in the loop, as it were. Now, what about this train?'

Thankfully, at this precise moment, the loud toot-toot of the steam engine whistle rang out and she was able to step forward with her dad to concentrate on the train as a plume of smoke rose up into the air.

'It's certainly been a labour of love for Bob and Eddie,' he murmured.

Her dad had been to school with Bob and knew the family very well. Not that her dad ever socialised these days, with Libby always making an excuse for him whenever they were invited anywhere.

'You don't want to stand out on the platform and watch?' she asked, looking back up towards the station, where a small group of people were beginning to gather.

Her dad shook his head. She wasn't surprised.

'Still, we'll get a good view here, won't we?' she said, gesturing at the low fence, over which they would get a grandstand view of the steam engine.

It was only a little white lie about finding another job, she told herself as they stared down the line back towards the station. Her dad didn't need to know about her two written warnings. And surely she'd find a job quickly, wouldn't she?

But the twinge in the pit of her stomach reminded her that her whole career might be over and she had no idea how she was going to earn a living from now onwards.

# 6

Ethan stood in the driver's cab of the steam engine and exchanged nervous but excited looks with his dad and grandad.

'So it looks like we're good to go,' Ethan told them both.

'Well,' said Bob, rubbing his hands together. 'No time like the present.'

'Aye, son,' said Eddie, nodding. 'Let's get this show on the road.'

The boiler was already packed with coal and with the water tank also full, the engine billowing out clouds of steam from its chimney. All it needed now was a release of the brakes for the train to move forward.

'Better give the folks another warning,' said Bob.

Eddie smiled. 'You do the honours.'

But Bob shook his head. 'Together, I reckon, Dad,' he said.

'All right,' replied Eddie. 'Together.'

So they both reached out to the chain hanging from the ceiling and gave it a hearty couple of tugs.

The train whistled and Ethan found that, despite the heat

from the nearby coal fire, he had goosebumps up his arms. It was really happening, he reminded himself.

He thought back to the early days of his childhood, riding the trains with his dad and grandad, then rushing home to play with toy replica models. But this was a real-life, full-size steam engine. He could hardly believe it.

However, there was no time to reminisce as Bob pulled a couple of levers whilst Eddie hung out of the side of the cab to check the wheels. With a small jolt and another large puff of steam, the locomotive began to move forward. It was a slow movement but enough for them all to exchange another brief round of smiles.

Slowly but surely, the steam train puffed its way forward into the bright sunshine.

They all kept checking the gauges for temperature and water levels, but all seemed okay as they drew nearer to the station.

Ethan glanced down as they went past, waving at Ryan and Katy, who gave him wide smiles as they waved back.

Everyone else on the platform was recording the journey on their mobiles. So Ethan stepped back to let his grandad smile and wave at everyone.

'How far are we going?' asked Ethan.

'To Cranley junction,' shouted Bob, above the noise. 'We can turn around there.'

The single railway track ran for ten miles until the main station in Aldwych town. Cranley junction was situated about halfway along. As the train chugged and puffed past the station, Ethan glanced out of the driver's cab once more and briefly saw Libby and her father standing at their back gate. Eddie gave a wave of greeting when he too saw them.

Seeing Libby standing there, Ethan absent-mindedly felt for

the bump on his head and smiled to himself. Libby still didn't come with a rulebook.

Then the train went past his new home, the old school, a little square box in the same sandy bricks that the whole village had been built in. Despite being an impulse purchase, he quite liked the feel of the place. The large rooms and high ceilings were a plus point and it overlooked the railway line and then the lavender fields and countryside beyond.

Besides, he had happy memories of that little school. Those had been happy, carefree times and he remembered playing outside with Ryan, Flora and Libby. Before they all grew up and life and hormones got in the way of their relationships, he thought, feeling his ringless wedding finger. Of all the things he had ever planned for his future, getting married had never been one of them.

He had been in Las Vegas for a work convention but had grown weary of his colleagues and had taken a walk along the Strip to clear his head. He had been shocked to come across Libby, of all people, watching the fountains in front of the Bellagio Hotel.

It had ended up being a crazy, drunken night in a glamorous, glittering city with Libby, his oldest friend. After the disaster of the prom, he'd thought they would never be able to get back what they had lost, but that particular evening, the bright lights and romance of Las Vegas, along with enough alcohol to fell a moose, had broken through the barriers that Libby had dramatically put up between them. All he wanted to do was take Libby in his arms and admit how he really felt about her. But something went awry in the haze of alcohol and one of his jokes had suddenly become reality.

For a man who hated the idea of marriage, he had to admit to himself that he had been the one to drag Libby into the wedding chapel. Suddenly, they were buying cheap rings, signing a licence and standing in front of a fake plastic altar. The only clear memory he had of that whole evening was slipping the ring onto Libby's finger. A sober Ethan would have been horrified but somehow he remembered feeling nothing but pure happiness in that moment.

Afterwards, they had drunk even more alcohol before passing out in his hotel suite. He had woken up to find himself alone, Libby's wedding ring left behind on the bedside table as the only evidence of the previous evening.

The marriage could have been easily and quickly annulled and yet he had never completed the paperwork. For some reason, a tiny part of him was happy to remain married to Libby and he still didn't know why.

Libby had never mentioned anything about the marriage and it was pretty obvious that she had regretted getting married to him. So to make things easier for them both, he had carried on as if it had never happened, even though he still carried with him a small sense of wonder that the whole night had even taken place.

The school was the last building at the edge of the tiny hamlet and as the train moved on, Cranfield was suddenly behind them and they were surrounded by the open countryside. It was slow progress as nobody wanted to max out the steam engine on the first outing. They had made a few tentative moves back and forwards within the confines of the train workshop, but this was the first time in the open air. And it was glorious, thought Ethan, shovelling in more coal. The sound was incredible. The hiss of the steam, with the clanging of the engine right ahead of them, along with noise from the air whooshing around them as it went past.

Time seemed to fly past until suddenly they were at the small junction near the village of Cranley. In the very far distance, just peeping out through the woods, Ethan could see Willow Tree Hall, the grand stately home, and figured that they must be right at the end of the estate.

The train slowed down as it neared a level crossing and they gave another toot of the horn to ensure that everyone in the vicinity knew that it was coming along the tracks. After the crossing, the train slowed down ever further until it ground to a shuddering halt with a hiss of steam coming up from all of the wheels.

All three men sighed a sigh of relief.

'It works,' said Eddie, with a huge smile.

'Of course it works,' replied Bob, laughing.

'Let's hope it works just as well in reverse,' said Ethan through gritted teeth. 'Otherwise we've got a long walk home.'

It had all gone too smoothly, he thought. Gone too well. He wasn't a superstitious person, but surely nothing was perfect?

A few levers were pulled so that the engine would be able to reverse back up the railway track the way it had come. More coal was shovelled and gauges checked and then, with another jolt, the steam engine puffed back into life and they were off and running once more, this time with the driver's cab at the very front.

Ethan was overwhelmed with what his dad and grandad had achieved over so many years, along with a bit of help whenever he returned home. His love of engines had all stemmed from these men standing beside him, both grinning from ear to ear like small children as they trundled along the tracks.

Soon, he could see the tiny hamlet of Cranfield along the tracks. The village was surrounded by rolling hills, all beginning to lose their green hues as autumn rushed in and replaced it all with its resplendent bright yellows, oranges and scarlet colours.

In the distance, just down the narrow path on the other side of the railway tracks was Cranbridge, the village split down the middle by the river. It had a well-stocked corner shop and a popular pub, The Black Swan Inn.

As they approached the station, the train slowed right down so that it crept along the platform. Then, with more steam, and the hiss and clanking of huge metal cogs and wheels, the steam engine ground to a halt just beyond the station.

Bob turned to look at his son and father, his teeth bright white against the sooty black-smeared face. 'We did it,' he said, with a laugh. But his blue eyes shone out with pride. 'It's been a dream come true to go out on the engine we've worked so hard on.'

Eddie nodded slowly, his eyes looking watery but he was smiling too. 'Well done us,' he said.

Bob and Ethan stepped forward at the same time to embrace Eddie and all three of them stood there for a moment, relishing the result of their ambition.

Even Ethan could feel his throat contracting with tears and emotion. 'That was amazing,' he told them both.

Bob nodded, still looking extremely stunned. 'Let's have a drink to celebrate!' he declared.

'It's only half past ten in the morning,' said Ethan, checking his watch and laughing.

'Yes, but we've been waiting twenty years for a pint to celebrate the first run!' said Bob with a grin.

## 7

'Cheers!' said Libby, as she and her friends clinked together their glasses that evening.

They were celebrating the success of the inaugural run of the steam engine earlier that morning. The cosy Black Swan Inn in Cranbridge was the perfect place, with its roaring fires and exposed wooden beams. Plus, it was only a short walk from Cranfield and so everyone had been able to come to celebrate after work.

Nearly everyone, thought Libby. Her dad had once more declined her offer to join them, preferring to stay at home with his radio for company, despite thoroughly enjoying watching the steam engine.

'Wasn't the steam train romantic?' said Harriet, with a soft sigh. 'I thought it was dreamy. Like something out of a movie.'

Everyone nodded in agreement.

'I just can't believe they got it going after all this time,' said Flora, shaking her head in disbelief.

'Oh, Eddie's always had a can-do attitude,' said Grams, with a nod.

Flora's elderly grandmother, Helen, known to most people as Grams, was eighty years old, but her eyes sparkled bright against her grey hair and rosy cheeks.

'And Bob definitely inherited that attitude from his dad too,' added Maggie, with a smile.

Maggie was one of Libby's neighbours on Railway Lane. She was a shy widow who had begun to come out of her shell over the past year, thanks partly to her skills in baking delicious cakes which were sold in Platform 1.

After the breakdown of his marriage, Bob had become friends with Maggie and they often went out for a walk at the weekend, followed by a drink in the pub.

'I'm so pleased for Bob and Eddie,' said Katy. 'Everyone in the coffee shop today talked of nothing else.'

Harriet nodded in agreement. 'All my customers in the lavender spa wanted to know when it's going to be running again as some people missed it.'

'Well, here's hoping we'll see it out and about again at some point,' said Grams. 'If not, it would be lovely to have it out on show for everyone to have a closer look. Maybe at the weekend when folks aren't working.'

'Talking of which, any good news about a job?' asked Flora gently, turning to look at Libby.

Libby shook her head. 'Nothing but my official redundancy letter,' she replied, almost unable to bear their pitiful looks. 'And at least it gives me more time to make some more chocolate, I suppose.'

'Good news for us,' said Harriet.

'Hopefully a new challenge job-wise will come up very soon,' said Katy, with a knowing smile and a wink.

Libby wasn't sure what Katy's plan was. She was a business whizz who was always coming up with somewhat hare-brained schemes that had all miraculously worked. But how she would find a job for Libby was anyone's guess.

She raised her eyebrows in question at Katy, who merely shook her head in reply.

'And think of all the spare time that you'll have now for all those hunky men you're always dating,' said Harriet, waggling her eyebrows.

'Exactly!' replied Libby, before taking another sip of her gin and tonic.

They all still thought that she had an amazing love life. When the truth was that she hadn't felt deeply for any man except Ethan. And look what a mess that had turned into.

Libby excused herself to go to the ladies' and avoid any further lies that she needed to tell her friends.

But, on the way, she came face to face with Ethan coming in the other direction.

He gave her his wide smile that had been so successful with the ladies over the years. 'I'll take a cold beer and a hot towel, please,' he said.

Libby rolled her eyes. 'You don't deserve anything. In fact, I would deliberately place you right next to the toilet at the back of the plane,' she told him.

He carried on smiling at her. 'Nice to see you too again, Libby. Despite still feeling the effects from your earlier visit.' He rubbed the top of his head and she felt a little sheepish about hitting him. 'I still can't believe your job is being nice to people all the time,' he carried on.

'Well, it's not,' she said, puffing out a sigh. 'Not any more.'

It was one of her many failings. Always outspoken, she could barely keep any secrets to herself. Except the most dangerous ones.

Ethan's smile quickly faded. 'You lost your job?' he asked, searching her eyes with his.

She shrugged her shoulders, trying to be as nonchalant as possible. 'Just been made redundant, as of twenty-four hours ago,' she told him, checking her watch.

The way he was searching her face, though, was making her uncomfortable, as if he knew how much pain she was carrying deep inside.

'So what are you going to do now?' he asked.

'Keep calm and drink gin, of course,' she told him before walking away.

Why on earth was she blushing? She never blushed.

She had made so many mistakes over her life, but getting married to him had been the biggest one. She hadn't seen him for at least three years since he had left college and moved away with his work. After the disaster of the night of the prom, she had barely said two words to him, such was the level to which he had broken her heart.

She and Ethan had never recovered their friendship after the disastrous prom and they had lived separate lives until that stopover in Las Vegas for work. She had bumped into Ethan in front of the Bellagio fountains. She had been shocked to see him, but he was, as usual, relaxed and carefree Ethan.

Stunned by how affected she had been to see him, she had let him buy her a drink and the evening had progressed from there. For once, the conversation had been awkward and they had both ended up drinking far too many cocktails with far too little eaten to soak it all up. They had soon begun to relax and regain the back-and-forth banter that they had always had. At some point much later, many hours into the evening and after way too much alcohol, they had ended up in a wedding chapel.

She had woken up the following morning in Ethan's hotel

room, wearing a cheap silver ring on her third finger. A glance next to her had confirmed that not only was Ethan in the bed with her, but he too was wearing a wedding ring.

For a brief second, she had been thrilled. Then the memory of the prom had reminded her how much pain he had caused her. She had thought that she could trust him, but she knew better. It had just been a silly, reckless mistake, that was all.

Besides, she was certain, given Ethan's long-declared hatred of marriage, that he would have regretted it and would not be able to bear to see his change of heart and regret in the cold light of day.

Embarrassed and severely hungover, she had silently got up to get dressed. Then she had slid the ring from her finger and left it on the bedside table before letting herself out of the hotel room without waking him.

The first time she had seen him after that had been a week later. They had been surrounded by friends and family in Cranfield for a birthday party and so neither of them had been able to mention that fateful night.

But what was there to say? She had left the wedding ring and the whole episode behind her and decided never to refer to it ever again. Ethan seemed to have got the message as he too had never mentioned it since. The marriage hadn't been annulled as neither of them had drawn up the paperwork and asked for a signature, but as far as she was concerned, it was best left in the past, much like her close friendship with Ethan.

However, sometimes, late at night when she couldn't settle her mind, she found herself wondering what on earth would have happened to their relationship had she not run out that morning? Had she been able to truly trust him, would they actually have managed to make a go of their marriage?

But it wasn't to be. The prom had been a disaster. Their

wedding even more so. Both had been colossal mistakes, which they both regretted. Or, at least, she assumed he did. In unguarded moments, she yearned for him. She missed their friendship. But he had moved on and she'd tried to do the same.

Her relationship with Ethan was better left in the past, wasn't it?

## 8

Ethan headed back to the bar, enjoying the celebration regarding the successful inaugural journey of the steam engine. Everyone inside The Black Swan Inn had been rushing up to shake his hand, along with his dad and grandad's. He had managed to snatch a few brief bits of conversation with his friends Joe and Nico whilst they stood at the bar with his brother. Meanwhile, Bob and Eddie had been relishing their success at a nearby table with a constant stream of well-wishers. Finally, when he had a moment free, Ethan joined them to sit down next to the roaring fire.

'What a day,' said Eddie, with a satisfied smile.

Ethan thought that it had been a long time since he'd seen his grandad looking so happy and proud of himself. The years of hard work had paid off for his dad and grandad. He was so happy for them both. They had achieved what had turned into a lifetime dream for them both. The steam engine had worked.

'It certainly was,' said Bob, before suppressing a yawn.

'At least we all get a lie-in tomorrow,' Ethan told them with a grin.

'You're joking!' said Eddie, before giving a hearty laugh. 'We've lots to do yet, lad.'

Ethan was confused. 'What are you talking about?' he asked. 'The train run was successful.'

'Yes, but it's not going to stop there!' replied Bob, looking at Eddie and rolling his eyes. 'These youngsters don't have much vision these days, do they?'

'Don't we?' said Ryan, as he sat down to join them. 'I think my successful coffee shop and pizza takeout service should cast any of your doubts aside.'

Bob waved his eldest son's comment away with his hand. 'We were talking about the train,' he said.

Ethan instantly took a deep intake of breath. He recognised that expression on his dad's face. It held the familiar sense of determination and obsession which only revealed itself when the train was being discussed. He exchanged a nervous look with his brother, who only gave a bewildered shrug of his shoulders in response.

'But we did it,' said Ethan in a faltering voice. 'You both did it. The steam engine ran successfully.'

So what came next? he wondered.

'We've had a little chat,' said Bob, glancing at Eddie, who gave him a nod. 'And we reckon we're ready for the next phase.'

'The next phase?' asked Ryan tentatively.

'Paying passengers!' announced Bob.

There was a slight pause at the table as Ethan and Ryan both leaned forward at the same time with a shocked look on their faces.

'Passengers?' murmured Ryan.

Ethan stared at his dad. 'What do you mean? You're not seriously thinking about taking out those old carriages at some point, are you?' he asked, flabbergasted.

Two old train carriages had been renovated and upgraded into Airbnb accommodation over the previous winter, to much success. However, there were two more large carriages still in the workshop, but they had never been touched as the steam engine had taken up the main restoration.

'Of course we want to hook up the spare carriages,' said his dad, beaming.

'Then everyone can enjoy the ride,' added his grandad.

Ethan thought back to when he had last looked at the old pullman carriages properly. As far as he could remember, they still had their seats and were fully fitted, but they hadn't been used for a very long time.

'That's a lot of hard work to get them sorted,' he said, not wanting to upset his dad and grandad. 'Maybe by the new year...'

'Oh no, lad,' interrupted Eddie, shaking his head. 'We need it to be up and running sooner than that. Anyway, it's not like we're scared of a hard day's work.' He sighed. 'You see, I've always had a dream that I could see a Christmas train on the railway line again.'

'A Christmas train?' Ethan's eyebrows shot up in surprise.

His grandad gave him a watery smile. 'I went on one with your grandmother many years ago. I'd love to see it run from Cranfield again. So it's been our secret little goal, hasn't it, Bob?'

Ethan's dad nodded in agreement.

'So we reckon now that the steam engine's up and running, we can move on and get it ready in time for Christmas,' said Eddie.

Ethan exchanged a look of despair with his brother. It appeared that his dad and grandad had replaced one obsession with another.

'That's a big ask,' replied Ethan carefully, his mind running through the potential pitfalls and long to-do list.

'And you're going to need things like public liability insurance because it will involve people's health and safety,' said Ryan, who knew about all of this thanks to setting up the coffee shop.

'We know that,' said Bob, with a chortle. 'And we've already applied for the proper licences. We're just waiting for them to come through.'

'The carriages are in a bit of a mess though,' said Eddie, frowning. He looked at Ethan. 'But we were really hoping for an extra pair of hands to get them up and running, restoring the paintwork and the internal fixings. Plus the train itself needs a new coat of paint.'

'I've got to head off to America for work at the beginning of next month,' Ethan reminded them. The contract had already been delayed, but there was every expectation that he would be needed from the beginning of November. There was a huge new shopping mall that required his skills as lighting technician.

However, to his surprise, his dad and grandad didn't seem concerned about him leaving the country.

'Well, that might work out,' said Bob, nodding thoughtfully. 'Because we were thinking of a trial run on the last day of October in any case, so you could always help us with that instead.'

'This month?' spluttered Ethan.

'You mean for Halloween?' asked Ryan.

His dad and grandad gave a cry of disbelief. 'Oh! Why didn't we think of that!' said Eddie, looking at his son with delight. 'A Halloween-themed train!'

'It's a smashing idea,' replied Bob, beaming from ear to ear. 'It could be a real-life ghost train!'

'That'll get the punters in for miles around here!' said Eddie, clapping his hands in excitement. 'And that was the idea because we plan to raise money for a local charity.'

They both looked across at Ethan, smiling broadly.

'You'll help, won't you?' asked Bob.

'Er, of course,' said Ethan, running a hand through his hair.

What choice did he have? His dad had been through such a tough couple of years and with his grandad saying it was a life-long dream of his, he didn't want either of them taking on too much. And yet, he felt trapped into a corner.

'Don't you think the end of month date is perhaps a tad ambitious?' he asked in a soft tone.

But his dad and grandad were too busy looking at the calendar on their mobile phones. 'It's perfect,' Eddie was saying. 'Halloween actually falls on a Saturday this year.'

'So no worrying about the kids needing an early night because of school the next day,' replied Bob. 'So they can go trick or treating first.'

'Or we can set up something on the platform instead,' added Eddie, beaming.

Ethan blew out a long sigh. It looked as if he had some serious work to do before he headed off to America in four weeks' time.

He just needed to get everything in place before he left, he decided. Then he could leave everything in his dad and grandad's capable hands.

The trouble was, neither of them were getting any younger and it was a big task they had set themselves.

He looked at his brother, who looked equally concerned.

'I think I'd better get another round in,' said Ryan, collecting the empty pint glasses. 'Whilst you've still got time to drink it.'

## 9

The following evening, Libby headed up the stairs to the apartment above the station, armed with a bottle of her home-made gin cocktail and a large box of chocolates.

When the front door was opened, it was Ryan who was standing there.

'Good evening,' he said, letting her inside.

'Excuse me, this is supposed to be a girls' only space,' she told him, with a grin.

'You're half an hour early,' he replied, as she shrugged off her coat. 'Katy's still in the shower.'

Libby felt a little sheepish. The day had dragged at home, without work or being able to make any chocolate, and so she had decided to arrive for gin night a little bit earlier than usual.

Libby sniffed the air. 'Something smells delicious,' she said.

'It's my garlic bread,' said Ryan, leading her into the large lounge. 'Don't worry. There's enough for poker night with the boys, as well as you ladies.'

'Glad to hear it,' said Libby, licking her lips. She knew how good Ryan's cooking was.

She had known the Connolly brothers all of her life. Ryan was like a big brother, always looking out for her. Her relationship with Ethan was always destined to be more complicated. Perhaps because they were too alike, she thought.

Ryan's smile slipped as he placed another log onto the fire. 'How are you doing, Libs?' he asked, as he straightened back up. 'I heard about your job.'

'I'm fine,' she said automatically.

He stared at her in response until her shoulders sagged. 'Okay. I'm not fine,' she confessed. 'But I will be. It was just a bit of a shock, that's all.'

The shock was still reverberating around her daily life, she realised and she'd only been unemployed for two days. She hadn't slept well, tossing and turning, fretting about where the money was going to come from to support her and her dad. Then she had ended up finally falling asleep at five o'clock in the morning and oversleeping. This upset her dad with his routine as she was having her breakfast when he was usually in the kitchen alone with his radio and the daily crossword in his newspaper.

It hadn't been the best of starts to Libby's new life being full-time back at home. Her dad hadn't said anything further about her losing the job but she was sure that he must have been disappointed in her.

'Will you go for another flight attendant job?' asked Ryan.

'If any come up,' she replied.

But the thought didn't bring her joy. Over the years, she had slowly begun to shut herself away from the parties and socialising that most of the crew enjoyed when they reached their destination. In fact, she had actually become what the rest of the staff called a 'slam clicker' on layovers, which meant that she would shut the hotel door when she arrived and didn't see any fellow crew members until they were ready to fly again.

In a way, it was the best part of the whole trip. This was her selfish time, where she could curl up and research bean to bar recipes and dream up new chocolate flavours. Sometimes, if they had landed in the right place, she would spend her free time looking around the local food scene to get ideas for different flavours, such as sweet nutmeg whilst wandering through the souks of Marrakech or dark rum when she was staying in Jamaica.

The thought of going back to work on an airplane depressed her however necessary it may be for her bank balance. But what choice did she have?

Katy suddenly appeared from their bedroom, wrapped only in a large bath towel.

'Tell me I'm amazing!' she announced with a huge smile on her face as she waved her mobile at them both.

'Do I have to?' asked Libby, rolling her eyes.

'I will if she won't,' said Ryan, leaning forward to kiss his girl-friend's lips.

'Mmm,' said Katy, giving Ryan a wink. 'But you already knew that, didn't you?'

Ryan leant back with a grin. 'So what have you thought up this time and how much work is going to be added to my already hectic schedule?' he murmured.

'Actually, this time it's all about Libby,' said Katy, turning to face her.

Libby gave a start. 'Me?' she said. 'What about me?'

Katy nodded. 'Well, I got to thinking about your delicious chocolate truffles,' she began.

'Right,' said Libby slowly, wondering where this was going. 'Is this about putting more chocolate in the coffee shop?'

'Actually, that's not a bad idea, but this was more about

making a living from your chocolate,' carried on Katy. 'So I think the best idea is that you upscale your business.'

'Upscale?' Libby blinked rapidly. 'I don't think you've got the space here, have you?'

'Unless you want to work outside,' said Ryan, glancing at the tiny corner kitchen. 'But you know that we'll support you no matter what.'

'Of course,' said Katy, nodding. 'But the amount of chocolates you need to produce probably wouldn't even fit in the old ticket office, to be honest.'

'What are you talking about?' asked Libby, completely nonplussed.

'If you're going to start a new business, you need a big client to start you off, don't you?' said Katy.

'Er, yes, I guess,' said Libby, exchanging a nervous look with Ryan.

'So I've been putting out a few feelers and I've come up trumps!' announced Katy. 'One of the hotel chains that I used to work for has just opened up a brand new swanky place on the other side of Aldwych. So I went to see the manager yesterday and it turned out to be someone I used to work with! Small world, eh? Anyway, bookings are still a little slow, so they're looking to add a few special touches, which is where you come in.'

Libby finally caught up. 'So you need me to make up a couple of boxes of truffles for them?' she asked.

That was doable, she thought. It would only take her a day or so.

But Katy shook her head. 'They've got a party for some local corporate players around Bonfire Night. There's going to be fireworks and loads of promotions apparently.' Katy broke into a winning smile. 'And here's the exciting news – on my recommendation, every guest gets a goody bag filled with some of Harriet's delicious products and your chocolate too!'

'Right,' said Libby, surprised. 'Well, thanks.' She smiled at her friend. 'That really will help me out a lot. So what do they want – truffles, bars?'

'Actually I gave them that spare box you brought round on our last gin night a few weeks ago,' replied Katy.

'You mean this?' asked Libby, holding out the box she had brought with her. It was the largest box that she produced, holding ten chocolates. The range of flavours included sea salt and caramel, alongside tangy raspberry, nutty pecan and even a zingy chilli dark truffle.

'That's it!' said Katy. 'Having tasted them yesterday, my contact was absolutely raving about it! Give them organic and fairtrade and they're over the moon. All with a special wrapper or box or whatever you think. We can work out those details later. Anyway, the main thing is that my contact loved the idea. So did everyone in his office! A fight almost broke out to get the last truffle! Honestly, you've got such a talent.'

'Thanks.' Libby was still reeling as she tried to work out what it meant for her. 'So this party is on the fifth of November?' she asked.

Katy nodded. 'To be held in their enormous ballroom to accommodate the many guests.'

'And how many boxes do I need to produce?' asked Libby.

There was a month to go, long enough to produce one hundred boxes of quality truffles. It would be hard work, but she was feeling excited at what it might lead to for her future business.

'How many boxes?' Katy glanced at her phone to check before looking back up. 'Five hundred.'

Libby wondered whether she had heard wrong. 'How many?' she asked, looking at her friend.

'Five hundred,' repeated Katy. 'They've put feelers out for loads of people in the area and—'

'Five hundred boxes!' exploded Libby. 'Each holding ten chocolates, is that right? That's five thousand truffles! I can't possibly make that many in time!'

'Of course you can,' said Katy in a soothing tone.

Libby was horrified and turned to look at Ryan.

'Don't bother,' he told her with a soft smile. 'I've found that whenever she's got one of her business heads on, you've got to just roll with it. Turns out she's got a good gut instinct for this kind of thing.'

From the coffee shop to the glamping site, normally Libby would agree with him, but this time, she reckoned Katy was way off base. She found she was shaking her head furiously. 'I can't,' she said, feeling the panic rising inside of her.

'Look, this is a great start for your business,' said Katy, reaching out to give her arm a squeeze. 'And wouldn't it be wonderful if you could do that for a living instead?'

'Of course,' said Libby.

It had been her dream for so long.

Perhaps, despite the tight deadline, there was something else now. Hope. That she might just be able to make a go of it.

## 10

Libby was still reeling from Katy's mad business idea. Could she really make five hundred boxes of chocolates in just under four weeks? Could she produce five thousand truffles, entirely from scratch, in that length of time?

For a second, she found herself thinking that if she knuckled down to some serious hard work, perhaps she could. Perhaps this time luck might be on her side.

But as her friend stepped back from giving her an enormous hug, Libby looked over at the tiny kitchen in the apartment once more and was suddenly struck with horror.

'I can't! I just can't accept the order,' she said, her heart plummeting as her dream sank as quickly as it had almost become reality. 'You'll have to say no.'

Katy looked at her with wide eyes. 'What are you talking about?' she asked. 'Why not?'

'Because I can't create chocolate on an industrial scale at home,' Libby told her. 'You know the size of the kitchen. It's not much bigger than yours. And then there's Dad. He doesn't even know that I make it and I can't upset him. There's just not enough time when he barely leaves the house...' Her voice trailed off. Well, the dream had been nice while it lasted, she thought.

Katy frowned. 'Give me a minute,' she said, tapping her chin in thought. 'There must be a solution.' She looked up at Ryan. 'Can you think of anywhere?'

He blew out a sigh. 'That's got a kitchen big enough to upscale Libby's business? What about the farmhouse? You know that Grams wouldn't mind.'

But Libby shook her head. 'It's always so busy over there, with Flora, Nico and Grams living there now. Besides, I'd only be in the way. No, I need somewhere empty. Or at least, a big kitchen owned by someone who doesn't like cooking!'

It was a joke, but as soon as she'd finished talking, Katy broke into a wide smile. 'I've got it,' she said, with a nod.

'Where?' asked Ryan, looking at his girlfriend in amazement.

'Your brother's new home,' she told him with a smile.

Libby gave a start as her friend's words sank in. 'Brother?' she gasped. 'As in Ethan? No way. No way on earth!'

'Think about it,' said Katy quickly. 'It's the only kitchen big enough in Cranfield. And it belongs to Ethan! He showed us around last night. It's huge and everything is brand new!'

Ryan was nodding along. 'Seriously, it's my dream kitchen,' he told her. 'It's amazing.'

'Yes, but it belongs to Ethan,' Libby told them slowly, trying to make her friends see the huge problem.

'You know, he's going to be crazy busy with this Halloween train idea,' added Ryan. 'They've got loads to do to get the train and carriages ready, so he's bound to be out a lot of the time.'

'Not helping,' muttered Libby, shooting him a scowl. 'I thought you were on my side.'

'I am, Libs,' said Ryan, looking at her with a soft smile. 'And I can assure you that my little brother won't be using that lovely kitchen at all, apart from the kettle and the toaster.'

'And that's still too much for my liking,' she replied.

'Do you want the business?' asked Katy, putting her hands on her hips and looking stern. 'Do you want to try to make a go of making your chocolates as a job? I thought this was your dream.'

'Of course it is,' Libby told her.

Katy stared at her for a moment before drawing out her phone. 'Then let's see if this might sway your mind,' she said, swiftly typing a message.

Libby's phone lit up. 'What's this?' she asked, looking at the text.

'It's the agreement that the hotel forwarded onto me last night,' replied Katy. 'Scroll down to that big number at the bottom.'

Libby did as instructed, somewhat confused by all the legal mumbo-jumbo until she saw the figure that Katy was talking about. She blinked and peered closer at her phone. No, she wasn't seeing things. That figure after the £ sign was as big as she thought it was.

'Wow,' she said, blowing out a big sigh.

Ryan leaned over her shoulder and let out a long whistle. 'Definitely wow,' he said. 'You can't give up that kind of money.'

It was a lot, she thought. Enough to keep her and her dad's bills paid up until the new year. Maybe even beyond that.

Katy smiled at her. 'Good job I've already agreed on your behalf. And I've just registered you as an official food business with the local council so you've got no excuses now!'

Katy was laughing as she drew her into a warm hug.

Libby relished her friend's embrace, but all the time she was wondering how on earth she was going to produce so many chocolate truffles in time for the deadline.

'Besides, what other job options do you have?' Katy carried on, when she stepped back.

And that was the problem, thought Libby. There was no other choice. She was literally stuck between a rock and a hard place. And she could see no way out of her predicament other than asking Ethan for a really huge favour.

And that was the worst problem of all.

## 11

Ethan woke up and, for a moment, wondered where on earth he was.

The unfamiliar surroundings soon took hold when he remembered that he was in the old schoolhouse.

Of course, it didn't exactly feel like a home yet, despite having had a few pieces of furniture delivered the previous day, such as a proper bed and a couple of sofas. Apart from that, he had quite a few boxes that he had finally brought out of storage a year after selling his apartment in Hong Kong.

In a way, it was nice to finally have a place of his own again, he realised. He had been living out of a suitcase for so long that it was good to put down some roots. Not that Cranfield would be a forever place as far as he was concerned. There were just too many bad memories hovering around every corner.

The apartment above the station where Ryan and Katy now lived was warm and welcoming, but it had been the family home when he was growing up and would forever be tainted with the past. His mum nagging his father over and over, all the time whilst young Ethan knew that she was seeing another man. Or men, plural, as it turned out.

He swiftly spun his legs out of bed, wanting to dismiss all thoughts of his mum and the past. They spoke occasionally and he was pleased that she was happy at last. But he would always put up invisible defences whenever he spoke to her, nervous of getting too close or hearing any more of her lies.

He sighed, shaking his head to wake himself up, and looked around. The school had always been small as it had only served a couple of the local villages. But it at least held happy memories for him.

There had originally been two classrooms when it was built in the Victorian era – one for boys and girls. Of course, by the time he had attended the school all that had changed. He smiled to himself as he remembered his early years, messing about with Ryan, who had been a couple of years older, as well as Libby and Flora. They were happy innocent days, that he could look back on fondly.

The classroom he had chosen for his bedroom was large and even with his order for a couple of wardrobes and other pieces of furniture, it would still be plenty big enough. Thankfully, the renovations completed by the previous owner had got as far as the en suite bathroom, with a huge bath and walk-in shower.

Ethan gave a shiver in the cool morning air. Getting the chimneys swept was high on his priority list, along with a new front door and, most importantly, a new electric circuit board. He was hoping there wouldn't be too much else to do. His spur-of-the moment decision to buy the old school would quickly turn into a money pit if he wasn't careful.

He quickly got dressed into jeans and a sweatshirt before making the bed and heading into the other half of the school, which was the living quarters. He crossed the floor, which was new oak boards, already sanded and waxed. The lounge area had a large fireplace, as did the small room on the other side. It was the old headmaster's study, which overlooked the railway line. It was a reasonable size and he was hoping to use it as his own workplace when he had finally unpacked.

The only other room was the oversized kitchen. He supposed at one time it had been used to feed all the school children, but it was excessive for his own needs. He could rustle up cheese on toast, but beyond that, Ryan was the brother blessed with all the culinary skills. Ethan possessed pretty much none.

The kitchen had also been renovated by the previous owner. It still needed a proper deep clean after all the time lying empty over the summer, but now that he had had a large modern fridge-freezer delivered, at least he had somewhere to keep the milk. The only thing that he needed to replace was the old stove, which the previous owner appeared to have wanted to keep for character. Whereas Ethan just thought it ugly and would be buying something far more modern as soon as he could.

He wandered over to his expensive but much-needed coffee machine and flicked it on, staring out of the back window. The view beyond the back railings was of the railway line and then onto the fields beyond.

But it was the railway line that caught his attention. He was still reeling from the idea that the steam engine and carriages would be up and running for passengers by Halloween. Then there was his grandad's dream of a Christmas-themed train. Ethan would be long gone by then and for a moment he wondered who would be helping out his dad and grandad with the train. Christmas was a super busy time and Ryan would be flat out in the restaurant. Besides, his brother didn't have the engineering skills required.

Ethan knew that the answer was staring him in the face. He

should be the one to help them out, but that meant staying in Cranfield and he couldn't face that. His plan, as always, was to head off as soon as he could, despite now having a home in the village.

On the plus side, at least while he was around, he could enjoy a few more poker nights with Ryan, Joe and Nico. He had enjoyed the boys' night the previous evening, despite only winning one hand of cards and it had reminded him of the pleasure of having real friends who knew him so well. Mostly working on the road for a living and staying overnight in hotels, he hadn't developed any close relationships outside of the village.

He was about to make himself a coffee when there was a knock on the front door.

Running a hand through his messy blonde hair, he headed to the hallway and wrenched open the front door that still needed replacing.

There, to his surprise, he found Libby on the other side.

'Good morning,' he said, raising his eyebrows at her. 'I'm surprised you knocked on the door. Last time you just barged into the place and cracked me over the head.'

'Good job there's no brain in there to speak of then,' she told him. 'Come on. Let me in. It's freezing out here.'

The temperature had dropped overnight and the northerly wind was whistling down Railway Lane and into the hallway.

Ethan stepped aside and gestured for her to step over the threshold. He wondered what on earth had been so important that Libby had needed to visit him.

Intrigued, he closed the front door behind her.

## 12

Libby stepped inside the schoolhouse, trying to act in front of Ethan as if she didn't have a care in the world, whereas the truth was vastly different and she actually felt hugely nervous.

This was a ridiculous idea, she told herself. Asking Ethan, of all people, for a favour.

But Katy's words ran through her mind. What choice did she have? If she wanted to take on the huge order for her chocolate truffles, then he was the only person she knew with a big enough kitchen where she could make them.

So she gave herself a little shake and concentrated on the inside of the school. She hadn't seen it in the daylight for many years, only in complete darkness when she had charged inside mistaking him for a burglar a few days before.

In the daytime, the tall windows at the front flooded the two large rooms with sunlight and it had a completely different feel. It felt both familiar as her old school and yet completely different now that it had been updated.

Looking right, she could see a bed and an awful lot of boxes and so turned left instead and found herself in a room with high ceilings and yet more unpacked boxes surrounding a sofa.

'Is this our old classroom?' she asked, staring around, trying to remember how it looked with all the desks lined up.

Now empty apart from the sofas, it was a large room, with an equally large fireplace. The walls were a plain white, but it had a warm and airy feel to it. When it was finally dressed with furniture and a roaring fire, it would be truly lovely, she thought.

She looked back at Ethan, who nodded. 'We spent many happy days messing around and not taking our lessons seriously in here, didn't we?' he remarked.

'Some of us have still retained that attitude,' she replied in a pointed tone.

'Some of us still don't care,' he told her with a grin. 'So are you here for a trip down memory lane, because if you are, I just want to reassure you that I haven't forgotten anything.'

For a second, the air in the room went heavy and Libby found herself gulping before swiftly pulling herself together.

'Nor have I because I can still remember you pulling on my pigtails all the time,' she told him. 'So, are you going to offer me a coffee as I'm a guest in your home?'

'An uninvited one, but yes, as it happens, the coffee machine is on,' he replied, walking towards a doorway in the far wall.

Libby walked across the lounge, noting the new leather sofas, as well as a book on steam locomotives. Ethan had always been interested in fixing anything with an engine for as far back as she could remember from their classes. She hadn't enjoyed any of her lessons, except cooking. But he had always been able to help make her smile with his jokes. She missed being friends, but their shared history was far too complicated for them to become close once more.

She followed Ethan through the doorway and found herself

in a large kitchen. It was even bigger than Ryan and Katy had said. The footprint alone was almost the same as the whole of her cottage.

The units were laid out in a U-shape on three sides. On the fourth wall were a couple of doors, one of which was the back door leading out into the small paved area which led to the railway lane through a small gate. The other, presumably to some kind of cupboard. In the middle of the room was a large central unit, covered with boxes.

She walked around, taking it all in. At some point, the original units had been replaced by ones with modern oak doors. In the fireplace, she could see what appeared to be a large vintage oven. The oak flooring was the same as the remainder of the house, as were the high ceilings.

'Latte?' asked Ethan, standing next to a modern and extremely expensive-looking coffee machine.

'Yes, please,' she replied. All the appliances appeared to be new, apart from the old oven.

'What's in there?' she asked, nodding at the second door.

'See for yourself,' he replied, picking up one full coffee mug and replacing it with an empty one.

As he pressed the buttons on the machine, Libby headed over and opened up the door. It led into what must have been the old pantry. It too had been painted white and stacked with plenty of long oak shelves. It was the perfect cool temperature for storing, for example, boxes of ready made chocolate, she immediately thought.

She closed the door and looked around once more at the kitchen, feeling a pit of excitement in her stomach. It needed a good clean and disinfectant, but it was perfect. Absolutely perfect for her needs to upscale her chocolate making temporarily.

Ethan was giving her a knowing look as he handed over a mug of coffee.

'What?' she asked.

'Much as I appreciate the house call, what's all this about, Libby?' he said, leaning against the worktop and studying her as he sipped his coffee. 'After all, you've barely said more than ten words to me in as many years.'

'Okay,' she said, putting down her coffee and taking a deep breath. 'I need a favour.'

He looked surprised but pleased. 'Of course,' he replied, after a beat. 'Anything for my dear wife.'

Libby took a sharp intake of breath and quickly looked around. Luckily, there was nobody else about. 'I thought we'd agreed that we would never mention that ever again,' she finally said, blushing.

To her frustration, he smiled as he shook his head. 'Nope. I don't recall you saying anything about that after you had literally run out of my hotel room the following morning. And we've never talked about it since.'

'Well, let's not start now,' she said, still feeling how warm her cheeks were. This was not how the conversation needed to happen and she tried to claw back control. 'Well, this favour I require from you is in no way to be accepted by you as a sign that I like you,' she carried on. 'I want you to bear that in mind. In fact, I insist on it.'

'You can insist all you like,' he finally said, his eyes glittering with humour. 'But until I know what it is that you need from me, I won't commit to anything.'

'Nothing new there then,' she retorted.

It had been meant as a joke, but at once, the memory of their getting married in a wedding chapel rushed to the front of her mind. And as she looked into Ethan's blue eyes, she knew that he was thinking about exactly the same thing. That one night eight years ago, they had committed themselves to each other.

Her cheeks beginning to grow even warmer, she pressed on, trying to maintain control. 'It's Katy's fault,' she began. 'Although I love her dearly. She was trying to help me out and has managed to get me a huge order for my chocolate truffles. It's good money. Great, in fact, and would really help me out now that I'm out of a job. The trouble is, it's a ridiculously large order to be made in a very short space of time. By Bonfire Night, in fact.'

'I see,' said Ethan, nodding thoughtfully. 'And you've come here to, what? Ask for my assistance because you remember how good I was in Home Economics?'

She rolled her eyes. 'All I remember is you stealing my perfect chocolate soufflé, passing it off as your own and getting an A for that particular assignment.'

He grinned. 'Oh yeah. I'd forgotten about that. So what did my effort get you?'

'A fail because it had sunk without a trace,' she said, scowling at him. 'So, no thank you. I most certainly do not want you as my catering assistant.'

'So what do you want?' he asked.

She took a deep breath. 'Your kitchen,' she told him.

Ethan couldn't have looked more surprised, she realised as she watched his blue eyes widen. '*My* kitchen?' he said, staring around.

'It's the perfect size,' she told him, feeling desperate. 'I can clean it and get it up to health and safety standards. But it's the space that I really need. Nowhere else has this much surface area, let alone a pantry where I can store stuff.' She hesitated. 'My kitchen is tiny and, erm, the situation's a bit complicated with Dad.'

'I see.' Ethan dragged a hand through his hair. 'How do you imagine this is going to work?'

'I don't know,' she told him honestly. 'It's only for just under four weeks.'

He nodded thoughtfully to himself before saying, 'During which time I'll be busy with getting the steam train up and running for this ridiculous Halloween thing that Dad and Grandad want to do.'

'In which case, I'll be here during working hours and then I'll disappear off so we don't even need to see each other,' she said, suddenly feeling somewhat hopeful that this crazy idea might just work.

'You mean I won't have the pleasure of hearing your soft and dulcet tones each and every day?' he asked, smiling.

'No,' she replied.

For a second, she wondered whether he would just make a joke and refuse her. After all, she was asking to use his home and it was a huge invasion of his privacy. But she was desperate for the money. Plus, a small part of her wanted to see if her business venture had any potential to earn her a living. She wondered whether she should confess as much to him.

But when she looked up, she found him studying her with a serious look in his eyes. 'Well, seeing as I'm going to get nothing but a clean kitchen out of the deal,' he finally said, breaking into the silence. 'How can I possibly say no?'

Libby blew out a sigh as her shoulders finally relaxed. 'Thank you,' she said, her shaky voice betraying her and showing just how much it meant to her.

'Let me dig you out a spare front door key and you can come and go as you like,' he said.

'Okay,' she told him, nodding. She was both surprised but pleased by the offer. Although having her own key would certainly make things easier than hanging around waiting for Ethan to show up to let her in each time. This way, she might not even have to bump into him.

She realised that he was still studying her and, as it had always been with him, it felt as if Ethan could see into her very soul.

Libby drew herself up to as high as her short height would allow before hesitating. 'This isn't going to be weird, is it?' she asked. 'Us being around each other?'

He shook his head and grinned at her. 'Of course not,' he told her.

However, deep down Libby knew the truth. It wouldn't be weird at all. It was going to be terribly, incredibly, horribly awkward.

But what choice did she have?

## 13

Libby asking for a favour had been surprising enough, thought Ethan after she had left. But her wanting to use his kitchen had been downright startling.

She had always given him the impression that to spend any length of time with him was out of the question and had been for years. Ever since their drunken nuptials in Las Vegas eight years ago, in fact.

Having more questions than answers about what had changed, he shrugged on a jacket and went along to Platform 1. There, Ryan and Katy confirmed what he hadn't let on to Libby about his suspicions. That she must have been desperate to ask him for anything in the first place.

Katy quietly confirmed that money was pretty tight for Libby as she tried to support both herself and her father after losing her job. He was proud of the way that she had stepped up to help out her father, despite the rocky relationship they had endured for so many years.

Katy had made him promise not to let on to Libby that he knew how bad things were and he had readily agreed. He knew how proud she was, perhaps more so than anyone he had ever known. She had always been like that, ever since he could remember. Never asking for help. Never letting on how much pain she was in. Only he had been able to get her to open up in their teenage years, despite Flora and Harriet, her closest friends back then, guessing the truth as to how much the strained relationship with her father had upset her. And she was still the same all these years later.

In a small way, he found that he was pleased that she had come to him for help. Perhaps at last he could start to make amends for letting her down at the prom and then suggesting they get married when they had been so drunk.

When she turned up that afternoon with bags of various cleaning materials, he made them both a coffee and then enjoyed watching her stride around the kitchen, that long pale hair of hers swinging behind her in a ponytail as she worked.

He had always been mesmerised by her hair. In fact, by all of her, for as long as he could remember. Pale soft skin that was so clear. Those blue eyes which flicked at him with such distrust and sarcasm these days. Only once since school had they looked at him any differently and that had been when he had finally held her in his arms that one night after they had married.

Once more feeling regret as to how things had worked out between them, he knew that he had lots to make up for and the loan of his kitchen for a few weeks was the very least that he could do.

'So, will it work?' Ethan asked, watching her open up various cupboards and close them again before feeling along the oak work surface.

She nodded slowly, deep in thought. 'I think so,' she said.

He gave a slight shiver. 'It's a bit cool though. As soon as I get the boiler serviced, it should warm up in here.'

But, to his surprise, Libby shook her head. 'Actually I'll work better in a cooler atmosphere. Not too cool, though.' She opened up the pantry and held up an app on her phone which appeared to be a temperature gauge. 'That's ideal,' she said, over her shoulder. 'Ideally storage should be between fifteen and eighteen degrees. Not so humid. And with these thick brick walls, I'll be able to store everything in here safely.' She frowned. 'Hopefully there aren't any mice in here.'

'Maybe I need the company,' he replied.

'Well, you always did have low expectations with the people you hung out with,' she told him.

'You're telling me,' he said, breaking into a grin.

'I was the exception,' she replied in a lofty tone, but she couldn't help shooting him a grin.

'To every rule,' he drawled.

She pretended to ignore him. 'Yes, this will do nicely.' She gave a firm nod. 'For once, you've exceeded my expectations and actually pleased me for a change.'

'Well, I've always known how to please a woman,' he told her.

He enjoyed watching her blush as she obviously battled the memories that they both shared of their night together.

Perhaps he had pushed it a bit too far, he thought, and made her uncomfortable. But just as he was walking out to the lounge to give her a bit of space, he heard her call out his name.

Ethan spun around and watched as she shuffled from foot to foot awkwardly. Eventually, she looked up at him.

'Thanks,' she muttered, giving him a sheepish look through thick dark eyelashes.

'You're welcome,' he replied. 'But just remember that this is my home, my rules and that I'm in charge, okay?'

Her beautiful face lit up into laughter. 'In your dreams,

Connolly!' she said, turning away but not before he caught her smile.

He too was smiling as he walked away. Perhaps it wouldn't be awkward, Ethan thought. But then he remembered how pleased he was to make her laugh again. It would be fine. He was just doing an old friend a favour. That was all, wasn't it?

# 14

Bright and early the following morning, Libby arrived at Ethan's home. She was anxious to finish cleaning the kitchen so that she could begin making inroads into the huge order of chocolates that Katy had found for her.

She was truly grateful for the money she would receive when the order was complete, but the sheer scale of work required was almost overwhelming.

She reminded herself it was all in the mind and that positive mental attitude would win through. But a tiny voice inside asked her how would she ever be able to make and pack five thousand chocolate truffles, all of different flavours, in less than a month? She tried to ignore it.

In any case, she wouldn't be able to do anything until the kitchen was absolutely spotless.

'Good morning,' said Ethan, opening the door with a yawn.

'Up partying all night again?' she asked, brushing past him.

'You know me, Libs,' he replied. 'I'd go to the opening of a barn door if there was a party afterwards.'

She looked at him. 'Are you at home all day today?' she asked.

He broke into a grin. 'Why? Are you concerned that I'll distract you with my devastating good looks?' He waggled his eyebrows at her.

In response, she shook her head. 'More like that you'll get under my feet when I'm trying to sanitise your kitchen.' She stalked ahead of him into the lounge.

'I suppose you want a coffee?' he asked, following behind her.

'Just show me how that fancy machine works,' she told him. 'And I might need a few extra mugs.'

'Are you inviting me to my own house-warming party?' he asked.

'Actually, it's a cleaning party,' she told him. 'I asked Flora to give me a hand as she had a free day.' She gave Ethan a sheepish look. 'I probably should have asked you first.'

There was a knock on the door in the hallway and Ethan looked at her. 'Probably, but at least I can trust Flora as the sensible one out of the two of you.'

He headed over to open up the front door and Libby spun round at the sound of a couple of familiar voices.

'Hiya,' said Flora, closely followed by Harriet. 'I found a pair of extra hands to help with the big clean-up.'

With a scrabble of paws, Paddington the dog rushed into the house.

'How good is he with a scrubbing brush?' asked Ethan, nodding at the golden retriever.

'Not as good as me,' said Harriet, with a grin, before staring around the room. 'Wow! I never saw inside this place before. I love those oak beams. It's really pretty.'

'I don't remember us saying that when we were stuck behind our desks,' said Flora, with a soft smile.

Libby and Flora had gone to school there, whereas Harriet had only ever visited Cranfield during the school holidays as her upper-class parents had insisted that she went to a private school, which she had absolutely loathed.

'Coffee?' asked Ethan, leading them all into the kitchen.

'Yes, please,' replied Flora.

'Oh, this will be perfect for you, Libby!' said Harriet, following him. 'It's huge!'

As Libby went behind her, she had to agree. But as she glanced at the large unit in the middle of the room, she gasped. 'Was this here all the time?' she asked, rushing up to the square island in the middle of the room and running her hand over the grey marble surface. She couldn't believe it and was almost mesmerised by how smooth it was under her fingers.

'Well, I didn't install it last night,' Ethan told her. 'I cleared it this morning as it had all my boxes of paperwork spread out everywhere. I figured you'd need the space. What's so special about marble anyway?'

'It's perfect for tempering chocolate,' she said, running her hand once more across the cool stone. She had dreamt of having a marble work surface for many years but had never had the opportunity. 'I normally have to use a machine instead.'

Once Ethan had showed them how the coffee machine worked, he said his goodbyes and left them to it.

'It's really lovely,' said Flora, running her hand over the oak work surface before staring at her palm in dismay. 'But you're right. It needs a really good clean or it'll never reach health and safety standards.'

'Absolutely,' said Libby.

'Right after I've enjoyed my coffee,' said Harriet, sipping her drink.

'No time,' said Libby. 'We'd better start cleaning this place or I'll never have time to make any chocolate.'

*And meet my deadline*, she added to herself in silent dread.

As they picked up the cleaning materials, Paddington the dog sprawled down on the floor to keep a watchful eye on them.

'By the way, I've told dad that I'm helping you out at the lavender spa, okay?' said Libby, looking at Harriet.

Harriet nodded. 'Of course.'

Libby had also had to tell her dad that Ethan had bought and moved into the empty schoolhouse. Her dad hadn't said anything in reply, merely silently nodded his head. Libby knew how much he missed teaching even though he never mentioned it.

She caught Harriet and Flora exchanging a look.

'Don't you think it's time for you to tell your dad about your chocolate making?' said Flora, in a soft tone. 'Isn't it time to be honest with him?'

Libby shook her head. 'Not now,' she said.

And perhaps not ever, she thought. The chocolate was too big a reminder of her mother's own skills and she couldn't bear to upset him any further.

Thankfully, Flora and Harriet were hard workers and so were able to concentrate on the task in hand. Pretty soon, the kitchen was starting to look a lot cleaner.

Naturally, it was accompanied by Harriet's only topic of choice, her wedding.

'No, I definitely don't want a vast wedding like my brothers and sister had,' said Harriet, giving an exaggerated shudder before she bent over to scrub the top of the vintage oven. 'Their weddings were so huge. And I just know my parents would invite all their fancy friends that would put me straight on edge. Joe and I just want everyone we love to be there and that's it. So we're happy with small and intimate.'

'Good job too, seeing as St Barnabus' Church only holds about sixty people at a push,' said Flora.

St Barnabus was the pretty but tiny church in Cranbridge, only a mile away.

'And Platform 1 will be perfect for our reception,' added Harriet, with a smile. 'It feels like home anyway. Although we don't want Ryan and Katy to have loads of extra work on that day. After all, they're best man and bridesmaid. Along with you two and Ethan, of course.'

'For a small wedding, you've got a lot of groomsmen and bridesmaids,' Flora told her, with a wink.

'Not sure Ethan is best at being anything,' added Libby, as she scrubbed the marble counter. It really was a revelation and she was itching to use it already.

'What about you and Ethan?' asked Harriet, frowning. 'Is this going to be okay with you being here? You've always gone on about how he ruined your prom, not that you've told us about it.'

Libby gave a shrug. 'It'll be fine. I can totally handle being here. It's just a business arrangement.'

She had definitely moved on and didn't need Ethan Connolly any longer. Just his kitchen.

So why did she feel so nervous all of a sudden?

She decided that the quicker she started making chocolate and lost herself in the process, the better.

She looked down at the marble surface once more. Perhaps it was a good sign. Perhaps it was a stroke of luck working in the old school. And perhaps she could put up with Ethan for the next three weeks too.

## 15

Despite appearing to be cool with it, Ethan had found that he was mesmerised by having Libby close by in his kitchen.

They had bumped into each other around Cranfield before now, of course. At various parties or even just grabbing a coffee from Platform 1. So he was used to seeing her around.

And yet, this was different. Closer. More personal, if anything, because she was in his home.

As he left Libby, Flora and Harriet cleaning his kitchen, he reminded himself that he had a very long to-do list to be completed over the next couple of weeks to keep both his mind and body occupied.

'Good morning,' he said to his dad as he headed inside the train workshop.

The steam engine was parked up inside the large hangar, away from the steady drizzle that was coming down. In the remaining space of the workshop, there were the two train carriages which his dad and grandad were so intent on getting renovated in time for the Halloween train run in a few short weeks.

'Morning, son,' replied Bob, poking his head out from behind a set of wheels underneath one of the carriages.

'How's it looking?' asked Ethan, going over to his dad to crouch down next to him.

'I reckon with a bit of grease, the mechanism should be all right,' said Bob, nodding.

'No bad rust?' said Ethan, running his hand over the metal.

'Not that I can see,' replied Bob.

Ethan was relieved that there was hope that the wheels might not have seized despite not being used for a couple of decades. 'Is grandad around?' asked Ethan.

'He had a bit of a lie-in this morning,' Bob told him. 'He'll be on his way shortly though.'

Ethan straightened up and looked along the length of the railway carriage and further to where the next one stood.

Long since abandoned when the train line had closed, they had remained in the same place for a couple of decades. Built in the 1950s, the classic green paint was a little faded but had still kept its shine. From the outside at least, they didn't appear to be in bad condition.

'I remember when these used to be full of people,' said Bob, coming to stand next to him.

'Let's hope they're up to the task now,' said Ethan, crouching down to peer at the underside of the carriage.

'At least they've been safe in here, away from whatever Mother Nature could throw at them,' remarked Bob, looking up at the windows.

Ethan straightened up and followed his gaze. A bit of new putty would help secure them in place, but who knew what other major renovations would be required.

'I guess we want to keep them feeling authentic,' said Bob as they walked towards the steps to the door at one end of the carriage.

'We want whatever it takes to keep the costs down,' commented Ethan.

They stepped cautiously inside the carriage, warily looking at the floor as they went. But to Ethan's surprise, and relief, it appeared to be pretty sturdy.

Immediately, it felt as if he were stepping back in time. It had such a different feel to the open, bright interiors of the modern day trains. Instead, a long corridor stretched out in front of him, half panelled with wood. On one side was a long line of outside windows. On the other were the doors to the individual seating compartments. Each one had two long upholstered benches facing each other. The cloth was the traditional British Railways blue checked design but, again, didn't appear too worn. Perhaps only being used on the short line into Aldwych, the wear and tear hadn't been too high.

'Good morning,' said Eddie, as he appeared at the end of the corridor, slightly out of breath.

'Morning, Grandad,' replied Ethan. 'We were just doing an inspection. Doesn't seem to be in too bad condition, although it'll need a proper once-over to ensure it's safe for everyone to come onboard.'

But his grandad didn't appear to be too concerned about the wear and tear as he looked into one of the compartments with misty eyes.

'Took your grandmother out for the day in a train just like this when we first started courting,' said Eddie, heading inside to sit down on one of the seats. 'I had big plans. It was almost Christmas and the snow was beginning to come down. We weren't sure we were even going to make it home from Aldwych if the snow began to pile up.'

'What happened?' asked Ethan. He had always enjoyed hearing about his grandparents' happy marriage, as opposed to his own parents' disastrous one.

'We made it, just,' said Eddie. 'And after everyone else had left the compartment, I made a big thing about having to tie my shoelace so I was already on one knee when I proposed to her.'

'Grandad, you're an old romantic,' Ethan told him.

Eddie nodded. 'That I am, lad. Or at least where your grandmother was concerned. I'm not a wine and roses kind of chap, but when it's true love you just know, don't you?'

'So that's why you're so set on getting the Christmas train up and running,' said Ethan, finally understanding.

Eddie sighed. 'I'd love one last journey in the snow. For old times' sake. I'd always dreamt of taking her out on a train on Christmas Eve.' His grey eyebrows knitted together into a frown. 'Too late now, of course. Time ran out and we didn't have the train ready before... you know, we lost her.'

Ethan felt a little choked up as he saw the grief etched on his grandad's face.

'Well, hopefully the Halloween train will be a good trial run for the future,' Ethan said softly.

He didn't want to disappoint his grandad, but there was still an awful lot of work to do before the thirty-first of October.

'Thanks, lad,' said Eddie, standing up and placing a hand on his grandson's shoulder. 'It would mean the world to me to see it one last time.' He nodded. 'Now, how about I put the kettle on?'

'Sounds good to me, Dad,' replied Bob.

As Eddie slowly climbed out of the railway carriage, Ethan took another look around. Of course, the seats would all need cleaning and the whole place would need a decent wax and polish. The main problem would be checking the rusty wheels to see if they all turned in unison.

But that wasn't his main concern.

He turned to look at his dad. 'Listen, are we really set on this Halloween train idea?' he asked in quiet tone. 'Because I'm not sure we can get all of this ready on time for the end of the month.'

Bob frowned. 'I know, son. It'll take a lot of work. But your grandad's set on it happening.' Bob hesitated before carrying on. 'He's been a bit tired recently. I thought that perhaps it might perk him up a bit.'

Ethan stepped forward to give him a brief hug. 'Okay, Dad,' he said. 'We'll do our best.'

Bob nodded. 'Course we will. We'll make it a Halloween to remember, eh?'

Ethan smiled and nodded along with his dad. But all the while he was just hoping it wasn't going to be for all the wrong reasons.

# 16

It took the whole afternoon until Libby felt that the kitchen in the old school was as clean as she was able to get it. It was more time out of the extremely tight schedule to complete the order and get paid, but she felt better when she arrived the following morning with all the boxes of cookware she had kept hidden away from her dad.

Of course, there was still the awkwardness of crossing paths with Ethan most days. But he seemed concerned with his own deadline as he explained about the idea for the Halloween train to Libby.

'Dad had the bright idea of it being some kind of ghost train, so it'll need to be suitably spooky,' he said, zipping up his jacket. He was wearing an old pair of jeans and sweatshirt, in deference to the cooler morning air. 'As well as actually being able to run a couple of carriages too,' he added, rolling his eyes.

'And they'll be paying passengers this time?' asked Libby.

Ethan nodded. 'Joe offered to help out with the marketing, so we've already got thirty people booked!' He frowned. 'How on earth we're going to get all this ready in time, I honestly have no idea. I've got my hands full just making sure that the whole thing runs safely.'

'Can you get any extra help?'

'I've blackmailed Joe and Nico to give us a hand with the carriages,' Ethan replied, glancing at his watch. 'Talking of which, I'd better get going as I'm meeting them there.' He hesitated before adding, 'Well, make yourself at home and all that.' He looked around at the now almost full kitchen, with every surface laden with bowls, measuring equipment and ingredients. 'What is all this stuff?' he asked, agog. 'I thought you just needed a mixing bowl and a wooden spoon.'

'This is everything needed to make a cocoa bean transform into delicious chocolate,' she told him, bending down to open up one of the sacks on the floor. She showed him the little nuggets of goodness.

'And that's a cocoa bean?' he said, picking one up before bringing it up to his mouth.

'Don't taste it yet!' she told him, laughing as she took it from his hand. 'They need roasting first!'

'Where did you get these from?' he asked.

'When I went to the plantation in Venezuela, I got their name and address. I would only ever order from a place with Fairtrade accreditation. It's fairer on the farmers and makes sure they get paid proper wage for their work harvesting.'

'I agree,' he said, nodding. 'So this lot has been shipped over from South America?'

'Yup,' she replied. 'Each country and area has its own unique flavour of cocoa bean, but I like these ones the best.'

He looked thoughtful. 'So, rather like a fine wine being made from a certain grape, you mean?'

She nodded. 'But rather than being crushed with your feet in a tub, the magic happens here instead.'

'And all this is magic?' he asked, looking at the many boxes around him.

Libby nodded. 'Absolutely. By the way, does that old oven actually work?'

'I think so,' he told her.

'Let's hope so,' she replied. 'I need it to roast the beans and then take their shells off. Then, the bit that's inside, called the nib, is ground into a thick paste using that fancy machine over there called a melanger.'

She involuntarily gulped. Before this week, she had used a tiny melanger but had spent the very last of her savings on a much larger one which should speed up the process. She was banking on getting the money back when she was paid by the hotel for the chocolate, but until then, things would be pretty tight.

Ethan looked confused. 'A melanger?'

'It grinds the nibs until it's liquid cocoa,' she told him. 'At that point, it just needs heating and cooling, or rather tempering and flavouring.'

'All that for one little truffle?' he asked, picking up one of the flat-pack boxes which she had ordered to place the truffles inside.

'I like to think mine are worth it once you taste them,' she said, in a proud tone. 'Besides, with my chocolate, I know every single ingredient and process that has happened to them from the moment that the cocoa bean is harvested. You can't say that about your mass-produced stuff.'

'And to think, you almost burnt down the physics lab when we were at school,' said Ethan with a sudden frown.

'The only thing I'll set on fire is your feet if you steal any truffles when they're made,' she warned him.

He grinned at her. 'And on that cautionary threat, I'll leave you to it. I've got two carriages to get renovated. See you later.'

'Only if I'm very unlucky,' she told him, before turning her back on him.

She decided that their back-and-forth banter was the only way that she would be able to get through the uncomfortable situation of having to use his kitchen. But she was pleased with the place now that it was cleaned, especially the marble counter on the centre island. It gleamed from many hours of polishing.

At least it now complied with the food hygiene regulations that she had learnt about online, in order to pass her inspection by the local officer. Katy had also helped Libby complete all the administration to set up as a self-employed business.

She glanced over at the large number of packets and small boxes on the far counter which would make up all the different flavours. There were sharp cranberries to contrast with a drizzle of sweet white chocolate, freeze dried orange pieces for a tangy bite in the darker chocolate and even bottles of champagne for a decadent tasting truffle.

Libby just hoped the hard work it was going to take to complete the contract would be worth it. Because she still had serious doubts that she would get five thousand truffles finished in time.

Feeling the pressure, she began to get everything ready.

# 17

Despite the pressure of working to an extremely tight deadline for the huge order for chocolate truffles, the first couple of days flew past for Libby. She was revelling in pure and utter enjoyment.

Working on making chocolate was a dream come true and she realised just how long she had been unhappy in her old job.

She felt especially proud when she passed the inspection from the local council with flying covers and was given the all clear to continue making chocolate as a business.

Best of all was the knowledge that she had control over the whole process, from bean to truffle.

The old oven, despite being a little tricky to figure out at first, turned out to be perfect for roasting the cocoa beans so that the nibs at their heart could be isolated. They were so rich in cocoa solids and cocoa butter that she had to stop herself from eating too many after they had been roasted.

Her expensive purchase of the melanger had also been a success as it easily ground out much larger amounts of the nibs than she had ever been able to do before. It sped up the long process, although there was still so much to do.

But the piece de resistance was the marble work surface on the central island of the kitchen. Once the nibs had been melted into liquid cocoa in a saucepan, she was able to pour the melted chocolate onto the cool marble and begin to work it back and forth until it started to thicken.

She would lose all track of time at that point, relishing the process that was the most traditional and had been around for so long. It was an amazing feeling to keep the older skills and artistry alive.

In fact, she enjoyed it so much that late one afternoon, she didn't even hear Ethan come in. It wasn't until he clicked on the overhead lights that she realised how dark it had become as the nights began to draw in.

'You don't use a bowl?' he asked, indicating the spread of chocolate all across the marble work surface.

She shook her head and carried on working her spatula back and forth, taking the melted chocolate with it. 'Not for tempering,' she told him. 'I need to cool it down before heating it back up again.'

'Why?' he asked, looking completely non-plussed.

'Because it will make it into the silky wonder that my chocolate is,' she replied. She took a nearby piece of greaseproof paper and scraped a small amount of chocolate onto it. 'See how shiny it is? That's what tempering does.'

'And I thought I was the only engineer around here,' he told her.

'What are you doing back so early anyway?' she asked.

His eyebrows shot up in surprise. 'It's six o'clock, Libs,' he told her.

She looked at him aghast. 'Six o'clock? Already?' She couldn't believe it. She glanced to the window and could see the inky black dark of the evening outside. 'I had no idea,' she said, looking back down to the chocolate she had been working.

To her dismay, it had bloomed. She groaned out loud.

'What's the matter?' he asked.

She sighed heavily. 'The chocolate has bloomed. See those white bits? I'll have to do it all over again.'

'In the morning, though?' he said. 'You look done in. You should go home and get some rest.'

Her eyes strayed to the large amount of flat-pack boxes not yet made up and empty of truffles. Time was marching on and she was so behind. Another day had passed and she didn't feel as if she had progressed as much as she had hoped.

'I should really carry on,' she said out loud, to herself more than Ethan. She then felt a bit sheepish. 'Sorry. I know it's your home and I'm taking over.'

'You know I don't care about that,' he told her, with a shrug. 'But I care about you looking whiter than that marble surface in front of you. Listen, have you thought about asking your friends for help?'

She immediately shook her head. 'They're all so busy. Besides, I'll be fine,' she said.

Ethan rolled his eyes. 'No surprise there,' he muttered.

It was one of her many failings, she knew. She never liked to show anyone that she wasn't in control. Besides, nobody else could make chocolate like she could.

The fact that Ethan also knew of the protective wall that she had built around herself for so many years reminded her of how close they had once been.

'What about your dad? Where does he think you are each day?'

'He thinks I'm helping out Harriet at the lavender spa,' she told him, avoiding eye contact. 'But I guess I'd better head home as it's getting late.'

'And because you look tired.'

She automatically shook her head. 'I'm fine,' she said quickly. 'Anyway, it's only five thousand truffles!' She felt the dull pit of anxiety as she said the huge number out loud.

'Listen,' he told her, coming around to stand next to her. 'I know you well enough to tell when you need to stop and I'm telling you right now that it's time. Stop.'

'You can't tell me what to do,' she said, fighting the fatigue which suddenly ran through every bone in her body.

'Turns out, yeah, I can,' he said softly.

To her surprise, he reached out and stroked her face. For a second, she was lost in his gaze, those blue eyes that she knew so well. Did he still care for her? Did he feel that they had unresolved business like she did? Like she had always done?

As he pulled his fingers away, she saw that they were covered in chocolate. She must have smeared her cheek at some point when she was working.

'Occupational hazard,' she muttered.

He smiled. 'Yeah, but what a way to go,' he told her.

They stared at each other for a moment more before she came to her senses. This was Ethan. Ethan who had walked out on her at the prom. Ethan who had married her and never talked about it. Ethan who had broken her heart just when she had needed him the most.

'Well, perhaps you're right,' she said. 'I should head home.'

'When have I ever been wrong?' he replied, with a smug smile.

'I lost count when it hit double figures,' she told him, before glancing around the chaotic kitchen. 'I'll tidy up before I go,' she said, aware that it was his home she was messing up.

'No need,' he told her. 'I'm going to pick up one of Ryan's pizzas so that'll be dinner sorted tonight.'

'Okay. Well, thanks.' She cleared her throat. 'Goodnight.'

'Goodnight, Libby.'

She grabbed her coat and headed out of the front door, but the fresh air did nothing to clear her muddled thoughts. She was trying so hard to hold Ethan at arm's length, to not get too close to him even though they'd been thrown together like this. But that was hard when he would stand so close to her that her pulse would thump and flutter in her throat.

It was nothing. She was just stressed, that was all.

And tired too, she had to admit.

But as Libby lay in bed that night, she tossed and turned, her mind still racing. Suddenly, she grabbed her phone and typed some numbers into the calculator app.

She had been making chocolate truffles for four days now. Okay, three, as she had lost one to cleaning Ethan's kitchen. And so far she had made the sum total of three hundred. By her calculations, she had to seriously up her game. There were twenty-two days left before her deadline. That meant she ought to be making over two hundred truffles a day!

Her eyes clicked wide open as she stared at her phone screen. Two hundred truffles a day! And even making that many meant that she would have to work seven days a week.

She couldn't do it, was her first thought.

But she had to, was her second thought.

The money was seriously good, and without a job, she and her dad needed the income. She just had to get faster, that was all.

Less enjoyment, more work, she told herself.

But it did nothing to stem the rising panic deep inside of her.

## 18

It felt to Ethan as if time had flown past and suddenly Halloween was less than a fortnight away. The trouble was, there was still an awful lot of chores left on his to-do list to ensure that everything would run smoothly for the passengers.

And there were going to be plenty of them, according to his friend Joe. Using his vast business experience, Joe had come up trumps with creating a website for the 'Cranfield Steam Train!' experience. He had also placed an advertisement in the *Cranbridge Times*, which had garnered quite a bit of excitement and the number of people promising to turn up was becoming quite daunting.

Having already cleaned and painted one train carriage, suddenly the second one would need to be used as well. That one was in a poorer condition so had needed extra work on both the floor and the windows.

When Ethan went to grab a much-needed coffee from Platform 1 one afternoon, he was bombarded with questions from Katy.

'Have you thought about what will happen when the passengers arrive?' she asked, glancing at the worryingly long list she had made on her phone. 'Are you going to put up some signs showing them where to go? And what about toilets and such. People will need facilities. What if it's freezing cold? Are we going to plan on opening late that evening?'

Ethan knew she was only trying to help, but he didn't need any more work to do.

'I was hoping to give everyone a hand with the train,' said Ryan. 'But I can't say that the additional income wouldn't be welcome.'

Katy nodded. 'Okay. Well, I can hold the fort here.' She bit her lip. 'Of course, we'll have to keep opening late when the Christmas train is up and running in any case.'

Ryan looked at her. '*If* the Christmas train happens,' he told her.

'If?' repeated Katy, looking surprised as she spun around to face Ethan. 'I thought it was what Eddie wanted?'

Ethan sighed. 'It is. But let's just get through Halloween first, shall we?'

'But what about...?' Katy began to ask once more.

Ethan held up his hand. 'It's a very short train ride of about thirty minutes. It'll be fine.'

He hoped he sounded more assured than he felt. His actual main concerns were about ensuring that the train ran smoothly and that the carriages were also deemed safe when inspected by the train inspectors later that week.

But as he looked around the inside of the old station waiting room, he realised that there had been a change since the last time he had been there. Katy had decorated around the door with an autumnal wreath of flowers. In addition, there was a mixture of carved pumpkins and greenery around some hurricane lamps, which had thick white candles in them on each of the tables. There were also swathes of nets with fairy lights across the ceiling, along with a few strategically placed fake cobwebs.

'What do you think?' she asked, following his gaze. 'I was going for a sophisticatedly spooky vibe.'

Ethan frowned. 'Right.'

He spotted an old wicker broom in a corner, with yet more fairy lights. There were black and orange tapered candles on the tables, too.

'Don't you like it?' asked Katy, catching his expression.

'Of course,' he replied, running a hand through his hair. 'But I've just realised that it's the one thing we haven't thought of. Should we be decorating the train?'

Katy laughed until she realised that he wasn't joking for once. 'You mean you haven't planned to decorate the train?' she said, with a gasp.

He shook his head.

'But it's a Halloween-themed train!' she spluttered.

'Who's talking about my famous train?' asked Bob, coming into the coffee shop.

'We haven't thought about any decorations,' said Ethan, looking round at his dad aghast.

'Well, there's plenty in the shops,' said Ryan. 'Just go and buy some.'

But, to Ethan's surprise, Bob was shaking his head. 'It's all right, son,' he told them. 'It's all in hand.'

'How?' asked Ethan, non-plussed. He could hardly imagine Bob and Eddie going online to order Halloween decorations.

'As it happens, your cousin has offered to help out and is going to bring it all on the day.' Bob smiled. 'Isn't that kind of him?'

But Ethan wasn't smiling. 'Dodgy Del is helping to decorate our Halloween train?' he asked slowly.

'For free!' said Bob, beaming. 'Isn't that marvellous?'

Ethan blew out a long sigh and mentally crossed his fingers that the Halloween train wouldn't end up being a horror show if Dodgy Del was involved.

Del was their cousin and a nice enough guy. He just had a habit of continually getting into trouble, normally leaving a trail of chaos and carnage behind him wherever he went.

'Apparently he knows someone in the party industry,' carried on Bob. 'So it's all sorted without any kind of price tag.'

'Will there be any price to pay though?' asked Ethan, thinking back to Del's other disasters.

Ryan grimaced. 'Let's hope not, bro.'

Katy was looking out of the window onto the platform. 'I can always get some more of our decorations and decorate the outside as well,' she said.

'Thanks,' replied Ethan. 'That would be a great help.'

'I shall think of it as a practice run for the Christmas train,' Katy told him, her eyes lighting up. 'Can you imagine dressing up the whole station for that? It's going to look amazing.'

'A big tree,' said Bob, nodding his approval.

'Wreaths and swags all lit up with fairy lights,' added Katy.

'I wonder if we could even get some fake snow from somewhere?' said Bob, thoughtfully.

Katy clapped her hands together. 'Wouldn't that be magical?' she replied.

As she and Bob carried on chatting, Ethan's heart sank a little.

He wouldn't be there. He would be in Seattle, helping create the lighting system for a sophisticated shopping mall, full of designer boutiques and fancy dining. It would be vastly different from tiny Cranfield in both structure and grandeur.

Normally, he would be grateful to be getting away around Christmastime. The memories of his mum trying to fake how happy she was stayed with him. Christmas had always made the sham of his parents' marriage seem even worse to Ethan and he had managed to stay away throughout the festive season ever since leaving home.

But things felt a little different now. Katy had blown in like a hurricane a year ago and had changed both his brother's life and the station for the better. There were more happy times now to be had in Cranfield for his family. In addition, he could feel himself growing closer to Ryan by spending more time in his company. They had always been brothers but were slowly becoming friends at last too.

Then he also had real friends now. Joe and Nico were also new to the area and weren't tainted with the bad memories of the past. He liked the men and was enjoying getting to know them better.

Finally, there was Libby. No longer travelling around the world, even she seemed to be content to be staying on in the village.

Christmas would arrive and perhaps there would be a steam engine puffing in and out of the station past an enormous Christmas tree. Ethan found himself hoping that someone would take a video to send to him if that happened.

But it was time to go, he reminded himself. He always left, didn't he?

However, this time, he felt a little wistful as he thought it.

# 19

As the days slipped by, trying as hard as she could, Libby still couldn't see a way to getting the contract for the chocolate boxes finished on time.

She was starting to feel incredibly anxious, not sleeping properly and then feeling tired all day. The trouble wasn't the process of making the chocolate, nor even the length of time that took. The problem was that there was just too much for one person to do. But everyone was busy and she liked to oversee everything, so it was all up to her. Besides, she had never asked for help before and wouldn't start now, she had decided.

However, she realised that no matter how much under-eye concealer she put on, it wasn't quite enough.

'Are you all right?' asked Harriet when she handed Libby a gin cocktail.

Gin night had rolled around again and this time it was being hosted by Harriet in her tiny cottage on Railway Lane.

'I'm okay,' replied Libby.

She had been hoping to work a bit later that day but hadn't

wanted to let the girls down so, once more, she hadn't quite made her self-imposed daily total of chocolate truffles.

She took a sip of her drink before curling her legs up under her on the enormous floor cushion she was sharing with Paddington the dog.

'You don't seem okay,' said Flora, who was sitting on the other side of her.

'We all get tired and cranky from time to time,' Libby told them. 'It's tough getting a business up and running with everything else going on.'

'Is there anything we can do to help?' asked Katy.

'Just keep filling me up,' said Libby, with a winning smile as she held up her gin glass before taking a huge gulp.

She felt her friends exchange worried looks but said nothing, deliberately making herself brighten up. Gin, she decided. Gin always helped.

She shuffled under the enormous weight of Paddington's heavy body, which was almost sprawled on top of her. 'I know it's your cushion,' she told the dog. 'But I do have to sit somewhere.'

As her friends began to chat about the wedding, Libby was thankful that they weren't pressing her too much that evening. For once, she just wanted to relax and not think about anything. She sipped her gin cocktail, just grateful for the alcohol slipping through her and numbing the pain.

Her dad had been extremely fretful since finding out about her losing her job. He hadn't expressed himself, of course. He never got upset these days. He didn't appear to feel anything. But the worry was most definitely there. So she spent any time with him being overly bright, optimistic and cheerful and felt absolutely exhausted by the lie.

She didn't want to lie to her friends either. They didn't need protecting, thankfully. But she still felt as if she were playing a part the whole time and it was tiring.

'So are you planning on bringing a plus-one to the wedding?' asked Harriet, suddenly turning her cheery face towards Libby.

Libby felt everyone look at her. Of course, she was the only single one amongst them now. They were all happy and loved up. She had been lying about the number of dates that she had been going out on for a couple of years now. A little white lie that she somehow couldn't control and now they all expected her to dazzle them with her amazing love life. But that wasn't true. She hadn't been on a real and meaningful date for years.

In fact, a tiny part of her wanted love and romance and all that her friends had told her felt so good. But, thankfully, it was mostly shouted down by the rest of her brain that reminded her about her failed marriage.

'You mean because I appear to be the last spinster around here,' she drawled, making a face.

'No! Don't think of yourself like that,' said Harriet quickly. 'Nobody else does.'

Harriet had a huge and generous heart and always liked to think positively of everyone and everything.

'Exactly,' said Flora, nodding. 'You have this amazing life travelling the world.'

Flora had stayed to run the family farm since her late teens and had never really left Cranfield for any length of time. She too had spurned all forms of romance until Nico had arrived from Italy last summer and changed everything for the better for her.

'I did have,' said Libby, reminding them of her job loss. 'Actually, I haven't yet decided which of the many men in my little black book will be the lucky recipient of being my date at your fabulous wedding,' she announced with a winning smile.

'Well, you wait until those bridesmaid dresses arrive next

week,' Harriet told her, with gleaming eyes. 'You'll have them lining up for a date.'

'Oooh, I can't wait to try mine on,' said Katy.

'As soon as they get here, I'll let you know,' said Harriet. 'We could make a day of it on Sunday, if you like. What do you think?'

As her friends all nodded their approval, Libby stayed silent. The thought of taking any more precious time away from making chocolate filled her with dread. Which was ridiculous because it was all about spending time with her friends. She had promised Bob and Eddie that she would help out with the Halloween train the next day, but she didn't want to finish work early. She didn't know what was wrong with her at the moment.

'I guess the dates might dry up a little if you're no longer around all those hunky pilots,' murmured Flora.

Libby gave her a look. 'Thankfully, there are many more fish in the sea,' she said before draining her gin glass. 'Fill me up, Katy.'

Katy raised her eyebrows at the speed with which Libby had drunk her gin cocktail but said nothing. Instead, she leaned forward to pour another large measure from the jug on the table.

Thanks to the gin, and only having time to snatch a piece of toast for dinner before she had arrived, the rest of the evening went in a bit of a blur, to Libby's relief. Conversations passed her by, but she was content to be a bystander, for once. She just wanted someone to invent a time machine to whisk her to when the truffle order was delivered and she could finally relax.

But, in the meantime, the gin was helping, she decided, draining her glass once more.

## 20

Ethan always enjoyed getting together with his friends and having a spirited game of darts in the Black Swan Inn. But, that evening, he found his mind kept wandering back to the Halloween train and the long to-do list to get everything done on time.

'Hey,' said his brother, taking the remaining darts out of his hands. 'Do you want to play properly or do you want to try and hit as many of us as you can?'

Ethan looked at him. 'What?' he asked, in a daze.

Ryan rolled his eyes. 'My point exactly. So put down the lethal objects and go get us all another round.'

Ethan wandered away to the bar but found his dad had been cornered by Dodgy Del.

'Just let me have a little drive of the choo-choo train and we'll call it even,' Del was saying.

Ethan and Bob immediately started to shake their heads. Del didn't have the best track record on driving any vehicle, let alone anything as big as a massive steam engine.

'I don't think that's a good idea,' began Bob.

'There's absolutely no way you can drive the train,' added Ethan in a firm tone.

'Aww, come on, Uncle Bob,' said Del. 'After all, I'm family. Kith and kin and all that.'

Bob looked at Ethan. 'I guess he could stand in the driver's cab for a while,' said Bob eventually.

'Whilst doing absolutely nothing and touching no levers whatsoever,' insisted Ethan.

'Great!' said Del, seemingly oblivious to their warnings. 'How about tomorrow morning?'

'Well, the train is all set for another run with the carriages,' said Bob. 'I guess you could come along then if you're free.'

'I'll make sure of it,' said Del, smiling. 'This is going to be amazing!'

'Maybe if we go early then it'll be too late,' murmured Ethan.

'In any case, I'd better not have anything else to drink tonight,' replied his dad.

'Yeah, you wouldn't want to be drunk in charge of a steam engine,' laughed Del.

Ethan also settled for a Coke Zero at the bar instead of another pint of beer.

When the evening was over and they had all wandered back along the path to Cranfield, he saw his dad safely home but almost bumped into Libby, Katy and Flora as he began to walk along the platform to the old school.

'Good evening,' he said to them all.

'For some of us,' said Katy, with a roll of her eyes.

She and Flora were holding up Libby in between them. She was swaying from side to side and looking quite drunk.

'Had a good evening, have we?' asked Ethan, with a grin.

'Too good,' replied Flora. 'She finished off most of the gin bottle, I reckon.'

Libby broke free of her friends' arms and staggered away to twirl and dance to some imaginary song.

When she nearly twirled over and onto the railway track, Ethan leapt forward to steady her.

'Hello,' she said, looking up at him with a wide smile. But her eyes were glassy with alcohol, he realised.

He couldn't remember the last time he had seen her that drunk.

'Hello yourself,' he told her. 'I think it's time we got you home.'

Luckily, her cottage was only a few short steps away.

But Libby went off in the other direction, running down the platform towards the station.

Ethan, Katy and Flora caught up with her as she crashed to a halt to stare up at the steam engine. It was all ready for its test run with the carriages, and apparently Dodgy Del too, the following morning.

'Show me your train!' said Libby imperiously to Ethan, as she spun back around again. 'I've not had time to see it yet.'

'Yes, ma'am,' he replied.

Ethan exchanged a look with Katy and Flora, who merely smiled at him and said their goodnights before walking away.

Once they were alone on the platform, Libby took off her coat and flung her handbag onto a nearby bench before giving another little twirl. Then she walked over to stand in front of Ethan.

'Show me the driving seat,' said Libby, almost tripping over her feet.

'You'll lose your licence in this state,' he replied, ushering her towards the driver's cab.

She struggled on the steps and almost fell backwards onto him. 'Whoops,' she said, laughing.

Finally they made it inside, where she stood very close and his senses reeled from the soft aroma of the cocoa that she spent all her time around. She tried to take in what he was saying about the various levers, but in the end, Ethan gave up as he could see that she really wasn't paying attention.

'Can I blow the whistle?' she said, reaching up to the cord.

'Not if you want to wake up the whole of Cranfield,' he said, grabbing her hand just in time. 'Come on. It's time for you to head home.'

But she began to shake her head. 'I don't want to,' she replied. 'I've let him down again.'

'Him?' Ethan wondered if she was talking about her dad.

He was so worried about her falling down the steps that he went first and lifted her down.

'So you don't want to go home? What do you want to do?' he asked. 'Make more chocolate?'

She groaned and shook her head. 'No more chocolate,' she sighed. 'It'll never be enough.' Instead she pushed him away slightly and staggered along to look up at the first railway carriage. 'What about the inside?' she asked.

'That at least is finished,' he told her, opening up a door and showing her inside. He was pleased with the result. The seats were clean and the woodwork as polished as it could ever be. It seemed to be holding up, with the odd spot of patching up here and there still needed.

Libby clambered up the steps and looked along the corridor. 'Wow,' she murmured, before staggering into the first compartment. 'This is amazing.'

'Yes, it is,' he told her, with a yawn. He had been working long days and was really quite tired now. 'Come on then. It really is time to get you home, ready for your hangover tomorrow.'

But, to his surprise, she sank down on the seat instead, with a miserable expression. 'But when I wake up there won't be enough chocolate again,' she told him, her words slurred.

He went to sit next to her. 'What's going on, Libs?' he asked. He couldn't make sense of what she was trying to say.

'It's all too much,' she said. 'I need a hundred more Libbys.'

'A hundred more Libbys?' he repeated, with a grin. 'What a terrible thought.'

But Libby wasn't smiling back at him. 'You didn't even want one of them,' she muttered.

'It was never about not wanting you,' he told her. 'It was about my own mess, not you. You were as perfect as you've always been.'

She shrugged her shoulders, her long blonde hair spilling all around him. Then she pulled her knees up to her chest, shivering in the cold air.

She seemed very sad, very low and he couldn't stop himself from hesitantly putting his arm around her and drawing her near. Just for a moment, he promised himself.

She leant her head on his shoulder and he was taken back to a time when he had held her just like that, after one of the many arguments with her dad in her teenage years. Back when he was still pretending to be her friend and yet wishing it was so much more.

He felt her move her head and look up at him in the almost darkness.

'I've missed you,' she whispered.

His heart lurched at her words before he reached out to remove a stray lock of her pale hair that had got caught on her long eyelashes.

Her face was so close, her lips so near to his. It wouldn't take much for him to lean forward and kiss her.

Ever since the prom, she had kept pushing him away, apart

from that one memorable night in Las Vegas. Finally he thought that they had been true to each other, that they both felt the same way. But when he had woken up, she had left and they had never spoken of it since then.

He had missed her too. Missed her so much that he ached inside for her. So just to hold her at that moment felt like bliss. A dream.

They locked eyes in the darkness before she moved once more, snuggling her head into his neck. He pulled her closer and wrapped his coat around them both. For a long while, they remained like that. Then, feeling her breath steady and slow, his eyes grew heavy and they both fell asleep in the darkness of the railway carriage.

## 21

---

Libby awoke with a start and immediately felt a blinding headache. She also had a stiff back where she had obviously lain awkwardly.

She became aware of someone lying next to her and turned her head to come face to face with Ethan.

She took a sharp intake of breath, trying to work out where they were and what had happened. For a brief second, it felt just like all those years ago in Las Vegas when she woke up after they'd got married. She even checked her ring finger, but thankfully it was bare. So where was she?

Ethan moved slightly and murmured, 'Good morning,' to her.

She gave him a half-hearted shove and sat up, staring around. She realised that they appeared to be in one of the old railway carriages, lying together on one of the long seats. What on earth had happened last night?

She had started off going to gin night with the girls but didn't remember a whole lot after that. She must have drunk an awful lot to block so much of the evening out. But perhaps there was a whisper of a memory of being with Ethan in the darkness. Was that in the train carriage where they'd somehow ended up?

She was just about to ask him what had happened when she became aware of a massive jolt that ran through her whole body. Was this the worst hangover in the world ever?

Then she realised that it wasn't just her. The whole of the compartment was moving.

They both sprang up at the same time and rushed to the window.

'We're moving!' said Libby, staring as the lavender fields on the other side of the railway track began to move sideways.

'Are you always this observant first thing in the morning?' asked Ethan, yawning.

He was maddeningly calm whilst Libby intended to keep freaking out.

'This train is moving!' she said, beginning to raise her voice. 'Why is this train moving? Who's driving it? Why are we in this carriage? And why is this train moving when you're the driver and you're here next to me?'

Ethan winced and held up his hand. 'Can you keep the yelling down to a dull roar until I work out what's going on?' he asked, leaning past her to pull down the window a couple of inches and try to peer out.

Libby patted down her jeans pockets before searching the floor for her phone, but she couldn't see it. 'Where's my handbag?' she asked. 'And what are we doing in here anyway?'

'I seem to remember you left your bag on the bench outside Platform 1 last night. You had an extremely good time at your ladies' gin night and then insisted on having a tour of the carriage when I bumped into you on the way home,' Ethan told her.

A cold draught whistled through the open window and around Libby's shoulders and she hugged her arms around her.

'And then what?' asked Libby.

'What do you mean?' replied Ethan, looking back at her with a grin. 'Are you asking whether you gave into the constant temptation that is my body?'

Libby rolled her eyes and glared at him.

He shook his head. 'Don't worry. You pretty much passed out on me as soon as we got in here. I guess I did too – more from weariness than the gin cocktails that you were enjoying.'

But Libby wasn't concerned about the past. She was more worried about the days ahead.

'Listen, Connolly, you'd better figure a way to get me off this train,' she snapped. 'I've got a tight deadline and a huge amount of chocolate truffles to make. I haven't got time for a magical mystery tour this morning! Where are we going, by the way?'

'I guess Dad and Grandad have decided to give it a test run without me,' he told her, with a shrug. 'I was supposed to be helping, but it looks like I overslept.' He patted his jeans pocket and brought out his phone before grimacing at the screen. 'And my battery's dead.'

Libby groaned. 'So what do we do now?'

Ethan leaned out of the small window as far as he could but was unable to make his shout of warning heard above the loud sound of the whistle being pulled from the driver's cab at the same time.

Libby blanched and held her head at the noise. 'Ow!'

But the train continued at its leisurely pace with no signs of slowing down.

'I don't believe this,' said Libby, looking out at the countryside. 'This is all your fault. You'd better work out a way to get this thing turned around!'

'We weren't planning on stopping until we get to Cranley junction which is five miles along the track,' he told her.

'Five miles!' Libby nearly screamed in frustration. 'What are we going to do until then?' she asked.

'Enjoy the journey,' Ethan told her.

'I don't have time for this,' she said, feeling decidedly grumpy as she slumped back down on the seat. The hangover wasn't helping her mood either.

'Listen, from what I've seen over the past few days, this is the first time you've seen daylight for a while,' he said. 'So just relax and enjoy the vitamin D, would you?'

She sighed heavily. 'I don't have time to relax.'

He frowned. 'Why is this order stressing you so much?' he asked.

'Because it's a ridiculously large order that I need to complete. I need the money since losing my job,' she told him. 'What else do you expect Dad and I to live on?'

'Perhaps you could ask everyone for help as I previously suggested,' he told her, raising an eyebrow at her.

But Libby automatically shook her head. 'I don't need help,' she said. 'Nobody else can make the chocolate.' She sighed. 'All I know is that I don't have time to sit and look at the countryside this morning.'

'Even when it's this beautiful?' he asked.

He had a point, she had to concede. From the large windows, she could see out across the fields, where the mist hung on to the cold ground and, in the distance, the hills rolled out to the horizon. The trees had begun to change to a kaleidoscope of golds, reds and orange as autumn went on.

Despite the many exotic places she had visited through her flight attendant job, nowhere had ever matched the beauty of her own village and surrounding area.

'See?' he said, in a smug tone.

'Just get us out of here,' she told him, not wanting to admit that he was right.

To her surprise, he walked over and sat next to her.

'You do this every time,' he said, his tone more serious. 'Ever since I first met you, in fact. As soon as you're in trouble, you isolate yourself away from your friends and don't tell us anything.'

She frowned at him. 'Us?'

He nodded. 'Yeah. I was your friend too, remember? Not just the girls. So I know the signs that you're struggling, Libby Jacobs.'

She shrugged her shoulders, not wanting to admit that he was right. 'It's always been a struggle,' she muttered. 'You know that.' She paused before carrying on. 'I only got through my childhood because of you.'

It was true. Ethan had always been there to cheer her up with some silly joke or to whisk her away into Cranbridge where they could spend hours messing about beside the river, being anywhere other than their unhappy homes.

'Right back at you,' he replied before he frowned. 'At least you took care of your dad when he needed you,' he carried on. 'I'm the weak one. I'm the one who kept running, leaving Ryan to deal with everything this past year.'

'You're back here now,' she said. 'That's the most important thing.'

'Only for now,' he reminded her. 'My next job starts after Halloween so I'll be gone again.'

She felt suddenly felt sad that she wouldn't be seeing Ethan on a daily basis for much longer.

'But I'm sure I can drive you mad whilst I'm still here,' he told her with a smile. 'As always.'

As usual, he was deflecting any sort of discussion about his own personal feelings with humour. He was the same, familiar Ethan that she had always known. The best friend that had been missing for so long in her life.

She gave a start as he covered her hand with his larger, warmer one and squeezed it. She blinked back the sudden tears that were pricking her eyes.

She couldn't stop herself from blurting out, 'I'm so glad we're friends again.'

He gave her a long look. 'Friends?' he said, raising his eyebrows.

For a second she couldn't breathe as she read the unspoken words in his eyes.

After a long pause, Ethan broke into a smile. 'Okay. Friends it is,' he said. 'Unless you want to make me a partner in that profitable chocolate business of yours?'

'The only thing I want you to do is stop this train,' she replied, swiftly moving her hand away from his and getting up to look out of the window once more, hoping the cool air would help lessen the heat that had flared up in her cheeks.

What concerned her most at that moment, even more than the chocolate sitting unmade in the school kitchen, was what had happened to her the night before. She had probably needed to blow off a bit of steam, but surely she'd have done that with her friends rather than Ethan?

Of course, the two of them had been friends once. So many years ago, he had been her everything. He knew her inside out, but the years had passed and they had grown apart. Or so she had thought.

Now, when she had let her guard down, he had roared back into her life. She didn't even know what they had talked about the previous evening. Apparently, she had slept in his arms too and she had absolutely no idea how she felt about that.

All she knew was that she was never drinking gin ever again.

## 22

Ethan had woken up feeling uncomfortable but happier than the first time in ages.

For a brief second, as he had realised where he was, he had relished having Libby in his arms. But then the train had begun moving and reality had brought them both down to earth with a large bump.

She was completely stressed about being stuck on there, but there was nothing he could do or say to calm her down.

Except for a brief moment, sitting together on the long seat, when the familiarity between them had returned. He had been unable to stop himself reaching out to take her hand in his. As always, the pain that she suffered was his to share. They had been through so much together when they had been growing up. It was only when they had become adults with real grown-up feelings that the problems had begun, he realised.

Finally, the train stopped at Cranley junction so that they could turn around and Ethan took the opportunity to leap out of the carriage and rush along the track to see who was there.

He was concerned about his dad and grandad taking the train

out by themselves as it was quite a responsibility to ensure the safety of the train and the surrounding area near the tracks.

Bob was just climbing down from the driver's cab to change the points so that the train could return to the station when he looked up with a start. 'What are you doing here?' he asked, looking around his son, seemingly to see if there were another train somewhere on the track.

'We hitched a ride unexpectedly,' Ethan told him.

'*We?*' asked Bob, his grey eyebrows rising up in amazement.

Ethan moved out of the way so Bob could see Libby climbing down from the carriage to carefully make her way along the tracks.

Dodgy Del poked his head out of the driver's cab and grinned down at his cousin. 'Good morning,' he said, as if there were nothing wrong with suddenly seeing Ethan standing in the middle of the railway line.

'Del! I might have known,' said Ethan, with a heavy sigh. 'What on earth are you doing up there?'

'Driving the train,' said Del. 'Uncle Bob here promised me that I could have a go.'

Ethan was horrified and stared at his dad.

'Your grandad's having a lie-in and I couldn't get hold of you on your mobile,' added Bob in a pointed tone. 'So I figured you'd overslept.'

'We did, sort of,' said Ethan, flicking a glance at Libby.

'Good morning, Bob,' she said, with a soft smile. 'We accidentally hitched a ride in one of the carriages.'

'What were you doing in there then?' asked Del.

'We wanted to see how smooth your handling of the train was,' replied Ethan, looking at his dad. 'Please tell me he didn't go anywhere near the gauges or actually anything that works.'

Bob shook his head. 'He just shovelled the coal,' he replied.

'Would have preferred doing the steering, to be honest,' said Del, who was looking a bit grimy and sweaty.

'And I'd have preferred you well away from our train,' Ethan told him.

'I didn't touch nuffink,' said Del quickly.

Ethan narrowed his eyes in response to his cousin's guilty tone of voice.

'Well, maybe just the whistle,' carried on Del. 'Anyway, what were you two doing back there?' he asked with a cheeky grin. 'Having a bit of alone time, were you?'

His lips curled into a leer, which made Libby give an exaggerated shudder.

'Just leave it, Del,' she snapped. 'The last thing I need this morning is your innuendo.'

'My what?' asked Del. 'Is that the new slang or summink?'

Libby rolled her eyes. 'How about we get back to Cranfield?' she asked. 'I've got a lot on my to-do list this morning.'

So Ethan helped with changing the points on the track before they all clambered into the driver's cab and began the journey back to the station.

Libby shivered with the cold early-morning air and Ethan offered her his coat to wear, which she took from him gratefully.

Ethan let Dodgy Del shovel the coal whilst he stood next to the open door with Libby. As the pace of the train increased, so did the noise in the cab. They almost had to shout to be heard above the din. The faster it went, the more coal needed shovelling. Which left Ethan and Libby on one side.

'It feels as if we're flying,' she said, her eyes sparkling with wonder as they sped along the tracks.

She looked relaxed for the first time that morning.

He smiled down at her, close enough to see the thickness of her eyelashes against her blue eyes.

She gave a start as they went past an old abandoned station. 'What's that?' she shouted.

'The old station at the far end of Cranley,' he told her loudly.

'It shut down the same time as our one in Cranfield,' added Bob.

'So why does it look in worse condition?' asked Libby, with a frown. The tiny station office was looking very dilapidated and uncared for.

'Because there wasn't a family like ours living in it,' said Ethan without thinking.

He gave a start. It was true, he realised. The station in Cranfield had been a warm and loving family home. There had been happy times, he reminded himself. If he searched long enough, he could recall opening his Christmas stocking with Ryan. Big family dinners, full of loved ones long since gone. But those happy memories were few and far between and the usual rows and arguments overcrowded them until he could barely remember anything but the daily arguments and tension.

He took a deep breath to rid himself of the past, but it was hard when Libby was standing so close to him. The sweet memory of holding her in the darkness the previous evening lingered in his consciousness, a strand of her pale long blonde hair on his jacket. He stood close to her all the way back, not really noticing the glorious views or even what Dodgy Del was saying in his excitement about the train.

All too soon, Bob slowed the train down until they were crawling past the old school and then along the platform, past the back gardens of the cottages.

With a hiss of steam and water, the steam engine finally ground to a halt.

'That was amazing,' said Del, the whites of his eyes gleaming in his pink, soot-covered face.

Ethan looked down at Libby, who was still standing close to him. He raised his eyebrows in question at her.

'It was okay,' she said, before breaking into a grin as she looked at Bob. 'Better than okay, actually. It was wonderful.'

'Thought you'd enjoy it, love,' said Bob, smiling back at her.

They all clambered down onto the platform, a few interested people had come out of Platform 1 to view the vast steam engine as it had pulled up outside the coffee shop.

Along with them was Katy, holding a handbag and coat.

'Good morning,' she said to them all. 'Libby, I believe these are yours.'

'Thanks,' muttered Libby, blushing.

'Do you want a coffee and to tell me all about it?' asked Katy in a pointed tone, flicking her eyes between Ethan and Libby.

'Later,' Libby told her. 'Can I use your bathroom? I've got soot in my eyes.'

With that, she rushed off, leaving the rest of them on the platform.

Whilst Bob answered a few questions from the customers and Dodgy Del declared himself the deputy driver, eager to take all the credit, Katy wandered over to Ethan.

'So, how did Libby end up on the train this morning? And why was her handbag and coat still abandoned on the platform?' she asked.

'I never kiss and tell,' Ethan replied her, with a winning grin.

She shook her head, but he could tell she was smiling as she walked away.

He too was smiling. Were he and Libby closer after their unexpected trip along the railway tracks? Maybe, just maybe, he decided.

And that hope that they might become friends again was

even more precious than the successful first run of the steam engine with the railway carriages.

## 23

After being stuck on the train and losing most of her planned early start, Libby hustled straight into Platform 1 and ordered a latte with an extra shot of coffee.

Katy smiled at her. 'I'm not surprised after all the gin you drank last night,' she said.

'It was our gin night,' Libby told her. 'That was the always the plan. Drink gin and be merry.'

'Except you didn't seem very merry,' replied Katy, giving her a hard look.

Libby shrugged her shoulders. 'There's a lot going on, thanks to the massive order for more chocolate than I've ever made in my life,' she said.

'Listen, if it's too much,' began Katy, 'let me help, or Harriet, or Flora. Even Ryan. Remember that he's actually a chef, so he'll be good at this kind of thing.'

But Libby automatically shook her head. 'It's fine,' she said, trying to offset her friend's concern. 'I'm grateful. Truly grateful for this. It'll really help me and Dad out.' She picked up the latte and paid for it. 'Listen, we'll catch up later, okay?'

'How about tonight?' asked Katy.

'What about tonight?' replied Libby.

'Why don't you come over to our place and have a nice hot chocolate and a proper chat,' said Katy.

Libby began to panic about the time already lost to complete the order. 'I'll see how the day goes, okay?' she said. 'Talking of which, I'd better get out of here. Laters.'

She rushed out, relieved to have got out of Katy's laser-vision glare. But as Libby headed down the platform towards home, she wondered when life had got so hectic that she needed to make up an excuse not to see her friends. She missed them terribly of course, but there would be plenty of time after the order was complete. She had an awful lot of chocolates to make in that time.

Libby found her dad already having breakfast in the kitchen.

'Good morning, Elizabeth,' he said, seemingly unaware that she hadn't been home all night. He didn't even seem to notice that she was wearing the same clothes as she had left in the evening before.

'Good morning, Dad,' she replied. 'I grabbed an early coffee.'

He nodded and looked down once more at his newspaper.

Libby was just about to go upstairs and change her clothes when he suddenly said, 'You're working long hours at Harriet's spa.'

Libby spun around, her cheeks blushing. 'Oh! Yes. She's got a bit of a busy time on, which is great for the business obviously,' she lied, her words coming out in a rush.

'Indeed,' he replied, nodding his head thoughtfully.

Libby gulped. She hated lying to him, but what could she do? The thought of telling him that she made chocolate was unbearable. He wouldn't understand and would just get upset. And she would never cause him more pain.

So she cracked a joke about needing a shoulder massage of her own, made him smile and then rushed upstairs to get changed.

After grabbing some toast for breakfast, she gave her dad a kiss and left the cottage for the old school.

Libby hesitated before knocking on Ethan's front door. She was desperate to get on with her busy day but somewhat apprehensive about seeing Ethan again so soon after their night together. There had been a moment of connection between them and it unsettled her to such a degree that she felt immensely grateful to find that he wasn't at home yet and had to bring out the spare front door key instead.

Presumably he was carrying on getting the train ready after the run earlier that morning. Her cheeks were still glowing at the thought of falling asleep next to him. She still couldn't believe that had happened.

Not only did she need to complete this order in time to get paid, she also needed to get it done so that she could stop using his kitchen. It was becoming too awkward, too weird to be around him all the time. And what was that about last night? It must have been the gin, she decided.

Thankfully, she was sober now and had a large latte to power her through the next hour.

Although a couple of hours later, she was wondering whether another gin might just sort out her hangover and also relax the panic inside. The days were beginning to fly past and she wasn't anywhere close to her daily target, let alone the five thousand total.

It looked as if she had a couple of hard weeks ahead of her and mentally rolled up her sleeves to prepare for the long days of work ahead.

But she would miss this lovely kitchen, she thought, looking around. And, she had to admit to herself, she would miss Ethan a little bit too.

Because he was leaving a few days after Halloween and then would be abroad for a couple of months. He had been kind enough to offer her the loan of his kitchen until the order was complete. And yet, she knew that it wouldn't be the same not having him around all the time. After their conversation on the train that morning, she felt that they had finally begun to get over the awkwardness that had shrouded their relationship for so many years. They could actually talk to each other, although it had only been about non-romance matters. For that she was grateful as it would only complicate things more.

It wasn't as if she had forgiven him for the prom, nor their disastrous wedding in Las Vegas. But she would miss him.

Libby shook her head as she focused on the chocolate once more. It must definitely have been the gin, she decided.

Because the last thing she needed right now was to fall in love with Ethan all over again.

**24**
_____

The last day in October dawned bright and chilly and, Ethan was glad to see, dry as well.

He spent an extremely busy day with his dad ensuring that the train was ready at the station, that all the parts were working properly and that the carriages were also ready to go. Eddie was also on hand but appeared to be struggling a bit with the workload, so Ethan made him rest before the busy evening ahead. The last few days had been manic and they all felt weary with the strain of making sure that everything was prepared.

Ethan returned to the station, just as the sun was beginning to sink down towards the horizon. It was only when he stepped out onto the platform and saw that Katy had been true to her word about giving the platform some properly sophisticated but spooky decorations that he remembered about the decorations for the train.

He sent a quick text to Dodgy Del and was relieved when his cousin replied that he was heading over with a van full of Halloween decorations. There really wasn't a moment to lose, thought Ethan. It was now teatime and there were already a few trick or treaters about on Railway Lane.

Ethan was pacing up and down nervously when his brother came out of Platform 1, dressed in a vampire costume.

'What's up?' asked Ryan.

'You're not here for a donation, are you?' said Ethan. 'Because it feels like all the blood has drained from my body anyway.'

He looked up as Bob and Eddie walked down the platform.

'Why aren't you all wearing costumes?' asked Ryan.

Ethan looked down at the blue overalls that protected his clothes from the smoke and soot from the steam engine. 'We're wearing what we always wear,' Ethan told him.

'Not much of an effort,' said Ryan, making a face. 'Have you seen Katy? She looks amazing.'

Ethan had to concede that his brother's girlfriend did look incredible as she headed out of Platform 1. She was dressed in a bright pink skirt suit with pink high heels and a blonde wig.

'You look very pretty, love,' said Eddie as they drew nearer.

'Thanks,' she replied. 'I've gone full Barbie.'

But Ethan wasn't in the mood for small talk as there was still no sign of Dodgy Del.

'Where is he?' he snapped, glancing at his watch and seeing that only another four minutes had passed since the last time that he had checked the time.

'He said he was on his way,' replied Ryan. But even he was looking a little concerned. 'It is getting a bit tight time-wise though.'

'He's never let us down before,' announced Bob, who appeared to be taking it all quite calmly.

'You are joking, right?' said Ethan, raising his eyebrows at his dad. 'Between trying to burn down a field, crashing a tractor and almost ruining the fireplace in Ryan's coffee shop, you mean?'

'Well,' said Bob, a small frown appearing on his brow. 'I never said he was perfect, did I?'

'He's here at last,' said Ryan, looking through the narrow alleyway onto Railway Lane, where an old van had just pulled up in a puff of grey smoke. They all quickly rushed to greet him.

'Nice van,' said Ethan, as Dodgy Del climbed out of the driver's cab.

'Does it always smell like that?' asked Ryan, wrinkling his nose.

'Yeah, but you get used to it,' said Dodgy Del, going round to open up the back of the van. It was full of boxes. 'There you go, Uncle Bob. You asked and I've delivered, as promised.'

'Thank you, lad,' said Bob, giving him a pat on the shoulder.

'Don't thank him yet,' Ethan told his dad. 'We need to get this lot up and around the train carriages sharpish.'

So they all grabbed a box and began to carry everything onto the platform.

'Shall I start to open them up?' asked Katy, pulling out a pair of scissors from her suit.

'Yes, please,' said Ethan, carrying the last box from the van.

'It's just like Christmas,' said Katy with a smile as she unpicked the Sellotape on the top of the box.

Ethan watched as she carefully opened up the lid before her smile dropped and she quickly closed it again.

'What is it?' asked Ethan, rushing over.

'I... I... I think it's the wrong box,' she stammered, beginning to back away with wide eyes.

Ethan immediately flung open the box that Katy had tried to close and stared down at what she had seen. Even he flinched at the sight before him.

'Del!' he roared. 'What on earth is all this?'

Del casually wandered over to see what all the fuss was

about, but his congenial smile faded into confusion as he took in the contents of the box. 'I dunno,' he said.

Ethan stared down again once more. The box appeared to be full of bloodstained sheets, as well as scary-looking zombie masks. 'Where are our child-friendly Halloween decorations for all the family?' asked Ethan slowly.

Still frowning, Del bent over the next box and opened it up. He tried to mask his small gasp of horror, but it was too late.

'What's in that one?' asked Ethan sharply, his stomach plummeting.

'Nuffink,' said Del quickly.

But he wasn't quick enough for Ethan, who nudged him out of the way and looked down to see a whole load of plastic severed limbs, all in various shades of deformity but all equally disgusting.

Katy, meanwhile, was ripping open a box and gave out a small scream of alarm.

'What is it?' asked Ryan, heading over to join her.

But Katy merely shook her head and closed the box up once more. 'Clowns,' she muttered. 'Really scary clown faces.'

Ethan turned to Del in despair. 'Del!' he shouted. 'The passengers are going to be here in less than an hour. What are we going to do?'

'Well, you asked for scary,' said Del, looking a little guilty.

'Del, this isn't scary,' Ethan told him, groaning. 'This is X-rated, Hammer House of Horror stuff rather than the Disney Halloween vibe we were going for.'

'Whatever's the matter?' asked Harriet, rushing out of the lavender spa with Paddington the dog next to her to see what all the shouting was about. She was dressed as a witch and Paddington had been turned into a large, fluffy pumpkin.

'It's Del, of course!' replied Ethan, rolling his eyes before turning back to his cousin. 'We've got little children coming! How are they going to react when they see...' He interrupted his rant to open up another box and grimaced. 'Disgustingly realistic squelchy body organs.' He gulped.

Harriet looked into a box and pulled out a life-size zombie doll that looked so realistic that Paddington took one look, howled and shot back inside the lavender spa.

Ethan groaned. It was a disaster.

'We'll send out an SOS,' said Ryan, getting out his phone. 'Ask for any help at all from everyone.'

As his brother sent out the distress call, Ethan turned to look at Dodgy Del.

'Well done,' he drawled. 'You've just replaced the classic *Nightmare on Elm Street* with what appears to be Nightmare on Railway Lane.'

'Might still be a big hit,' muttered Del.

'I suggest you get out of here sharpish,' warned Ethan. 'Otherwise, the only thing being hit will be you, dear cousin. How could you do this to Grandad on his big day?'

Del shot a sheepish smile at Eddie, who just shrugged and smiled. He did seem a little quiet that evening, thought Ethan. Perhaps the strain of getting the Halloween train ready on time was showing.

As Del rushed out of the station, Ethan wondered just how quickly they could decorate the train for their paying customers. And, as a heavy drizzle began to rain down on them, whether the evening was a disaster before it had even begun.

## 25

Libby had had no time to sort out a Halloween costume as she had been working flat out on the chocolates around the clock. So she had opted at the last minute to wear her flight attendant's uniform which the airline had never asked her to return. It had felt a bit strange to be getting back into her old clothes, along with making sure her hair was in a perfect bun. She hadn't realised just how free she had felt being able to wear her own clothes every day.

Arriving on the platform and catching up with the last-minute panic, Libby thought that it was particularly true to form that Dodgy Del's van wouldn't start so he ended up staying to help, although that meant keeping out of Ethan's way. He seemed very stressed that evening and she just wanted to help him however she could.

Thanks to Ryan's quick thinking, all the friends rushed to help decorate the train carriages with whatever they could lay their hands on that was child friendly.

To everyone's relief, it turned out that a couple of the boxes of decorations that Del had given them weren't quite so extreme as the rest. They were able to use the plastic skeletons and some netting, although they all decided that the fake tarantulas were far too realistic and would give the adults nightmares, let alone the children.

Inside the train carriages, Libby and the others added various decorations, such as fake velvet pumpkins, witches' hats and the odd broomstick. It wasn't much, but it was better than nothing, they thought.

'We should have handed out hot chocolate,' said Libby. 'Or at least some trick or treat bags.'

But at least the train would be running in the darkness outside, despite the meagre decorations. Wouldn't that be enough ambiance for a spooky night for everyone?

Just before six o'clock, all the families began to arrive. Unfortunately, a slight drizzle had turned into a torrential downpour. But at least everyone was still in a good mood as they oohed and aahed at the train, despite the bad weather.

Tom, the editor from the local newspaper, *The Cranbridge Times*, was also in attendance to record everything with the promise of a front page spread including photographs.

As Bob, Eddie and Ethan climbed into the driver's cab to get ready, all the passengers went onboard and Libby joined them.

She heard the train whistle to signify that the engine was ready and called out, 'Here we go!' down the corridor.

Everyone looked around excitedly and then, with a lurch, the carriages began to very slowly move.

'This is great!' said one man, smiling at Libby from his seat. 'I haven't been on a steam train in years.'

It was certainly charming, despite the tacky decorations, thought Libby.

She looked out of the window as they passed the end of the platform and saw her dad waving from the back fence in the semi-darkness, holding an umbrella against the rain which was now lashing down. She waved back and smiled, thankful that he seemed to have at least taken an interest in this special outing.

She had, of course, invited him along but he had inevitably declined. There had been no change in her dad's withdrawn personality since she had been back full-time. She was beginning to think that things would never change at home for either of them.

They had just left Cranfield behind and were in the middle of the dark countryside when suddenly the overhead lights went out. For a second, all she could hear was the heavy rain on the roof of the carriage. But then there were a lot of screams, from both young and old.

Libby called out for everyone to hold on tight, wondering if this was part of the event. What was going on?

She quickly text Katy, who was in the next carriage. Her swift reply confirmed that their carriage was also in darkness and that it was most definitely not planned.

The screams began to magnify and Libby peered around in the darkness to try to work out what was upsetting everyone so much.

The tacky fake skeletons and witches they had retrieved from Dodgy Del's boxes had looked pretty harmless in the light. However, in the darkness, Libby quickly realised that they were downright frightening. Because what nobody had spotted were the words written in illuminous paint, which was only now showing up in the pitch black. The skeletons had the words 'Death To All' scrawled on them and the witches had the word 'Kill' written over and over in what appeared to be fake blood.

There was a lot of crying now and Libby desperately tried to cover up the awful words. But as she tugged at the skeletons, it seemed to trigger some kind of ghostly sound effect. The witches, meanwhile, were beginning to cackle and scream.

Then, just when she thought it couldn't get any worse, the whole train braked hard and abruptly stopped. What had happened now?

Then, just to add to everyone's fear, she could hear thunder rumbling nearby. Only a second after they had stopped, there was a crackle of lightning across the nearby hills. It would have been funny if it had been a fake effect, she thought. But it wasn't.

Worse news was to come as suddenly she heard Bob's voice over the tannoy.

'Sorry about the abrupt stop, everyone. Unfortunately, it looks as if there's a fallen tree up ahead. We can't get past it, I'm afraid. So the only thing we can do is reverse back to the station. We will of course refund your tickets.'

And so the train slowly made its way back to the station, only minutes after it had left.

All the passengers were looking unhappy as they climbed down from the carriages with some of the younger children looking downright terrified.

'I can make everyone a hot chocolate, if you'd like,' offered Katy in a cheerful tone.

But most people wanted to head home as the rain lashed across the platform from the open fields beyond.

'What a disaster,' muttered one man as they went past.

Katy and Libby looked at each other with worried glances.

'I thought it was the scariest thing ever!' said a young girl, looking thrilled.

'Excellent!' replied Libby, nodding in fake enthusiasm.

But the majority of people looked disenchanted and miserable.

Once they were alone on the platform, Libby looked at Katy.

'I was sort of hoping it would be like Harry Potter on the Hogwarts Express. This was more like a Stephen King movie.'

Katy grimaced. 'Trick or treat?' she said, giving her a weak smile.

Libby blew out a sigh. Between Dodgy Del and the weather, it definitely hadn't turned out to be a treat. It had been a disaster, not only for Ethan but for the whole family. It was likely the idea for any further Cranfield Steam Engine train rides might be over after their very first run.

* * *

Ethan stood in the driver's cab and saw that all the passengers had left the station.

'They've all headed home,' he said to his dad and grandad.

His dad and grandad nodded but didn't reply. They didn't need to, thought Ethan. The disappointment of having to abandon the very first train ride had depressed them all.

Ethan looked back down the track, making a mental note to clear the fallen tree the following day.

As he looked out along the dark track, he realised that given his own skills with lighting, he should have thought harder about how lights could have helped the atmosphere. The train was in darkness, but he could have lit it outside somehow. Of course, it was too late now, but he wondered if he could make a few suggestions for the Christmas train. If it ever ran, of course.

Ryan and the rest of their friends gathered on the platform, no doubt to give their sympathies at the disastrous outcome. Ethan was grateful for their support and help that evening and realised how much he would miss his brother and friends when he flew off to America after the weekend. He had been looking forward to escaping at first, but the help and support that he had received that evening had made him appreciate just how lonely he often felt when he was away from home.

He looked at his dad and grandad and realised that they too would be needing some support. The disappointment might well mean that the Christmas train wouldn't run. Their dream was over. It seemed a bittersweet anticlimax to what had been such a driving force in both of their lives for such a long time.

For once, there was no excited chatter as Ethan, Bob and Eddie began to shut the train safely down for the night. His grandad was particularly pale and quiet, thought Ethan. Probably the shock of the disastrous evening.

Once all the checks had been made, Ethan climbed down the steps first. He looked across at Libby, and even from a distance away, he could feel her sympathetic gaze. He knew then more than ever that it wasn't just his family he would miss when he left on Monday.

Bob climbed down next with a heavy sigh before turning to ensure Eddie stepped down safely from the cabin.

However, Eddie's foot slipped slightly and Ethan rushed over.

'Steady there, Grandad,' he said, holding Eddie upright with both his hands until his grandad was safely standing on the platform.

He figured that Eddie was probably a bit overwhelmed by the whole evening. And that he must also be exhausted from the final few months of pushing to get the steam engine working in time for their self-imposed deadline.

But as Ethan stepped around to face his grandad, he saw something else in Eddie's eyes. Pain and confusion.

And before he could react, his grandad collapsed onto the platform.

## 26

Hours later, Ethan still couldn't believe what had happened. One moment they were preparing to commiserate with each other after the disaster with the Halloween train. The next, his grandad was being taken in an ambulance to the hospital after a suspected stroke.

Eddie was still having the medical checks and scans required, so Ethan and the rest of his family were sitting nearby in a waiting area of the local hospital, anxiously waiting for the results.

'Here you go,' said Katy, arriving back from the vending machine with some plastic cups of tea. She handed one to Bob, who was sitting next to Ethan. 'I'm not sure it'll taste very good, but at least it's vaguely warm.'

'Thanks, love,' said Bob, with a grateful smile.

Katy handed Ethan the other cup before sitting down next to Ryan on the only other available chair. Ethan watched as Ryan immediately put his hand in hers and squeezed it.

Ethan had always been grateful as he had watched Katy make his brother so happy, but that night he was even more thankful.

As soon as she had seen Eddie collapse, Katy had been straight on her mobile phoning for an ambulance, while the rest of them had been too shocked to think straight. Then, once they had got to the hospital, she had conjured up a flannel from somewhere so that Ethan and Bob could clean their faces and hands of all the soot and dust from the train. She had also packed away their dirty overalls in a carrier bag.

Ethan glanced at his dad, worry etched on his face as he slowly sipped his tea.

'You were right,' Ethan told Katy after taking a gulp of the hot drink. 'It does taste pretty dreadful.'

She gave him a tremulous smile at his half-hearted joke. But nobody was in the mood for talking. Katy looked at her phone and told them that all their friends back in Cranfield were sending their love.

To Ethan, it felt as if Cranfield, and even the steam train, were a long way away. His world had suddenly contracted into the small area he was sitting in, waiting anxiously for the results.

He had always been close to his grandad. Eddie's enthusiasm for all things to do with trains had been evident for a very long time, ever since he was stationmaster. Ethan had seen the photographs, although he had been too young to remember those days. Eddie looking so proud in his stationmaster uniform with the buttons shining so brightly and the cap set at exactly the right angle, his hand full of the flags ready to signal the safe departure of the train.

The trains were in Eddie's soul. They were a part of him and had inspired Ethan's own love for engineering. Together they had built their own train sets and even, to his mother's horror, a go-kart with an engine, which had resulted in a sprained wrist and a few bruises for the young Ethan, as well as a ticking off for Eddie.

But Ethan hadn't cared. He had loved tinkering with the

engines, something that he now realised he had lost along the way with his work. Creating light shows still interested him, but he wasn't getting his hands dirty the way he had done on the steam train these past few weeks.

He glanced at his hands, where his nails still showed traces of the soot from the coal. Had it only been a few hours ago that the train had puffed its way through the countryside, tooting its whistle as they went? It seemed like a lifetime ago.

For a brief while, he had relished in standing alongside his dad and grandad in the driver's cab. They had all worked hard to ensure the steam engine had run properly and he had felt both grateful and proud of what they had achieved together. It had been a brand new happy memory for him to cherish, a reminder of the strength that his family had through their love for each other.

As he looked around at his loved ones at that moment in the waiting area, he knew that it would be that strength and love that would be needed more than ever in the coming hours and days.

A short while later, the nurse led them back into the curtained cubicle where Eddie was lying in bed.

Katy immediately headed over and kissed him on the forehead and Ethan was grateful to see his grandad sleepily give her a somewhat lopsided smile in reply. Looking teary, she stepped out of the way so that Bob could go over and squeeze his father's hand.

Then the consultant came into the small area and Ethan found that he was holding his breath, braced for any bad news.

'The scans have shown that Mr Connolly had a blood clot

which caused a small bleed on the brain, causing the stroke,' he began.

Ethan gulped.

'The good news is that we think that the bleeding is contained and has been stopped,' carried on the consultant. 'We're going to keep him here for a few days for observation, but we're happy that he's stable and out of immediate danger.' He paused and looked around the family. 'The result of the scans does give me cause for optimism regarding his recovery.'

Everyone took a moment before seemingly sighing their relief in unison.

'Thank you, doctor,' said Ryan, stepping forward to shake the consultant's hand.

'We'll get him transferred onto a ward just as soon as we can,' replied the consultant.

After he and the nurse had left, the family exchanged tearful smiles.

'Well, Dad,' said Bob, giving Eddie's hand another squeeze, 'it sounds like you'll be back on the trains before you know it.'

Eddie smiled in response, although his eyelids closed almost immediately and he seemed to drop off to sleep.

'I was reading online and it says that being very tired is normal after a stroke,' whispered Katy.

Bob nodded but stayed still, holding his father's hand.

Ethan watched as Ryan turned to look at Katy with tears in his eyes and she swiftly drew him into a hug to comfort him.

Watching his brother lean on his girlfriend's shoulder, for a brief moment Ethan felt very lonely. He had been single for so many years, resolutely determined to be independent. But right then, he would have given anything to have someone to lean on. And the only person he yearned to have their arms wrapped around him was Libby. On the platform earlier, he had felt a hand squeeze his and he had looked around to find it was Libby. Then the moment had passed, but it had been enough for him to draw comfort and he was grateful for her support.

Ethan looked at his grandad asleep in the bed once more. His grandad had proposed to their grandmother on that steam engine. It had been his dream to see it carry passengers once more and Ethan had failed. He should have stepped up more. He should have given more and the guilt weighed heavily on him.

He couldn't leave for America now. There was no way he would leave his family at this awful time.

That meant that he would stay in Cranfield until probably Christmas at the earliest. But he had a sudden determination. That the Christmas train would run. That he would fulfil his grandad's dream.

Now Ethan understood why Ryan had stayed on to take care of their dad when his parents' marriage had fallen apart the previous year. The responsibility of his family was all encompassing. But it was time for Ethan to step up too.

The bad memories were still there in Cranfield. But he had to stay and help take care of his family. Perhaps it might just help him face up to the past as well.

## 27

Libby shivered, despite being sat next to the fireplace in the lounge of Harriet and Joe's cottage on Railway Lane.

It had only been two hours since the disaster of the Halloween train. But it turned out that a greater disaster had been waiting to reveal itself.

She had been watching Ethan after he had climbed down from the driver's cab and had been wondering what she could say to cheer him up about the passengers being so disgruntled about having their journey cut short. But suddenly he had rushed over to Eddie, who had collapsed onto the ground with his stricken-looking family surrounding him, and everything else had been forgotten.

Not wanting to interrupt them but desperate to know that Eddie was okay, Libby had headed over to stand with Harriet and Joe, who were quickly joined by Flora and Nico, along with Grams, Flora's grandmother.

'Stroke or heart,' Grams had whispered, her eyes still on Eddie. 'I'd put money on it.'

Grams had known Eddie since their school days, both born

and bred in Cranley, and was suitably upset by seeing her friend so stricken.

Libby could only look on anxiously whilst they had waited for the paramedics to arrive. She had found her eyes seeking out Ethan, who was drained of all colour as he crouched down next to his grandfather.

When the paramedics had arrived, they had appeared to confirm Grams' diagnosis of a stroke before carefully taking Eddie away on a stretcher. Bob went with him in the ambulance, whilst Ryan, Katy and Ethan were to take their car to the hospital.

Katy and Ryan had received brief hugs from their friends before they'd sprinted upstairs to grab the car keys. Ethan had waited downstairs on the platform, his face set in stone.

Libby had gone over to where Ethan stood a little away from everyone else and took his hand in hers.

He had given a small start as he felt her touch and looked down at her in a daze. But as Katy and Ryan had returned to head off to hospital, Libby had felt him give her the briefest of squeezes with his own hand before letting go and rushing off with them.

Words weren't necessary, thought Libby. That was Ethan's way of thanking her and she was grateful to have brought him some kind of temporary respite.

She knew that hours of waiting lay ahead for him, as she too had endured the long wait that Ethan would now be trying to get through, knowing that life wouldn't ever quite be the same for Eddie or the family ever again.

Everyone left behind had then silently dismantled all the Halloween decorations inside the train and on the platform, as if nobody could bare to look at them any more.

'Here,' said Flora, pressing a hot mug of tea into Libby's hands. 'You look done in.'

'I'm okay,' said Libby briskly. 'Just a little cold.'

She wasn't okay, of course. Eddie's stroke was bringing back all sorts of bad memories as to when her dad had suffered the same trauma. But she was grateful for the furry warmth of Paddington the dog, who had just wandered over to sit right next to her and place his heavy head on her legs. She was pretty certain he just wanted to hog the heat from the fire, but the dog was a welcome comfort nonetheless.

She moved the mug to one hand so that she could stroke Paddington's soft head with the other.

'Hmmm,' said Flora, giving her friend a look of disbelief, but she didn't say anything. Instead she checked her phone one more time. 'So, it sounds as if Eddie's going to be transferred to a ward later tonight,' she said.

'That's good,' said Harriet, who was sitting on the nearby sofa looking upset. Whereas Libby could hide most of her innermost feelings, Harriet was the complete opposite. Sitting next to her was her fiancé Joe, who wrapped his arm around Harriet and pulled her into him.

Grams sat down next to them and patted Harriet's hand with hers. 'He's in the best place for now,' she said.

'Should we do something? Send something?' asked Nico, Flora's boyfriend.

Grams shook her head. 'The best thing we can do is give them all a little space as they try to come to terms with it all. It's been a shock for everyone, least of all Eddie, of course.'

Nico nodded. 'We can help out when he comes home,' he said, with a firm nod.

Grams nodded her agreement. 'That's what friends do. Rally round where they can. I'll start whipping up a few dishes that he and Bob can pop in the microwave for ease.'

'A bit of your home cooking is medicine all by itself,' said Nico, giving Grams a soft smile.

Grams' cooking was excellent and she had rustled up a box of her home-made biscuits from somewhere. She held out the box towards Libby.

'Sugar is always good for a shock,' she said.

But Libby shook her head. 'And absolutely no use for my skinny jeans unfortunately,' she replied. But even she could tell her tone was too bright, too loud as it betrayed her shaky frame of mind.

'Then take a couple home for your dad,' said Grams gently. 'You can both enjoy them later. They'll keep for a few days.'

'Thank you,' said Libby.

She had updated her dad on Eddie's condition before heading to Harriet's cottage, and right now she just wanted to head home and give her dad a hug.

So, after quickly downing her sweet tea, she went home.

She thought her dad might have gone up to bed, but instead she found him waiting in his armchair, over an hour after his usual bedtime.

As they locked eyes, she realised that the evening's events had triggered bad memories for them both. His soft blue eyes held tears as he looked at her.

There were so many things she could have said in that moment, but all she could think of was to tell him how much she loved him as she rushed across to kneel next to his armchair and wrap her arms around him.

She was grateful for his head on her shoulder, for the pat on her back with his good hand and for the murmured I love you in return.

As they held and comforted each other, Libby wondered how much the stroke would impact Eddie. Would it change his life completely as it had done for her father? She sincerely hoped not. After all, surely lightning couldn't strike the same place twice, could it?

Then her thoughts turned to Ethan and her heart went out to him as she knew how upset he would be. She realised that it didn't matter about their disastrous secret marriage, nor even the prom any more. It didn't matter about her pride or even a broken heart. Nothing was more important than a loved one and she wished that she could take away the pain that he was surely in at that moment.

**28**

---

Ethan felt absolutely exhausted by the time he got home from the hospital in the early hours of the morning and fell asleep in the same clothes that he had been wearing when he had driven the train almost twelve hours previously.

Despite the late night, he still woke up early, his mind was whirring after the events of the previous day.

The first thing he did was text his brother to find out if there had been any updates on their grandad overnight. Ryan sent a swift reply that Eddie had apparently slept well and that they could visit him in hospital later in the afternoon. He then invited Ethan to a family brunch at Platform 1, telling him that their dad was already there. Ethan replied that he would be along in a while.

He sat up in bed for a moment, but the house was silent. The peace wasn't helping to settle his mind and so he swiftly got up to take a long shower.

After getting dressed, Ethan faced up to the next problem. He had been due to leave for America the following day, however he needed to cancel the job contract in order to stay close to his family.

After calling his business contact, he was grateful that they accepted his apologies that he couldn't give them any kind of start date, especially whilst his grandad was still in hospital. He hated to break a professional commitment but there was no way he could leave Cranfield now. Family had to come first in such an emergency.

With that piece of difficult business concluded, Ethan took a moment in the old school, but it was still too quiet, especially without Libby pottering about in the kitchen. The aroma of cocoa hung in the air and the worktops were still full of all her ingredients and equipment. But he found himself missing their everyday banter that he had got so accustomed to over the past couple of weeks. The house felt empty without her presence.

Ethan grabbed his coat and headed outside. He looked down the railway line briefly. At some point, the tree would need to be cleared from the railway line, but first he needed to see his family, so he turned in the other direction and walked along the platform towards the coffee shop.

There was a real chill in the air as he realised that it was the first of November. The temperatures had dropped, promising a cold winter ahead.

Pushing the door into the coffee shop, he realised that by referring to family, Ryan had meant their close friends as well.

After sharing a hug with his brother, Dad and Katy, Ethan then found himself embraced by all of their friends as well. Except one, he realised, as he sat down next to Libby.

He turned to look at her and found she was already watching him.

'You okay?' she murmured.

He nodded. 'Sure,' he lied. 'Not working today?'

She shook her head. 'It's not important,' she told him. 'I didn't think you would want to be bothered after last night.'

'I don't mind,' he replied, thinking back to the empty, quiet schoolhouse.

Ethan looked over at his dad who was sitting on the opposite table, He gave a start as he realised that Maggie was holding his hand and talking softly in his ear. He liked Maggie and knew that she had his dad had become close friends over the past year. But when had it blossomed into something more, he wondered, and how had he missed something of such significance in her dad's life?

He was amazed that his dad was able to trust and become close to anyone ever again, after the way that his wife had treated him. And yet, there he was, nodding and looking back at Maggie with fondness.

As Katy passed Ethan a large mug of coffee, he stared blankly around, focusing on the station memorabilia from a time when the station had been open. From the old ticket station to the posters and even the stationmaster's hat up on the wall, it felt warm and cosy.

'Here you go,' said Ryan, placing a large basket of muffins and pastries on the table for everyone to help themselves.

Ethan automatically took one of the still-warm breakfast muffins but found he had no appetite and put it down in front of him.

'It's one of my best recipes,' Ryan told him in a pointed tone, standing over him.

Ethan looked up at his brother but couldn't find the words. Luckily, they knew each other so well that they didn't need to speak. Ryan just placed a hand on his shoulder and gave it a brief squeeze before moving away to sit next to their dad.

'Eat,' ordered Libby, giving Ethan a nudge with her elbow. 'You'll feel better for it.'

However, Ethan wasn't sure that anything would make him feel better. He had let his grandad down at the worst possible time. The Halloween train had been a complete disaster and being back in the station only merely reminded him how terrible it had been.

'People were very kind about the fallen tree on the line,' he heard Katy tell Joe and Harriet.

'You know, some of the people absolutely loved the really scary decorations,' said Harriet, trying to put her usual positive spin on the situation.

'And you really can't blame the weather, can you?' added Nico to Bob. 'The problem with the fallen down tree could hardly lay at your door.'

'No, the main problem was letting your nephew get involved,' Ryan said to his dad, rolling his eyes.

'You didn't see the worst of it,' said Katy with a grimace. 'When the lights went out when the power failed, all the decorations had Die! and Kill! written on them. I screamed along with everyone else. Talk about a nightmare!'

'Everything Del does gives us nightmares,' muttered Libby. 'Honestly!'

Ethan had listened to them all in silence, but he couldn't bear it any longer.

'Well, it's too late now,' he said, running a hand through his hair. 'It was my lack of care that made the whole thing a disaster.'

'You couldn't have stopped the tree falling on the tracks,' said Joe with a frown. 'That was just bad luck.'

'But I could have ensured that the train was decorated properly,' said Ethan, shaking his head. 'It's not like I don't have skills with lighting, is it?' He took a shaky breath. 'I let Grandad down.'

'He won't think that,' said Bob softly. 'Nobody does, son.'

'Exactly,' added Ryan, frowning with concern at his brother. 'All's not lost, bro.'

'So why does it feel like it is?' said Ethan, before gulping back the emotion caught in his throat. 'It was Grandad's dream and now...' He sighed heavily.

There was a short silence in which he jumped slightly at the feel of a warm hand slipping into his. He looked up into Libby's concerned face and she squeezed his hand.

She didn't need to say anything, just like when they had been growing up she could read his mind. She knew the pain he was in and, just like in the early days, his pain was less because she shared it with him.

Ethan glanced around the room, where everyone was trying to avoid looking at him and concentrating on their breakfast. Ethan glanced at the wall next to him and realised there were a couple of newer photographs that he didn't remember.

'They're new,' he murmured.

'I found those when we were clearing out the loft in the apartment,' Katy told him, following his gaze. 'Thought they'd look great down here.'

He concentrated on the nearest one. It was an old black and white photograph, in the time of the steam trains. There was snow on the platform but he could see the lights twinkling on a large Christmas tree on the platform. Even back then, the steam train had run at Christmas, its engine decorated with a large holly wreath on the front.

The same steam train that his grandad had proposed to his grandmother on.

And then it struck him. 'You're right,' said Ethan, looking across at his brother and nodding at him.

'Of course I am,' said Ryan, smiling for the first time that morning. 'About what this time though?'

'That all's not lost,' Ethan told him. 'We'll do it again and do it better. Much much better.' He looked at his dad. 'We're going to have a Christmas train right here in Cranfield, just like Grandad wanted. And it's going to be the best one this village has ever seen!'

Bob was nodding in tearful agreement. 'That'll be just the tonic your grandad will need, son,' he said.

'But...' Katy was looking confused. 'But aren't you leaving tomorrow? For work, I mean?'

Ethan shook his head. 'I've cancelled the job,' he replied, before looking at his brother. 'This is the most important thing in my life right now,' he carried on.

Ryan raised his eyebrows in surprise but merely gave him a nod of approval in return.

There was a short pause before everyone started talking all at once in excited tones. Ethan turned to look at Libby, who nodded and squeezed his hand once more.

This time, the train idea would work, he promised himself. This time, he would throw every ounce of effort that he could to make it a success. He would give it one hundred and ten per cent and not let his grandad down.

Of course, he would need help and input from his friends and family. And he would also have to accept that he would stay on in Cranfield longer than he had planned. But he owed it to his grandad, and to prove to himself as well that he could contribute. That he didn't need to run away and let his family down again.

He might not believe in the magic of Christmas, but he could provide it for everyone else, couldn't he? And hopefully a little magic might just rub off on him too, he thought, looking down at Libby's hand in his once more.

## 29

Before leaving Platform 1, Libby had sheepishly asked Ethan if it was okay for her to use his kitchen that day. She felt bad about asking, even though he had told her that it was fine and she believed him. But he had already been through a dreadful evening after Eddie's stroke and she hadn't wanted to burden him further.

The fact was, though, that she had a week to her deadline and time was racing on. She had somehow managed to complete over half the order, but there was still a huge amount of work to do to get it done on time.

Ethan had been out all day, after his announcement in the coffee shop that morning about staying on in Cranfield to run a Christmas train. She had been surprised but pleased. She knew how much it would mean to his family and she was also happy that she would see him more often as well, although she tried not to dwell on the reasons why that would please her.

For the past couple of hours, she had knuckled down in the kitchen, working quickly. But despite the hard work, Libby found she couldn't stop her mind towards thinking of Eddie. Ethan and

Ryan had taken Bob to visit him in hospital and, according to the text she had just received from Katy, they were pleased with Eddie's progress so far. Relieved, Libby forwarded on the news to her dad by text.

Libby put down her mobile, and looked around the kitchen. She was still way behind on what she needed to get done. She had made more chocolates but the flat-pack boxes were still in their packaging nearby, so she had to store the truffles in layers. She could box them up last, she decided. The main thing was to get the chocolate finished. Although that was still such a tall order that she could almost cry at the thought.

She looked at the time. It was already half past four and she knew that Ethan wouldn't want her there when he got home from the hospital. She had maybe two hours before needing to finish her work for the day. She could feel the hysterical laughter bubbling up inside her. She was just tired, that was all. It had been an emotional twenty-four hours.

Libby checked her phone once more and suddenly weariness washed over her. She swayed a little on the spot and shook her head at herself. *Just sit down for five minutes*, she told herself. *You just need to rest for a short while and then you'll have more energy.*

Everything would be better just as soon as she'd had a little rest.

So she went over to the sofa, her phone in her hand and sank down. As soon as she was sitting, she felt her eyes droop. Maybe a power nap would be best, she decided. What was it that she had read recently? Twenty minutes was the optimum time to give the best results. Twenty minutes and the nibs would be ready in the oven. That was it. That sounded perfect.

Libby went to set the alarm on her phone to wake her up as soon as the twenty minutes was up, but she fell fast asleep before she had a chance to press the Set button.

* * *

It had been a long day, but Ethan was glad that they had been able to visit Eddie. The doctors were pleased with his progress and Ethan, Ryan and Bob had been grateful to find him weary but still the same old Eddie that they knew and loved.

'Wish you hadn't cancelled your job,' he'd said when he'd found out that Ethan was staying on. But even Ethan could tell that Eddie was pleased that the Christmas train would become a reality. 'That's great, lad,' he had murmured, squeezing Ethan's hand with his before falling asleep.

After dropping off Bob, Ryan and Ethan chatted outside for a short while.

Ethan suppressed a yawn. 'Sorry, bro,' he said. 'Long day.'

'Me too,' said Ryan. 'But it was good to see Grandad looking all right. He was, wasn't he?'

Ethan nodded. 'Early days, like the doctors said. But yeah.'

They both exchanged a concerned brotherly look as they stood by the front gate. Lights were beginning to be switched on in each cottage as dusk started to fall.

Ryan stepped forward to give his brother a hug before he headed home. But as he slapped Ethan on the shoulder, Ryan suddenly took a sharp intake of breath.

Ethan looked at his brother, but Ryan was frowning over his shoulder.

'Hey,' he said, squinting into the semi-darkness. 'Is that smoke coming out of your house?'

Ethan spun around and followed his brother's gaze down to the old school. He too could see a grey cloud pouring out of the open window of the lounge in the front of the building.

With sudden dread, he broke into a sprint towards his home.

Ryan raced alongside him as they both leapt over the small fence that separated the front yard from the lane.

Ethan ran up to the front door, noting the smell of burning coming out of the kitchen window as well as thick smoke. He threw open the door, grateful that it wasn't locked. But he realised with horror that it meant that surely Libby had yet to leave to go home as she always locked up each night. Therefore she must still be inside somewhere.

He rushed inside, immediately engulfed in grey smoke. 'Libby!' he shouted, trying to get his bearings through the acrid cloud. It was hard to see anything.

He went to switch on the overhead light, but Ryan stopped him. 'Too dangerous,' he said, bringing out the torch on his phone instead to shine a light around the lounge.

'Libby!' shouted Ethan again.

The brothers raced to the kitchen, feeling their way around. As the smoke billowed out of the open front door, Ethan felt his heart in his mouth as he looked for Libby.

Finally, to his absolute relief, he heard coughing nearby.

'Libby?' he shouted, heading in the direction where he had heard her.

It was then that he found her, sitting up on the sofa and coughing endlessly.

Feeling shaky but fired up on adrenaline, Ethan quickly picked her up in his arms and raced out through the front door. He headed down the path and lay her on the overgrown patch of grass, still holding her in his arms.

'Libby?' he said, his voice croaky with emotion and smoke. She looked tiny, her beautiful blonde hair covered with a layer of fine soot, as well as her face.

She tried to say something but began another round of coughing.

Ryan joined them, panting heavily. 'I've turned off the oven and opened up some more windows and the back door. How is she?'

'Fine,' said Libby, her voice tiny and raspy.

But when she began coughing yet again, Ryan drew out his phone and said, 'I'm calling the doctor.'

Ethan instinctively drew her closer to him, his heart thumping in his chest. Another hour and perhaps the outcome wouldn't have been so good, he thought. And the thought that he might have lost Libby made him hold her even tighter.

## 30

It was later that evening and Libby was tucked up in her bed, still trying to take in what had happened.

Apparently she had fallen asleep, but rather than only napping for a short time as planned, she had been told that she had been asleep for almost two hours. Which was plenty long enough for the cocoa beans in the oven to not only burn but catch alight.

'So is the school burnt down?' she asked, her voice still a croak from all the smoke.

Somehow she had slept through the smoke filling the old school until a moment before Ethan had suddenly rushed in and carried her outside. According to the local doctor who had already checked her out, that blast of fresh air had been the reason that she wasn't in hospital that night.

Katy shook her head. 'No, thankfully, it's just smoke damage. The building is still intact. The only fire was in the oven.'

Ryan had rung Katy for support as soon as they knew that the place wasn't on fire. She had stayed with Libby whilst the doctor had completed his checks, as well as helping her take a shower to wash away all the soot and grime.

Now Libby was in her pyjamas and squeaky clean, at least on her skin. Her throat and lungs would take a little while before they recovered.

She had a terrible thought. 'What about the chocolate?' she asked.

Katy sighed. 'Ryan took a look in there after the smoke had cleared. Unfortunately, anything out on the work surfaces in the kitchen is ruined, but luckily there wasn't a fire or it could have been much worse.'

Libby gasped, which brought on a further bout of coughing. She had made such a mess of things.

'But the pantry wall is inches thick and pretty air-tight,' carried on Katy. 'So it seems as if the truffles that you've made already are safe. You'll have to check them, but fingers crossed, it looks okay.'

It was a small consolation considering she'd almost ruined Ethan's kitchen, thought Libby with a grimace.

'Don't worry about anything for now,' carried on Katy, watching her closely. 'Remember what the doctor said.' She sighed heavily. 'You were so lucky that it's just the effects from the smoke inhalation for you to deal with. Now there's cough drops there on the side, next to the water, to help soothe your throat. For now, you just need to rest.'

'But...' began Libby, her mind thinking through everything that wouldn't happen if she had enforced rest.

'No buts,' said Katy, standing up. 'Just try to get some sleep tonight. Everything else can be sorted out tomorrow.' She hesitated. 'Your dad wants to see you, but he said Ethan could visit you first.'

'Ethan's here?' Libby was shocked. 'In my house?'

'He wanted to know what the doctor said. But he also wants to speak with you briefly.' Katy leaned over and kissed her on the cheek. 'I'm so glad you're okay,' she said, tears filling her eyes. 'Harriet and Flora send their love too. As well as everyone else in the village.'

'Everyone?' Libby's red eyes clicked wide.

Katy nodded. 'No secrets in Cranfield,' she said with a soft smile. 'Get some rest.'

As she went outside, Libby closed her eyes briefly. They felt gritty and sore, but Katy had rustled up some eye drops from somewhere which would help.

Hearing the creak of the floorboard, she looked up from her prone position in the bed and there was Ethan. He still looked sooty and grubby but, most of all, he looked extremely tired.

'You look worse than I do,' she croaked.

He appeared to try to smile at her joke but failed. Instead, he sighed and shook his head. 'Libs,' he began, with a groan.

'I'm so sorry,' she said. 'You were already worried about your grandad and now this! I hope I haven't completely ruined your lovely house.'

'To hell with the house!' snapped Ethan, before sinking down on the bed. 'I don't care about that! I care about you! When I think what might have happened if Ryan hadn't seen the smoke...' He ran a hand through his hair which was more black than blonde and a shower of sooty dust landed on the duvet cover. He tried to brush it off but ended up making it worse.

'It doesn't matter,' she told him, reaching out to take his hand in hers. 'I'm okay.'

He looked down at her hand, so pink compared to his, and squeezed it. 'You so nearly weren't okay though. I should have checked the batteries on that fire alarm. It's my fault.'

'It's not,' she told him. 'Anyway, I'm alright. So shut up.'

'Well, I'm not going to shut up,' he told her. 'I told you that you needed to ask for help.'

'I don't need any help,' she said automatically.

This at least raised a small smile from him. 'Sweetheart, you nearly burnt my house down,' he reminded her.

She looked so sheepish suddenly that he burst out laughing.

'Okay. So I have my faults,' she told him.

He raised his eyebrows. 'Am I allowed to list them?' he drawled.

'No. Not tonight.' She sighed. 'But yeah, maybe I can finally admit that I need help.'

'Do you know what your problem is?' he asked.

'I'm sure you're about to tell me,' she said.

He shook his head and finally looked into her eyes. 'You keep telling me that you're fine. And don't say that you are because tonight has proven spectacularly that you most definitely are not managing, are you?'

The tears welled up and made her eyes even more sore, but she didn't care. 'Nobody else can make the chocolate and we need the money, okay?' she said, feeling the tears roll down her cheeks.

Ethan groaned. 'Don't cry,' he said, reaching out to stroke the tears away from her cheek. 'I hate it when you cry. Listen, it'll be okay. We'll think of something.'

She sniffed. 'We will?'

'Absolutely.' He gave her a soft smile. 'I think between us we can cause everyone enough trouble, don't you?'

'It's been a while,' she reminded him.

He nodded. 'Yes, it has.' He leaned forward to kiss her on the forehead. 'Your dad wants to see you now.' He stood up from the bed and looked down at her. He went to say something else but shook his head instead, at himself. 'Get some sleep,' he told her.

Then he turned around and walked out of the bedroom. Libby closed her eyes, comforted by Ethan's visit and how much closer they were becoming after so many years apart.

# 31

Libby took a sip of the water from the glass that Katy had left on her bedside table and sank back against the pillows.

She still couldn't believe she'd been so stupid as to fall asleep whilst leaving the cocoa beans roasting in the oven. What an idiot! She felt bad for Ethan, who had effectively handed over full use of the kitchen and what had she done? Filled it with smoke and almost burnt it down!

She shook her head. Now she had to ensure the chocolates weren't ruined. And what if they were? Without the order for the chocolates, there would be no more income for her and her dad for the rest of the year, unless she found a job and fast.

She heard her dad's soft tread on the floorboards on the landing and looked up as he came into the bedroom.

He looked pale and drawn. All her fault, of course. He had already been upset about Eddie's stroke and now she had made things even worse for him by giving him something else to fret about.

'How are you, Elizabeth?' he asked, standing formally by her bed.

'I'm fine,' she croaked. 'Everything's fine, Dad. You don't need to worry about me.'

He looked surprised. 'Of course I worry about you,' he told her.

Libby sighed and shook her head. 'Only because I give you cause to,' she replied. 'I've always been a pain, making everything worse, making you ill and now look what a mess I've created! I nearly burnt down Ethan's home!'

She felt the tears prick her eyes once more and closed them to try to stop the emotion from overcoming her. She opened them as she felt her dad sit down on the bed next to her.

His blue eyes looked at hers, confused. 'What are you talking about?' he asked, his eyebrows crossed into a frown. 'How did you make me ill?'

'You know how,' she blurted out, the shock and fear from the evening's traumatic events finally coming to the forefront of her emotions. 'Your stroke, Dad! You think I don't know that it's all my fault?'

Her dad look horrified. 'What do you mean?' he said. 'Of course, it wasn't.'

She shook her head. 'I know you're trying to protect me, but it's true. All that stress I caused you when I was messing about growing up and that triggered something. I know it. I promised Mum I'd take care of you and look what happened! I failed her. And you.'

There was a short silence whilst Libby lay there, the misery almost overwhelming her. She had made such an almighty mess of things.

So she was shocked when her dad suddenly reached out to take her hand. She looked up at him surprised. He avoided her eyes for a while, merely looking down at the contrast between her smooth skin and his wrinkled one. Then, finally, he looked up.

'I had no idea that you've been blaming yourself all these years,' he said, with a shake of his head.

'Of course I have,' she replied. 'You're so sad all the time, Dad. It breaks my heart to see you like this when you were always so passionate about your teaching.'

'But it's not your fault,' he said, frowning. 'That's on me. I've been so stuck in my own misery that I hadn't seen what it had done to you. I was always too selfish. Too wrapped up with my job and my career to see what a special daughter I had.'

'Rubbish,' muttered Libby. 'I've been a pain to you since day one.'

'Now who's talking rubbish,' replied her dad, a smile touching the corner of his eyes. 'What a terrible job I've done as your father to make you feel like this.'

'Dad,' she began.

But he held up his hand. 'Let me get all this out. First of all, it was a blood clot in my brain that caused the stroke. That was it. And there is no way that you could have caused it.'

Libby gave a start at his words. Was it true?

'I've researched the subject since then and, believe me, I am right,' he carried on. 'Second, I don't know where you get the idea that you're a terrible daughter.'

Libby rolled her eyes. 'Have you conveniently forgotten how lazy I was at school, messing about and too busy rebelling to get any kind of qualifications?'

'All I know is that you've had a fire inside of you since the day you were born,' he replied. 'Qualifications aren't everything.'

Libby was shocked. 'But you always said that they were,' she reminded him. 'That education was the be-all and end-all.'

'May I add a small amendment to my original statement?' he asked, with a sad smile. 'Education is necessary and hopefully a good grounding for adult life. But some things are more important. Kindness. Generosity of heart. Vitality of spirit. All of which you have in abundance, my dear daughter.' He hesitated before carrying on. 'If I have given you cause to think that I'm not proud of you, then let me state my feelings once and for all. You've worked so hard to keep a roof over our heads, taking endless plane journeys at all hours of the day and night. I am very proud to call you my daughter.'

Libby couldn't hold back the tears any longer. 'But, Dad, I've made such a mess,' she said, with a sob. 'I lost my job and now I can't even use Ethan's kitchen. I won't reach my deadline and we won't get paid!'

'Don't worry about that now,' he told her, squeezing her hand. 'By the way, you lied to me about where you've been. You didn't tell me that you were making chocolate.'

Her shoulders sagged. 'I didn't want to upset you. It was something that Mum always did.'

'I know and I had no idea that you've inherited her talent,' her dad replied. 'I wish you'd have told me.'

Libby sighed. She really had made an awful lot of bad decisions lately, she realised.

'And I just wanted to say...' His voice drifted off and he frowned to himself.

Figuring that he had lost his train of thought, she said, 'It doesn't matter, Dad. It's late.'

He looked at her with a fierceness in his eyes. 'It matters very much and I need to say this. Thank you. Thank you for taking care of me all these years.'

She took a sharp intake of breath. 'I would never have left you,' she told him. 'Ever.'

'I know.' His eyes softened. 'Anyway, I've spoken to both Ethan and Katy tonight,' her dad carried on. 'You're not alone. You never were, although you obviously felt that you might be. And that's all on me. My fault. My error. And I'm so very sorry for it. But from tonight, that changes. We both need to start asking for help. Reaching out to people. To stop closing ourselves off from the world. Because it's not done either of us any good, has it?'

Libby couldn't speak and so merely shook her head and closed her eyes as the tears streamed down her cheeks.

She suddenly felt herself being pulled gently forward and found herself held against her dad's chest, his one good arm stretching out around her and patting her on the back.

'There, there, my dear darling Elizabeth,' she heard him say. 'Everything's going to be different now. Everything's going to be okay.'

She sighed with something akin to relief as she tried to take in what he was telling her. Perhaps it really was a new beginning for the both of them.

He gently released her and she sank back against the pillows. 'Now, doctor's orders were that you rest, so try to get a good night's sleep.' He stood up and gave her a sad smile as he looked down at her. 'By the way, when you're better, I'd like to taste some of that chocolate of yours.'

'You would?' she murmured.

'Of course,' he told her. There was a short pause before he added, 'I love you.'

Libby gulped away more tears at the words so rarely spoken between them.

'I love you too, Dad,' she said, her voice croaky from emotion as well as the smoke.

He reached out to give her hand another squeeze before he headed over to the door. 'We'll keep this open tonight because I want to keep an eye on you.'

She felt like a little girl but, for once, was grateful not to have to be the strong one, to let someone else take charge.

Suddenly overcome with exhaustion, her eyelids grew heavy. 'Goodnight, Dad,' she murmured, snuggling down under the covers.

'Goodnight, my dear,' she heard him say, before sleep pulled her into its arms.

Her dad stood watching her for a very long time until he was certain that she was peaceful and asleep before he quietly left the bedroom.

## 32

Libby woke up late in the morning to find the daylight streaming through a gap in the curtains.

It took her a moment to work out exactly what had happened the previous night to make her feel so groggy and croaky and then she remembered it all. She wondered how bad the smoke damage was in the rest of Ethan's home and immediately felt a wave of guilt of how she had almost destroyed his kitchen.

She was contemplating getting up, but, despite having slept for twelve hours straight, she still felt absolutely exhausted.

So it was no small relief when she heard footsteps and saw her dad come into the bedroom holding a small tray with his good hand.

'Good morning,' he said, with a smile. 'You're awake at last.'

'Morning,' she replied, sitting up in bed despite it feeling like a real effort. 'I can't believe I slept for so long.'

Her dad carefully placed the tray on the bed next to her. Libby looked down to see it was holding a mug of coffee and a couple of delicious-looking muffins, along with various envelopes.

'I'm glad you slept well,' he told her. 'You must have needed it. So I thought it was about time I brought you breakfast in bed.'

'Thank you,' she replied.

'I can't take credit for the muffins as apparently they're Helen's special recipe,' he said, sitting down on the other side of the bed.

'Grams made this?' asked Libby, her stomach growing in anticipation.

Flora's grandmother's baking was excellent and so she took a bite almost immediately. The sweet muffin exploded the flavours in her mouth, along with the tangy sharpness of blueberries.

'Mmm,' she murmured in pleasure.

'Helen dropped off a basket this morning crammed full of various pastries and pies to keep us both going,' her dad told her.

'How nice of her,' said Libby, before taking another bite.

'And the cards are all from our neighbours wishing you well,' he carried on.

'Seriously?' Libby was amazed. 'How kind.'

'Indeed.' Her father studied her carefully. 'Now, how are you feeling? Any soreness in your chest or throat? Has it got worse?'

His concern touched her. 'It's no worse,' she told him. 'I still feel a bit parched but just weary after all the excitement, I guess.'

'Then another day of rest should do you the world of good,' he said.

Libby immediately began to shake her head before she saw the look in his eyes and shot him a sheepish grin. 'Old habits die hard,' she muttered.

'Yes, they do,' he said. 'Anyway, your friends are all due to come and visit you any minute now, so you can't go anywhere, even if I were to let you.'

'They're coming here?' asked Libby, somewhat alarmed. Her

dad had always expressed his dismay at any visitors coming to the cottage so they had stopped arriving many years ago.

'I invited them.' Now it was her dad's turn to look sheepish. 'You're not up to going out and they were all expressing their concern for you, according to Helen. So I thought it would cheer you up to see them.'

'Thank you.'

'I also got a telling-off,' he said with a grimace.

Libby giggled. 'From Grams?'

'Yes, well, perhaps she felt it was overdue,' said her dad. 'Anyway, she told me that as I'm young enough to be her son, she felt that a "good nagging" was necessary to get me to pull my weight around the home.'

'Gosh.' Libby cleared her throat. 'Look, Dad, don't worry about that. As soon as I'm up and about again, then you can leave all that to me.'

'But she's right.'

Libby stared at him. 'She is?' she asked tentatively.

'I've been stuck in neutral, I think she said, for so very long. Almost revelling in the misery of the stroke that I've let it become more than it should have been.'

'Yes, but you're not the same as you were before,' Libby told him quickly.

He nodded thoughtfully. 'True, but I'm not sure I should let it define me either. And it was a huge burden on you when I really could do a bit more. I mean, look. I made you a cup of coffee.' He smiled proudly to himself. 'When was the last time I did that?'

'It's been a while,' she murmured, with a soft smile which she was pleased to see him return.

Just then, they both heard a knock on the front door.

'Your adoring masses appear to have arrived,' he told her. 'I'll go and let them in.'

'Thanks for the coffee,' she called out as he went.

By the time she had eaten her muffin and drunk half of the coffee, Katy, Harriet and Flora had all climbed the stairs and rushed into the small bedroom, immediately filling it up.

'Oh, you've got more colour today!' said Katy, rushing over to give her a kiss on the cheek. 'That's good.'

'Yes, only the croaky voice to get rid of,' replied Libby.

'I dunno,' said Flora, next up to give her a kiss. 'I think husky and quiet suits you.'

'A quietish Libby? Never,' said Harriet, giving an exaggerated shudder.

They all sat down on the bed on either side of her and then there was a short silence.

'You silly sausage,' said Harriet, eventually breaking the silence and looking tearful.

'I've aged about ten years,' said Flora, with a heavy sigh.

'Me too,' said Katy, checking her dark hair in the camera of her mobile. 'Do I have any grey hairs? It feels like I should have.'

'Thank goodness you're okay,' said Harriet, reaching out to take her hand.

'I'm fine,' Libby told them. 'Which is more than can be said for Ethan's kitchen.' She grimaced at the thought. 'How bad is it?' she tentatively asked.

'Nothing that a bit of scrubbing of walls and a new splash of paint won't sort out,' said Katy quickly.

'The men are all going over there to help clear up the smoke damage,' said Flora. 'They've all dropped everything to help out.'

Libby blew out a long sigh. 'Is Ethan very mad?' she asked.

Katy looked non-plussed. 'Ethan? No, of course not. Only with the thought of you hurting yourself. You know what he's like. He doesn't care about material possessions like that.'

Libby nodded thoughtfully. 'Yes, but I don't mean to pile

more stress on him when he's already got so much on his plate with Eddie and the Christmas train.'

'Oh, that's all going to be sorted out tomorrow,' said Katy briskly. 'Plenty of time yet if we all lend a hand.'

'Anyway, he'll be okay,' said Flora. 'It's Ethan. If he were to be any more laid-back, he'd be horizontal most of the time.'

'From his long list of girlfriends over the years, perhaps he has been!' added Harriet, laughing.

But Libby didn't join in. Ethan had had a string of dates over the years. And so had she, she reminded herself. They were equal partners in being footloose and fancy free. But the thought of him being with another woman didn't sit well with her that morning.

*It must just be because you're so tired*, she told herself, before taking a sip of her coffee.

As she relaxed back against the pillows, a dreadful thought occurred to her and she sat bolt upright.

'The deadline!' she said, before a bout of coughing took over once more.

Harriet and Flora leaned forward in united concern.

Katy, meanwhile, waited until Libby could catch her breath before she spoke. 'It's fine,' she said.

'It's not,' croaked Libby. 'I'm running out of days.'

'We know,' said Harriet.

'But you have us,' added Flora.

Libby blinked at them, trying to comprehend what she was being told.

'What we're saying is that we're all going to help make the truffles, along with Grams and Maggie,' said Katy. 'We're heading over to the old school now to clean everything up ready for your instructions this afternoon. But, for this morning, you're going to rest. And that's an order.'

'We'll have everything done on time, okay?' added Flora. 'So don't fret. Just rest for now.'

Libby leant back against the pillows once more and smiled at her friends, the tears pricking her eyes. 'Thank you,' she whispered.

They all smiled back at her.

'What are friends for?' said Harriet, reaching out to squeeze her hand.

## 33

Ethan was still feeling very rattled by Libby's near escape.

After a restless night spent in Ryan and Katy's spare bedroom, he headed back to the old school to survey the damage with his brother.

Ryan whistled as they stared around the lounge. 'I was hoping it wouldn't look quite so bad in the daylight,' he said.

Ethan nodded, feeling quite depressed. 'Me too.'

The lounge and kitchen, unfortunately, were not looking good, nor smelling great either with the acrid aroma of smoke still in the air. Soot covered the sofa, floor and walls and every surface that it had been able to settle upon. Thankfully, the door into the bedroom had been closed and therefore the smoke hadn't got in there, but the rest of the mess was almost over-whelming.

'On the plus side,' added Ryan. 'Because you're such a lazy so-and-so, you hadn't unpacked, so that's worked in your favour as most of your decent stuff is still in boxes. So that saves us a bit of work.'

Ethan looked at Ryan. 'Us?' he asked. 'Haven't you got work to do?' He glanced at his watch and realised that it was almost opening time at Platform 1.

But, to his surprise, Ryan shook his head. 'No way,' he said. 'Today my brother needs help. So Katy's put a notice on the door about a family emergency and we're closed for the day.'

Ethan felt incredibly touched. 'Great. Cheers, bro.'

Ryan appeared to hesitate before giving him a slap on the shoulder. 'Some things are more important than profits.'

Ethan nodded. 'Yes, they are.' He paused before carrying on. 'Dad said that the update from the hospital was positive this morning.'

'Grandad's got almost all his movement back in his hand which is good news,' replied Ryan.

'We should be focused on grandad and not all this,' said Ethan, waving his hand at the mess in front of them.

'We can do both,' Ryan told him. 'And besides, there's nothing we can do for Grandad at the moment. He's in the best hands with the doctors and nurses. So let's get things straight back here before he gets home.'

'Okay.' Ethan blew out a sigh. 'It's going to be a busy day.'

'I agree.' Ryan gave him a smile. 'Thankfully, many hands make light work.'

Ethan looked at his brother questioningly, but then he heard the chatter of people outside.

'Here's your workforce, right on cue,' said Ryan, going over to the front door and inviting whoever it was inside.

Ethan was surprised but pleased to see Joe, Nico, Bob and even Dodgy Del all standing outside.

'We're free but we come highly recommended,' Nico told him with a grin as they came inside. Although his smile faded a little when he saw the smoke damage.

'Thank goodness everyone was okay,' said Bob, staring around the room before heading over to give Ethan a hug.

'Blimey,' added Del. 'Bit of a mess, ain't it?'

'Nothing that a bit of elbow grease won't sort out,' said Joe. 'So it's just the soot and smoke to clear?'

Ethan nodded. 'I guess so.'

'Luckily, I know all about it,' Dodgy Del told them. 'Had a few burnt kitchens in my time.'

'Having tasted your cooking once, that doesn't surprise me in the least,' replied Ryan.

'First thing is to get everything outside, give it a good air,' carried on Del. 'Then we need to wash down the ceiling, walls and floor. With all the windows and doors open, this horrible smell will soon shove off as well.'

'Well, I never thought I'd say this, but we'll follow our cousin's plan,' said Ryan, raising his eyebrows at Ethan.

But Ethan had wandered over to look at the kitchen and was horrified to see all of Libby's chocolate equipment covered with soot.

'You're definitely going to need a new oven,' said Joe, coming to stand next to him.

'I was going to replace that old one anyway,' replied Ethan. 'But what about all of this?' He waved his hand towards the work surfaces, piled high with all of Libby's bowls, mixers and boxes.

'That's in hand too,' Ryan told him, coming to stand next to his brother.

At that moment, Katy, Flora and Harriet arrived at the back door, their eyes clicking wide open at the sooty mess in front of them.

'Wow,' said Flora, blowing out a sigh. 'It could have been so much worse.'

Harriet shook her head. 'Let's not talk about it,' she said with a shudder.

'Then let's keep busy,' said Katy, stepping forward. 'The chocolate truffle business is temporarily moving to Strawberry Hill Farm, so everything needs to be packed up and delivered there this morning.'

'I've got my van outside,' announced Dodgy Del. 'You can get it all in there and it will only take one trip up to the farm.'

For a second, Katy hesitated. They all knew that Del's smoky, spluttering old van was a health hazard all on its own.

But, to Ethan's surprise, Katy looked at him and smiled. 'Del, that would be a great help,' she told him.

Ethan watched his cousin beam from ear to ear before turning to his brother. 'Miracles are happening all over the place this morning,' he murmured.

'Well, you know what they say,' murmured Ryan. 'It takes a village to build a community.'

Ethan nodded thoughtfully. He had automatically pushed against the idea of becoming one of Cranfield's permanent residents for so long that he had never considered what it would really mean.

But now he thought about it, he wasn't quite so sure that doing up and selling the old school would be his plan going forward. After all, he realised, looking round at the family and friends that had gathered round to help him in his hour of need, perhaps he needed them.

He couldn't help but feel grateful as everyone began to clear and clean up his home.

# 34

After a morning of enforced rest, Libby was picked up in Harriet's car and driven the short distance to Strawberry Hill Farm.

Her dad had made them both lunch before she had left and she was struck by his sudden change of heart and outlook. He seemed, dare she think it, more positive. He had even told her that he was planning on visiting Eddie in the hospital that afternoon, once he'd checked it was okay with his family.

She had thought long and hard about what he had said the previous evening and perhaps he was right. Perhaps she wasn't to blame for his stroke. It was still hard to overcome her feelings of guilt but maybe she should try to believe him and then they could both start moving forward with their lives at last.

As Harriet turned left onto the narrow lane towards Strawberry Hill Farm, the view was a welcome sight. Autumn was in earnest now and the colours of the trees lining the avenue were beautiful in their golden and crimson hues. The rustling of a few dry leaves underfoot as Libby walked along the potholed lane reminded her that the crisp cold days of winter were only just around the corner.

A cool breeze whistled across the open courtyard in front of the farm as she reached the turquoise front door and knocked on it.

It was quickly flung open by a smiling Flora. 'Hello! You look so much better!' she said, stepping forward to give her a hug. 'Come on in.'

Harriet had told her that Flora and Grams had kindly offered the use of their kitchen to complete the chocolate order. They were also insisting on helping, a concept that was still somewhat new to Libby.

The door led directly into the large kitchen. It was a comfortable, welcoming space with a very large oak table in the middle and the homely aroma of coffee and freshly baked bread.

But that day there was also the sweet telltale smell of something far more familiar as well – cocoa.

To Libby's surprise, all of her chocolate-making equipment was already laid out on every work surface, along with the ingredients and the few flat-pack boxes that had been saved.

Also filling up the kitchen were Grams, who stepped forward to give her a warm embrace, as well as Katy, Harriet and Maggie.

'What are you all doing here?' asked Libby, delighted to see them.

'We're all taking some time off work to give you a hand,' Harriet told her.

'After all, it's all my fault that you got this big order,' added Katy, biting her lip in worry. 'So the least I could do is help you with it.'

Libby was touched and, for a moment, the tears pricked her eyes.

'It's all right to ask for help every once in a while,' said Grams softly.

Libby nodded.

'Now, everything has been cleaned and washed with lots of soapy water,' Flora told her. 'So how much is there left to be done?'

'I'm not sure,' said Libby. 'I'll have to have a count up and see.'

'You do that and I'll get the kettle on,' said Grams, with a firm nod.

Flora showed Libby into the pantry, where the completed boxes of truffles had been safely put away. Libby counted them up and realised that she still had over a third of the order left to do in only a couple of days.

She went back into the kitchen to let everyone know the state of play.

'It's okay,' said Katy, with a firm nod. 'Once we've set up the equipment properly, you can get all your ducks in a row.'

But at that point, Libby decided that if she was going to be honest with everyone, she really ought to start now.

'Actually I don't have my ducks in a row,' she confessed. 'I'm not sure I even have any ducks. Maybe I only have a couple of naughty squirrels who have legged it and are off partying somewhere.'

Her friends giggled.

'Truth be told,' carried on Libby in a far more serious tone. 'I don't think I was ever going to meet the deadline on my own.'

'Well, you're not on your own now,' insisted Katy.

'Absolutely,' said Maggie. 'Put us to work. We'll soon get up and running.'

Libby hesitated. 'Are you sure?' she asked.

'Of course we are!' said Flora. 'After all, look what happened last time you tried to do it all by yourself!'

'I was just a little bit tired,' muttered Libby.

'Well, thank goodness for Ethan,' said Harriet.

Libby was still embarrassed about the huge furore that she

had caused by falling asleep. But at least Ethan had been gracious afterwards, not letting her take the blame for the smoke damage when she knew that it was all her fault, her wretched pride that had caused the accident.

'The boys are still over there, helping clean up the soot from, well, everywhere,' Katy told her.

'Looks like everyone needs a hand this week,' announced Grams. 'So let's get the coffee and tea flowing and get going.'

Libby explained her process of making her truffles, all the way from the cocoa bean to the final chocolate truffle. They split the work down to individual tasks. Grams was put in charge of timing the roasting of the cocoa beans in her oven. Flora was measuring all the ingredients out in preparation, Maggie was in charge of the melanger, which, thankfully, had survived the fire, Harriet was rolling out the truffles and Katy, who had absolutely no cooking skills whatsoever, was putting the flat-pack boxes together as well as ordering more to cover the ones that had been lost to smoke damage.

They all began to work steadily but quickly, the conversation washing over Libby as they made inroads into the amount of chocolates still left to be made.

Perhaps, thought Libby, glancing around at her friends, some good could come out of something so awful. And that asking for help wasn't such a bad thing after all.

## 35

As the day went on, Ethan had to agree with Ryan that it was a good thing that he hadn't had time to unpack as the majority of his stuff was still in boxes and therefore immune from the soot.

But they still carried everything outside to give it a good airing, along with the leather sofas and the old oven, which had been disconnected and would be taken to the rubbish tip later.

At least, with all the ceilings and the walls having been scrubbed, the soot was beginning to be removed. The kitchen was still a work in progress as every cupboard needed wiping down, inside and out.

In the middle of the afternoon, there was a tentative knock on the front door despite it being open to continue to air the place.

Ethan headed over and was amazed to see Philip standing there, looking nervous.

'Hello, Philip,' he said. 'Is everything okay? Is it Libby?'

Philip gave him a tentative smile. 'She's fine, thank you. Safe with all the ladies up at Strawberry Hill Farm,' he replied. 'Actually, I was going to ask if I could do anything to help.'

'That's very kind,' Ethan told him.

'Not at all,' replied Philip. 'I think it's the least I can do when you saved my daughter's life last night.'

Ethan gulped. The memory of those few seconds when he didn't know what had happened to Libby still played over in his mind.

'It sounds more dramatic than it actually was,' he said, wanting to allay Philip's fears.

Philip glanced over Ethan's shoulder and a look of dismay crossed his face. 'It certainly looks quite dramatic,' he said, taking in the wall next to the fireplace which was still smeared with soot.

Ethan stepped aside to let Philip inside.

Philip had been the infant school headmaster when they had been growing up, as well as the strict father that Libby had spent so long rebelling against. They hadn't really spoken since Ethan had left Cranfield so it felt a little strange to be doing so at that moment. But perhaps time was the great healer that his dad had always told him it was.

Philip looked around thoughtfully as he went. 'Goodness, it's been years since I've been in here,' he said.

'Bit of a mess now,' said Ethan, with a grimace.

'Nothing that a lick of paint won't sort out!' shouted over Nico, as he continued to wash down the ceiling.

'The oak beams were from a local tree apparently,' said Philip, looking up to the ceiling. 'I always liked them.'

'Me too,' replied Ethan.

But Philip was frowning as he looked around once more. 'I think I never really appreciated this place until I lost my job,' he murmured.

Ethan looked at him in surprise at this confession but didn't say anything, letting Philip say what was on his mind.

'You see, I gave up what I thought was the pinnacle of my

career to be here,' carried on Philip. 'I was headmaster of Chantries Grammar School for ten years.'

The shock on Ethan's face must have shown because Philip gave him a nod of his head in confirmation. Chantries was a highly exclusive private school on the outskirts of Aldwych town.

'You and Libby were too young to remember back to that time,' Philip told him. 'It was the most prestigious school in the area even back then.'

'So why did you move jobs back here?' Ethan couldn't help but ask.

'Because my dear wife's illness had begun to make its unwelcome appearance,' said Philip with a soft sigh. 'We didn't tell Elizabeth for many years that her mother was unwell. And, for the most part, we were able to keep it hidden. Elizabeth was so young, you see. But Diana needed me more and more and so I took this job instead so that I could be close by.' Philip shook his head, almost at himself, it seemed. 'I'm afraid I took my frustrations of the backwards step in my career at any unruly behaviour in the classroom.'

Ethan shrugged his shoulders. 'Some of us most definitely deserved it,' he said, remembering the many times that he played the clown to impress Libby.

But Philip was still frowning. 'You were only children. It was wrong of me.'

'But you were hugely encouraging too,' Ethan told him, truthfully. 'You know, a lot of kids are where they are today in their careers because of your guidance and help.'

Philip placed a tentative hand on Ethan's shoulder. 'I was so glad Elizabeth had a friend like you growing up. Someone who understood her.'

Ethan raised his eyebrows. 'Are you sure about that?' he asked, with a smile. 'We got into a lot of trouble.'

But Philip merely shook his head. 'You're a good man, Ethan. And I know you care for her. How much, is down to what's in your heart.' He hesitated for a moment. 'How is your grandad?' he asked.

'Fine,' said Ethan. 'He's still very tired, but his speech has certainly improved over the past couple of days.'

'When do they think he'll be home?' asked Philip.

'According to the doctors, next week hopefully,' replied Ethan, holding up his crossed fingers. 'Here's hoping, although there's various tests and things to sort out before then.' But then he paused before carrying on. 'He just seems so different. Dad and I weren't sure if he's a bit depressed, to be honest.'

'That's totally understandable,' replied Philip.

'Hopefully we'll find him in better spirits this afternoon,' said Ethan. 'Ryan was just about to head over for visiting time. I'll head over tomorrow when all this is cleared up.'

Philip nodded slowly before seeming to come to a decision. 'Actually, would it be terribly intrusive if I came with you tomorrow?' he asked. 'Perhaps I may help, having been through the same thing myself, that is.'

Ethan was pleased. 'Of course,' he said, with a smile. 'I'm sure Grandad would welcome a change of conversation from me and the rest of the family.'

Philip smiled. 'Excellent,' he said. 'Now, what can I do to help around here?'

'How good are you with a scrubbing brush?' asked Bob, coming over to join them.

Philip held up his one good hand. 'I'll do my best,' he replied.

'Excellent,' said Bob. 'I'll lead the way.'

As they headed into the kitchen, Ethan found that he was surprised but pleased that Philip had come to join them. He knew that Libby's dad had been something of a recluse since his own stroke, but perhaps he was finally coming to terms with what had happened to him. And maybe he would help Eddie through these early days and weeks as well, although the family had already agreed that they wouldn't tell him about the dramatic events of the night before.

'You know,' said Nico, who was kneeling down to scrub the skirting board. 'I don't think this is going to come up too badly once we give it all a lick of paint.'

Ethan nodded. The feel of the place was much better, he thought. And the smoky smell would eventually disappear too.

The truth be told, almost losing the school wasn't anything like the thought of what might have happened to Libby. And yet, despite his initial reservations on buying somewhere in Cranfield, he actually liked the old school. It had felt more like home than anywhere he had lived for a very long time. Probably since he'd left the family apartment above the station all those years ago. He'd kept running all these years, except coming full circle back to Cranfield hadn't been quite as painful as he'd imagined. If anything, he was enjoying the company of his friends and neighbours even more than he would ever thought possible.

He wondered briefly how Libby was feeling that afternoon before distracting himself by picking up a mop and began to clear the soot from above the fireplace.

## 36

After another busy day, and with the help of her friends, it looked as if Libby was actually going to make her deadline for the large order of truffles. There was only a small amount left to do after everyone had clubbed together to get the order fulfilled.

'I never had any doubt that you could do it,' said Katy, beaming from ear to ear as she packaged up a box of glossy truffles with a red bow.

'I did,' said Libby, with a brief grimace.

Thankfully, her throat was entirely free of smoke damage and she felt much more like her old self.

She concentrated on rolling up the truffle she was holding in the tray of cocoa powder that she had placed on the kitchen table.

'So, what next?' asked Flora, sitting down at the table whilst she began to stick the printed labels that Katy had produced on each box.

'I sleep,' said Libby, with a smile.

'And then what?' asked Harriet. 'You're not going to give up making chocolate, are you?'

Libby laughed. 'Never! But I may just decide not to try to burn down any more kitchens,' she added with a grin.

'Let's hope not!' laughed Katy. 'Not that Ethan seems to have minded about that too much.'

'He never did where Libby was concerned,' murmured Flora.

Libby looked at her. 'What are you getting at?' she asked.

'Is there something you want to tell us about you and Ethan?' said Flora, in a pointed tone.

'Your eyebrows are telling all,' replied Libby. 'And yet there's nothing to tell.'

Harriet rolled her eyes as she dried up a couple of trays on the draining board. 'You always do this,' she said.

'Do what?' asked Libby.

'You don't really tell us anything,' Harriet told her. 'Not anything deep anyway.'

'And look how that turned out!' said Katy with a grin.

Libby blushed. She didn't think she'd ever get over almost burning down the old schoolhouse.

'So let us in,' urged Flora.

Libby shrugged her shoulders but could feel the blush spreading across her cheeks. 'I told you, there's nothing really to tell.'

'Yes, there is,' said Harriet.

Libby took a sharp intake of breath. Was it possible that they knew about her and Ethan's secret marriage in Las Vegas?

'The prom,' added Flora, to Libby's semi-relief. 'You always say he ruined it, but you've never really explained why.'

'All we know is that one minute you were as close as we all are to each other, the next you hated him with a passion,' said Harriet. 'Any time we asked you, you just brushed it off.'

Libby hesitated. Perhaps she could just give them the truth for once.

In the end, she decided to just go for it. After all, these were her best friends and she trusted them.

'Okay,' she began. 'So I was all dressed up, but when he came to pick me up, he was completely and utterly miserable. Snappy and cold. It was so unlike him.'

'Why?' asked Katy.

'No idea,' said Libby, shaking her head. 'He wouldn't tell me. But it carried on like that for the first hour of the prom. No dancing. Not even any conversation. He was just morose and sulky and nothing I could say could bring him out of his bad mood.'

She certainly hadn't had the first kiss with him that she'd been wishing for and dreaming of.

'That's not much to go on,' said Katy, still frowning.

'Exactly,' agreed Harriet. 'So he was just in a bad mood?'

'Worse,' Libby told them. 'He got steaming drunk and then just left me there. Alone! At the prom!'

There was a short, shocked silence.

'Why didn't you come and find me?' asked Flora, looking upset.

'I didn't want to ruin your night as well,' Libby told her. 'So I danced my high heels off, snogged the captain of the football team and then threw up in a bush on the way home.' She grinned at her friends. 'Epic.'

Harriet was still looking confused. 'But how can it be epic if you said he'd ruined it for you?'

'He did ruin it for me!' replied Libby, hotly. 'Because he shouldn't have left me. It wasn't supposed to be like that. It was supposed to be the start of something...' Her voice trailed off and she looked down to stroke Paddington the dog, who was lying under the kitchen table as usual. Anything to avoid the eye contact from her friends after she had said too much. In reply, Paddington thumped his furry tail on the floor in delight.

'It's us,' she heard Harriet murmur. 'You should have said something.'

'I agree,' added Flora. 'We were, are, your best friends. You're supposed to tell us everything.'

Libby took a deep breath as she straightened up. 'Well, I didn't see him for a couple of days after the prom because I was in a strop with him, quite rightly so in my opinion. And then Mum began to get ill and other things were more important.' She paused before carrying on. 'He came for the funeral.' She recalled a hug from him but nothing more. 'Then he disappeared off to college, barely came home in the holidays either, so that was the end of a beautiful friendship.'

Katy looked at her. 'So you were close one day and not the next? Didn't you want to know what happened?' she asked. 'Why he was so upset that evening?'

'No.' Libby shrugged her shoulders. 'Anyway, I know what happened. He's the same idiot he always has been.'

It was the first lie that she had told her friends since starting the story. Her biggest fear was that he just didn't care for her the way she'd always cared for him. That she'd misread his feelings and it had been all regret on his part for even asking her to go with him. That perhaps he had wanted to take someone else.

'Maybe you could ask him?' asked Flora.

'Or not,' Libby told her. 'It's ancient history, isn't it? Bloomin' prom. Those things are so lame anyway.'

Flora smiled to herself. 'Yeah, that's why you got all dolled up in that gorgeous dress.'

'Oooh!' Katy's eyes gleamed. 'Colour?'

'Dark blue,' Harriet told her. 'Like a midnight blue. And it sparkled under certain lights. I was with her when she bought it.'

'She looked amazing,' added Flora, nodding.

'Says the prom queen,' said Libby, giving her a nudge with her elbow.

Katy looked at Flora delighted. 'You were the prom queen?'

'Her dress was red,' said Harriet, misty-eyed in memory. 'She was so beautiful.'

'She still is,' said Nico, coming into the kitchen.

Flora blushed and the conversation moved on.

While her friends chatted with Nico about the progress of cleaning and painting the school, Libby waited for the inevitable regret about finally telling her friends about what had happened at the prom, after all these years. But the regret never came. Only the warmth and support that true friends could bring.

And perhaps they were right. Perhaps one day she would find out what had actually happened that evening to make Ethan so upset as to break up their close friendship. Then maybe they could begin to heal the past and move on at last.

## 37

After picking up Bob and Philip, Ethan drove to the hospital to visit Eddie.

'How is your home looking today?' asked Philip.

'Better thanks,' replied Ethan. 'Ryan, Joe and Nico are giving the whole place a second coat of paint and then I think it'll just be a matter of airing it out, although the smell has almost gone now.'

He was grateful for his friends' help and would be moving back in there the following day. Ryan had already helped him pick out a brand new oven and Katy had insisted on another order of new bedding, cushions, curtains, tea towels and towels for the bathroom. She had also added table lamps and other furnishings.

'All the nice things,' she had told him. 'So you can stop living like a student at last!'

Despite grumbling, Ethan was grateful for her input as he really had no idea about such things.

Once they had parked outside the hospital, Ethan and Bob

slowed their normal walking pace in deference to Philip's slower speed as he limped alongside with them.

Ethan was still surprised that Philip had offered to come along, but he was hoping it would be a positive visit for his grandad to see an old friend.

A short while later, they were with Eddie in the small ward.

'So how are you?' asked Philip, as he sat down on the chair next to the bed.

Eddie nodded. 'Not bad,' he replied, his congenial smile still a little wonky.

'I'm sure it's been a great shock,' said Philip, nodding. 'I know it was to me.'

Eddie looked at him. 'Yes. It was. I knew I'd not been feeling right but couldn't quite put my finger on it.'

'Things will still seem a little awkward for a while,' Philip told him. 'A silly thing like making a cup of tea could take forever in the early days. Now, I've got used to using my other hand.' He lifted up his left hand. 'Of course, being right-handed I've had to learn to do everything again.'

Eddie looked down at his hands. Thankfully, he had kept the majority of his mobility, both in his hands and feet. 'I guess I was lucky,' he said. 'If you call it that.'

'I'm not sure I would,' replied Philip. 'But here we are anyway. Survivors the both of us.'

Both men shared a smile and the fact that they weren't alone in going through their ordeal.

'I hope you can learn by my example,' said Philip. 'In what not to do, I mean.'

Eddie looked at him in surprise. 'What do you mean?' he asked.

'The fact was that,' began Philip, taking a deep breath. 'I was embarrassed. About being incapacitated. I felt less of a man, I guess. I lost my job, my freedom. But it turned out that I was the only one keeping me a prisoner, nobody else. I was too proud. Defined by how other people would perceive me.'

Ethan and Bob exchanged stunned looks. He had never expected Libby's dad of all people to admit some kind of failing. But it seemed to be what Eddie needed to hear as his grandad was nodding along with him.

'That's what I keep thinking,' said Eddie. 'I keep thinking folk will think me stupid if I can't think of the right word.' He frowned. 'I keep getting a bit muddled or sometimes just can't find the thing I want to say.'

'Yes. A stroke can do that,' said Philip. 'And sometimes, when you're tired, it gets a little worse in my experience. My advice would be to accept that you're going to have bad days and don't push yourself too hard when you do. Take each day as it comes.' He hesitated as he glanced up at Ethan suddenly, his eyes blazing with emotion. 'Your loved ones help. They help very much indeed.'

Ethan knew that he was talking about Libby and nodded in reply.

'And you've got the perfect goal to aim for,' added Philip, before looking up at Ethan. 'Elizabeth told me that you're pressing ahead with the plans for the Christmas train.'

Ethan nodded. 'Definitely,' he said. 'We're going to make it one of the best ones ever.'

'You shouldn't have had to cancel your work though,' said Eddie.

Ethan shook his head. 'I've told you, Grandad, it's fine,' he replied. 'They've found someone else to take on the project. In the meantime, we've got a big family meeting tonight to thrash out all the details. You're going to be there too, thanks to video calling.'

They looked at Eddie, who appeared a little emotional at the talk of the Christmas train. Ethan went to lean forward but found that he was beaten by Philip reaching out to pat him on the hand.

'That'll be something, won't it, Eddie?' he said. 'I was a small child when the last one went off, but I can still remember the thrill of seeing it all lit up in the darkness of winter.'

'So can I,' replied Eddie in a gruff voice.

'Well, it sounds like it's in good hands,' said Philip.

'Aye, it does,' replied Eddie, before a small frown crossed his forehead. 'But I'm still worried about the ballroom dancing.'

Philip looked back at him surprised at the change of topic. 'Pardon me?' he asked.

'Grandad's been going each week with Grams,' Ethan told him.

'I'm just not sure I'll be up to it after all this,' said Eddie, gesturing at his hospital bed.

Philip smiled. 'Do you remember that I used to love cycling?' he asked.

Bob spoke up. 'I do,' he said.

Philip nodded. 'I used to love cycling, going round all the lanes, up and down the hills. Hated to give it up.' He looked at Eddie. 'Look, you might be able to go back to an old interest. But that doesn't mean that you can't turn your hand to something new.'

'New?' asked Eddie.

Philip shrugged his shoulders. 'Well, the world's your oyster, as they say,' he told him. 'But perhaps we can both discover some new experiences together. I've got a few plans of my own that I'd like your input with.'

'I'd like that,' said Eddie.

'So would I,' said Philip. 'I could do with making some

friends. I've been cut off from too many people for too long. And I worry about the effect it's had on Elizabeth as well.'

'She's fine,' said Bob.

'I hope so,' said Philip.

'And you've always had friends,' added Eddie.

As the three men exchanged a smile, Ethan smiled to himself. Perhaps out of something so terrible like a stroke, something good could also appear, he thought.

'Elizabeth wanted me to give you some of her chocolates,' said Philip, handing over a box to Eddie.

As Ethan took a breath, he could smell the familiar aroma of cocoa and instantly thought of Libby. He hadn't seen her since that fateful night of the accident and had missed her. He couldn't wait any longer and decided to go and see her when they returned to Cranfield.

## 38

Libby was pleased to find her dad in good spirits when he returned from the hospital after visiting Eddie with Ethan and Bob.

'It'll take time, of course, but I can see him back on the train before too long,' announced Philip, when Ethan dropped him off.

'That's great news, Dad,' replied Libby before looking at Ethan.

'I'm here to convey an important message from my grandad. He wanted to say thank you for the box of chocolates.'

Libby shrugged her shoulders. 'It wasn't much, but I thought it might be something more tasty than hospital food.'

'And possibly healthier too,' added her dad, to Libby's surprise. 'I've been reading up on cocoa. It's packed with antioxidants.'

Ethan grinned. 'Perhaps you should have taken science more seriously, Libs, and become a doctor instead,' he told her.

'Perhaps not,' said her dad, with a twinkle in his eye. 'For the sake of the patients.'

'Hey!' protested Libby, but she too was smiling, amazed that her dad was making jokes. Perhaps they really had turned a corner at last, she thought.

'Listen,' carried on Ethan. 'I've called a family meeting tonight over dinner to discuss the Christmas train and would appreciate your input. As you know, time is getting a bit tight.'

'Me?' replied Libby. 'But I'm not family.'

Ethan rolled his eyes. 'As good as,' he told her. 'So how about it? Ryan's doing the cooking, if that's what you were worried about. You're welcome to come as well, Philip.'

But Libby's dad shook his head. 'That's very kind, but I'm a little weary tonight. You two go.'

'Are you sure, Dad?' asked Libby, concerned. 'If you're tired, I can stay here with you.'

'I won't be going too far, my dear,' he replied. 'So don't worry.'

After she had sorted out his dinner, Libby wandered along to the old school. Although Ethan had told her that the meeting would be held in Ryan and Katy's apartment, she was anxious to see how the house was looking after a couple of days of cleaning and so had invited herself along early.

She had just followed Ethan inside when she stopped short. 'Wow,' she spluttered. 'You have worked hard.'

She looked around but could see the walls had all had a new coat of paint. There was none of the acrid smell that her friends had told her about. But there were other changes as well.

'You've got cushions and lamps,' she spluttered, somewhat amazed.

He nodded. 'Katy made me order them,' he told her, with a roll of his eyes. 'Apparently I've got to act like a grown-up now.'

'That would be a first,' she said, following him into the kitchen.

She turned to apologise again to him about almost destroying the place when she found that he was pointing to the ceiling. She followed his gaze and saw that there was also a brand new smoke alarm fitted.

'Just in case,' he said, with a smile.

'I'm so sorry,' she told him.

'Like I said, I don't care about all that,' he replied.

'Well, the place looks great.'

'I'm glad you like it.'

'I do,' she told him, nodding.

The new oven caught her eye. It was silver, double fronted and looked expensive.

'Wow,' she muttered, heading over to have a proper look at it.

'Will it do?' she heard him ask.

Libby spun around. 'Do? Do for what?' she asked.

He gave a shrug of his shoulders. 'I'm not likely to use the kitchen apart from to make my morning toast and coffee,' he replied. 'I figured you were going to be making your chocolate again at some point, so why not have the perfect oven for your cocoa beans?'

'You did all this for me?' she asked him. 'Why?'

'Because I wanted to see your face light up like it's doing now,' he said, taking a step forward so that they were almost touching. 'Because chocolate means so much to you. Because I liked having you in my kitchen those weeks when you were here and I've missed you ever since.' He took a deep breath. 'And because I've missed you these past fifteen years too. I miss my best friend.'

Now it was Libby's turn to take a deep breath. She stared up into the face that she knew so well. 'Me too,' she told him.

'And if I've learned anything this week, it's that everyone can have a second chance to make amends,' he said, reaching out to hold her face in his hands.

She gulped, trying to concentrate on what he was saying, but the feel of his fingers on her skin was so good.

'I figure it's time,' he told her.

'I suppose fifteen years is long enough since the prom,' she said, with a small smile.

'My thoughts exactly.'

He was so close now that she could feel the pulse jumping in her throat. But just when she was thinking and wishing that he was going to kiss her, his phone buzzed with a text and he gave her a rueful smile.

'Dad's ready to be picked up. So this is to be continued,' he told her softly, before letting go of her face and walking away.

Libby was left standing in the kitchen feeling breathless. She could deny it no longer to herself. She had wanted him to kiss her. And she had wanted to kiss him right back. She found herself hoping that they might just have the second chance that Ethan was talking about after all.

## 39

After they had all enjoyed one of Ryan's delicious dinners in the apartment above the station, Ethan called everyone to gather on the sofas and chairs around the fireplace. Paddington the dog settled down in front of the hearth whilst everyone made themselves comfortable.

Ethan had been somewhat surprised when Bob had brought Maggie with him that evening. She too was included as part of the family, showing just how close they had become over the past few months. He was pleased for his dad that he appeared to have found happiness at last.

'Thank you for a lovely dinner, son,' said Bob, with a smile, rubbing his full stomach.

'Remind me to bill my brother for the cost later,' said Ryan, shooting him a grin. 'People pay a lot of money for my food.'

'Only people who don't share our surname,' replied Ethan.

'Well, I enjoyed it too,' said Libby.

'It would make it more believable if you didn't get mates' rates,' Ryan told her.

Libby smiled and, for a second, all Ethan could think about

was how he had been so close to kissing her in the kitchen before his dad had texted him.

'So how about we start this meeting,' said Ryan.

'Hang on,' Ethan told them. 'I'm just about to bring in our star guest.' He dialled on his phone and, a short while later, Eddie was waving at them all from his hospital bed.

After a few minutes of greetings and blown kisses, Ethan wrangled the meeting back under control.

'Right,' he began. 'We've got less than a month to get the Christmas train up and running and I'm going to need all your help and input to get it ready.'

'When's the first run?' asked Katy.

'The first of December,' replied Ethan. 'As it falls on a Saturday.'

'And what's the theme?' asked Ryan. 'Father Christmas?'

Ethan hesitated. 'I'm not so sure about that,' he said. 'I mean, I know the children will love it, but we want to appeal to everyone.' He leant back in his chair. 'So what other Christmassy themes can we think of?'

There was a long silence as everyone thought hard.

'Any ideas, Grandad?' asked Ethan, but Eddie merely shook his head in reply.

After another long pause, it was Libby who spoke in a dreamy voice. 'I always enjoyed *The Nutcracker* at Christmastime.'

Katy turned to look at her. 'Isn't that a ballet?' she asked.

'It's wonderful,' said Maggie. 'Really enchanting.'

Libby nodded. 'Mum took me every Christmas to the theatre in Aldwych.'

'I never saw it,' said Katy.

'It's Tchaikovsky,' said Bob in a knowing voice. 'But I don't really know the story.'

'Oh, it's lovely,' said Libby, smiling. 'It's about Clara whose favourite toy, a nutcracker, comes to life on Christmas Eve.'

'Thanks to her magician godfather,' added Maggie. 'Clara and the nutcracker head off to where there's a battle against the evil Mouse King. Which they win, of course.'

'And then they go through the Land of Snow to the Kingdom of Sweets, where there's lots of celebrations,' continued Libby. 'It's very Christmassy there, with an enormous tree and lots of sparkle and sweets.'

'Then she wakes up back at home and it was all a dream,' said Maggie with a dreamy sigh.

'Except her godfather's nephew looks just like the nutcracker!' finished Libby.

'It's a very traditional story actually,' said Maggie. 'You know, according to German legend, nutcrackers bring good luck and protection to a family and its home.'

Ethan's immediate thought was that luck and protection was exactly what his family needed at that moment.

'Then that's our theme,' announced Eddie, with a nod.

Ethan looked at him on the camera and smiled. 'Okay, Grandad. It's your show.'

Paddington the dog thumped his tail on the floorboards as if he too was confirming his agreement for theme and everyone laughed.

'So it's going to be *The Nutcracker* story?' asked Ryan, who was frowning. 'How are you going to fit all that on the train?'

Ethan shook his head. 'It doesn't go inside the train, dummy,' he told him. 'We can decorate the banks either side of the tracks and light them up into individual scenes.' There was a gasp of surprise around the table, to which Ethan rolled his eyes. 'I'm a lighting specialist,' he reminded them.

'Oh!' cooed Libby, her eyes lighting up. 'So there'll be a show outside of the train that everyone in the carriages can look at?'

Ethan nodded. 'That's the idea.'

Libby screwed her face up in thought. 'But what about the Kingdom of the Sweets?' she asked. 'That's quite a big bit to fit alongside the railway tracks.'

There was a brief pause where Ethan began to doubt himself. Perhaps it wasn't right after all. But the talk of protecting one's family and bringing good luck had struck home with him.

'The old abandoned station,' said Eddie, into the short silence.

'At Cranley? Oh, that's a great idea, Dad!' beamed Bob, nodding enthusiastically at the phone.

'Oh, that would look so pretty all done up!' said Katy, clapping her hands.

But Libby was frowning. 'But how are we going to decorate all of this?' she asked.

'Mainly with miles of lights but also many assorted decorations. Plus a lot of elbow grease,' Ethan told her. 'I need someone to explain to me the various stages of the story so we can plan what it can look like. In a simplified version, of course. Libby? Can I count on you for that?'

'Yes, sir!' she said, with a mock salute.

A smile twitched on his lips before he carried on. 'Someone else needs to check out that old station to see if it's safe.'

'We can do that,' said Bob, looking at Maggie, who was nodding her head in agreement.

'I'm still not sure what the story entails,' said Ethan. 'Not being a great lover of the ballet, that is.'

'Me neither,' said Ryan, frowning. 'So how will any passengers understand what's going on if they don't know the story either?'

'A handout with a description?' suggested Bob.

'How will they read it in the semi-darkness?' replied Libby. She suddenly gave a small gasp. 'There are speakers in the carriages, aren't there?'

Ethan nodded. 'Yup. Why?'

Libby broke into a smile. 'Then how about we get someone to read out a simplified version of the story over the speakers as the train moves along? It can be pre-recorded so it tallies up with whatever's outside of the window at the time.'

'With some of the music playing as well!' added Maggie, to more murmured agreement.

'That's a great idea!' said Katy. 'Who's going to read the story?'

Libby gave them a sheepish smile. 'Actually, I was wondering if you'd mind if my dad gave it a trial run? He was always good at reading aloud.'

'That's a grand idea,' said Eddie. 'He was always the narrator at our school concerts. He's got a smashing voice for that kind of thing.'

Libby looked at Ethan, who nodded his agreement.

'Then I'll ask him later,' she told him.

Ethan was pleased. 'It sounds as if it's going to be a bit of a village effort to get this thing ready in time,' he said.

'Well, the clue was always in the name,' said Eddie. 'After all, it's the Cranfield Christmas train, isn't it?'

'Yes. It is, Grandad.'

Ethan was warmed by his grandfather's words, as well as the thought of the steam train being a community effort. Not only would it need everyone's help to get it ready in time for December, in a way, he could see how much it meant to everyone sitting around the table that evening.

He finally understood the legacy that the trains had within

his family. He felt it deep inside, woven into his very blood. He couldn't let anyone down. Not now. Not ever.

And then he had to admit that it meant something to him too. That being born and bred in Cranfield still meant something to him. That not all of the times he spent there were bad. And perhaps there were future happy memories just around the corner as well, he thought as he looked across at Libby and found her smiling back at him.

## 40

After the meeting was over, Libby and Ethan walked Bob home.

As Libby only lived two doors away, a few moments later they stood by her front gate.

'That all sounded really positive,' she told him.

But, to her surprise, he actually looked a little sheepish. 'I need you to describe this nutcracker story to me again. Otherwise I can't begin to plan out the lighting. This is how I normally start off with my clients.'

'And I'm your client?' She gave him a wide smile. 'Excellent! How much does it pay?'

'Not very much at all you'll find,' he drawled, leaning against the front wall.

'Okay,' she began. 'I would start off with the scene on Christmas Eve as that's how the ballet begins. So you need a big tree, lots of twinkly lights and presents underneath the tree. I know! You could make that bit at the station, so when everyone arrives, they're immediately immersed into Christmas and the start of the story.'

He nodded and made some notes on his phone. 'Got it.'

'But you're going to have to highlight one toy somehow,' she told him. 'Have one of the larger boxes open to reveal a nutcracker doll, all dressed up in its smart uniform.'

He made some more notes.

She tapped her chin in thought. 'Then, as the train gets going, there would need to be a bit of shazam.'

'Shazam?' he asked, his eyebrows going up.

'You know, that something magical is happening,' she said. 'Because presto! The nutcracker doll comes to life.'

He nodded thoughtfully. 'Shazam,' he muttered to himself as he typed into his phone. 'That we could probably manage.'

'Then there's the big scene where the nutcracker doll has to fight the evil Mouse King in order for there to be peace in the realm,' she carried on. 'So it's like a big battle. You know, fighting, explosions. That kind of stuff.'

He frowned. 'Not sure we can have actual big explosions, but perhaps I could rig something up. Lights flashing, smoke machine, that kind of thing.'

She nodded. 'That would do it. After all, it's only as the train goes past. Then, when the battle is won, they go through the forest of the fir trees. That's normally to the "Waltz of the Snowflakes" in the ballet.'

'That we can do,' he said, suddenly animated. 'Lots of fake snow, icicles, that kind of thing.'

She clapped her hands enthusiastically. 'Perfect. The second act is where they arrive at the Kingdom of Sweets, which is a big celebration. The famous Sugar Plum Fairy dance, but really there's lots highlighting different sweets and food, such as coffee, tea and chocolate.'

He was deep in thought for a moment. 'If we simplify it but still make it magical with narration and perhaps some of the music, then that might work.'

'And the Kingdom of Sweets could be set up at Cranley station, if it's allowed,' she added.

He grimaced. 'It's all going to be pretty tight time-wise,' he told her. 'So how does the story end?'

'Back at home when Clara wakes up,' she told him. 'It's where she realises that her godfather's nephew looks just like the nutcracker doll come to life! But we could have that scene along with a big Merry Christmas sign to finish off just before the train gets back into the station.'

'Okay.' He blew out a long sigh as he scrolled through his notes. 'There's an awful lot to get done.'

'Yes, but everyone's going to pitch in,' she reminded him.

'They're going to need to if we want to get everything done on time,' he told her, with a worried look. 'The first of December isn't that far away.'

She hesitated to say what was on her mind before looking up at Ethan. He was studying her.

'Just say whatever's on your mind, Libs,' he told her. 'You always have done.'

'So you're staying on to get this done,' she replied. It wasn't a question. The very fact that he was planning to be so heavily involved with the Christmas train meant that he was.

He nodded slowly.

'Because of your grandad?' she asked softly.

'A little,' he admitted. 'This Christmas train idea is so important to him that I've got to get it right.' He was quiet for a while, but she knew that he was going to carry on, so she waited patiently. 'And, I guess, it's time for me to stop running.'

She was shocked to see pain in his eyes.

'What is it?' she asked, reaching out to take his hand in hers. 'What were you running from?' She gulped. 'Was it me?'

He looked fiercely at her. 'Of course it wasn't you. It was never you.' He gave a long sigh before he carried on. 'It was Mum. You see, she had affairs before the very last one when she finally left Dad. And I knew all about them.'

'You did?' she gasped. 'How?'

'Let's just say Mum was never particularly discreet,' he drawled, rolling his eyes. 'Anyway, I knew from the age of thirteen that my parents' marriage was a lie. That Mum kept having affair after affair.'

Libby was stunned by his revelation and suddenly realised why he too had been rebelling throughout his teens. 'Did Ryan know too?' she asked.

Ethan shook his head. 'No. Not until later... Not until the day of the prom.' He looked at her with a sad expression.

'So that was it,' she said, with a heavy sigh. 'You were so distant that night. So angry.'

'I thought I could carry it by myself,' he told her. 'I thought it was best that only I knew, not Dad or Ryan. But we saw them as we went into Aldwych and Ryan was, well, shattered. He'd never even guessed and then, boom, it was something we both had to suffer. But I'm sorry I was so miserable with you.'

'You should have said something,' she said. 'You should have trusted me instead of walking out that night.' She felt the tears prick at her eyes. 'I thought we were friends.'

'We were,' he said, squeezing her hand in his. 'We *are*. But you have to understand that it wasn't my secret to share. Mum's poison about how love was wrong, not to be trusted, I heard it over and over. Those kind of words remain with you.' He gave her a humourless smile. 'Especially when I came back later to apologise and tell you the truth and you were making out with that idiot Garth.'

Libby gasped. 'You saw that?' She blushed. 'You knew I never liked him like that. I was just hurting so much.'

'I know. It was all on me,' he told her. 'But when I saw you, I thought you must be just like Mum.'

She shook her head. 'Of course I'm not,' she muttered.

'I know that now,' he said. 'But at the time it just reinforced my feeling that women couldn't be trusted.'

'You can trust me,' she said in a fierce tone.

He reached out to stroke her face. 'I know that now,' he said. 'But at the time I had Ryan to think of as well. Then your mum got sick and you had other priorities.'

'We both had to grow up fast,' she said.

'You did,' he told her with a grimace. 'I just ran away from everyone, including you.'

'So did I,' she said. 'Why do you think I was a flight attendant? I couldn't wait to get away.' She shook her head. 'All those wasted years,' she said, thinking back to the pain that they had both suffered.

'I know,' he said. 'But we were always a pair of idiots.'

She giggled. Despite everything, he always knew how to make her smile.

'But we were always friends too,' he added. 'And hopefully friends again now.'

As he looked into her eyes, she found her breath caught at the intensity that was there.

'Just friends?' she whispered.

Ethan stared down at her, his eyes unreadable in the darkness of the night.

But she knew. She knew him so well, almost as well as she knew herself.

They came together instantly in an embrace, stepping forward so that their lips met at the exact moment that their arms wrapped around each other.

Libby moaned against his mouth at the feel of his lips on

hers. It was the same as it had been in Las Vegas. She had waited for this for so long.

She knew he felt the connection too. She knew from the way his lips covered hers, the way he was holding her against him. This was everything.

Finally, they broke apart, both breathless and wide-eyed as they stared at each other. Her lips were still bruised from their passionate kiss. And yet, she could feel him holding back from her and deep down she knew why. His mum had broken his trust in all relationships and he still didn't believe in them. At least she now understood but it didn't make her feel any better.

Her self-defence mechanism kicked in. 'Well, I'll have a chat with Dad about the narration,' she told him, reaching for her front door key in her handbag. 'Talking of which, I'd better get inside and make sure he's okay.'

She felt him watch her go down the short front path.

'Goodnight, Libby,' she heard him say as she opened the front door.

'Goodnight,' she replied before walking inside and closing the door behind her.

Nothing had changed in the years since their secret wedding. Her feelings for Ethan were exactly the same. Just friends? She shook her head. Nothing could be further from the truth, as far as she was concerned. And yet, sensing Ethan holding back from her, she wondered whether they could ever be anything but friends, despite her yearning for so much more.

## 41

Despite her confused personal feelings for Ethan, Libby was still feeling excited about her idea for the theme for the Christmas train over breakfast the following morning.

'So the meeting went well last night?' asked her dad.

She nodded, as she took a sip of her coffee, trying to dismiss the thought of Ethan's lips on hers when they had kissed. Something she had tried and failed to do all night. 'There's lots to do, but we've all promised to help come up with ideas for the decorations. But I came up with the theme!'

Her dad looked impressed. 'And what have you decided upon?' he asked.

'*The Nutcracker*,' she told him. Suddenly, she hesitated. It was another memory linked with her mother. Perhaps it was too painful a reminder. 'You see,' she stumbled on. 'We used to go to the ballet when I was younger and—'

'I remember.' Thankfully, rather than looking upset, her dad was smiling as if to himself. 'You know, it was me you have to thank for that.'

'Why?' asked Libby, surprised.

'Because your mother used to hear me playing Tchaikovsky's marvellous music and wanted to know what the story was behind it,' he told her. 'So I explained the story and she immediately got the both of you tickets to see the ballet.'

'And it became a Christmas tradition,' said Libby, heartened by the reminder of their happy marriage. 'I had no idea you loved it too.'

'Indeed.' Her dad nodded. 'I must say, it's been many years since I've heard the music. I must bring out that CD of mine.'

'Actually, you may need to dust it off a bit quicker than that,' said Libby, suddenly feeling nervous.

'Elizabeth,' said her dad, inclining his head to one side as he studied her. 'You have that exact same look you had when you told me that you had reversed the family car into a bollard.'

She grimaced. 'I'd forgotten about that!' She gave a small giggle. 'And I'd still swear that the bollard moved, not the car.'

'Now what were you saying about *The Nutcracker*,' prompted her dad.

'Well, Ethan's going to decorate the railway line with different scenes and they're going to play some of the music over the speakers,' said Libby, her words coming out in a bit of a rush as she realised the magnitude of what she was about to ask him. 'But not everyone will know the story, so I suggested having someone narrate it over the speakers to explain what happens as we go along. Pre-recorded in advance, of course.'

Her dad nodded. 'Sounds marvellous,' he said. 'But I'm still failing to understand your nerves.'

She took a deep breath. 'Well, I suggested that you might be the perfect person to record the story as a narrator,' she told him.

Her dad's eyebrows shot up in surprise.

'Of course, if you don't want to do it, then everyone will understand,' said Libby quickly.

'Why would you think that?' replied her dad, breaking into a smile. 'In fact, I'm very flattered that you even thought of me.'

'I remembered how much you always enjoyed reading stories aloud.'

'Thank you, my dear,' said her dad, reaching out to pat her hand. 'Then I accept.'

'You do?' Libby was thrilled.

'Of course,' said her dad. 'Shall I try to find a transcript online?'

Libby got up from the table. 'That would be great,' she told him. She was so pleased that he had agreed to narrate the story. It felt like another huge step forward for her dad's recovery. 'I'd love to help but I've got to rush off. I've got the last truffles to box up in order for the delivery to the hotel in time for the party tonight.' She couldn't quite believe it, but she was almost there with the huge order.

'Then it sounds as if we've both got a busy day ahead,' said her dad, with a smile.

At last, she thought, as she watched her dad pick up his iPad to start searching for the transcript, it seemed as if things were finally coming together for the both of them.

* * *

Later that morning, Libby looked at the huge stack of boxes that held her chocolate truffles. 'Well, we did it,' she said, shaking her head in disbelief. There had been times when she hadn't thought that they would make it, but thanks to a group effort, the order was complete.

'Clever girl,' said Grams, stepping forward to give her a hug.

'I only made it on time thanks to you and everyone else

helping me,' Libby told her. 'I owe you all a huge drink tonight, if you're all free.'

'You're on,' replied Harriet, smiling. 'And we were happy to help.'

'I never doubted you for a second that you wouldn't get it done,' said Katy, with a grin.

'And you can always carry on using our kitchen,' said Grams.

'Thanks,' replied Libby. 'But I know how busy you're going to be with all the Christmas pudding orders that you've got already.'

'Can't we work alongside each other?' asked Grams. 'It's been so nice having another cook in the kitchen.'

'Ahem,' said Flora, in a pointed tone. 'So what does that make me?' she asked.

It was a fact that Flora hadn't inherited her grandmother's skill of baking.

'The best granddaughter in the world,' said Grams. 'Who gets an A for effort.'

'And a D, maybe a C minus for results,' added Libby with a grin.

'Very funny,' said Flora before sticking out her tongue. 'Why am I helping pack up all this if you're just going to keep insulting me?'

'Because that's what friends do,' Libby told her.

'Who's insulting mi amore?' said Nico, coming into the farm-house kitchen.

'One of my so-called best friends,' Flora told him. 'Apparently I can't bake!'

She looked at him, waiting patiently for Nico to reply.

He gave her a gracious smile and took her in his arms. 'You are a wonderful painter, an amazing girlfriend and the love of my life.' Flora's hands crept up to his shoulder as he gave her a gentle kiss. 'Who cares if you can't bake?' he added, once they'd finished their embrace.

Flora gave him a playful smack on the shoulder whilst Grams and Libby laughed.

But seeing the happy couple reminded her of Ethan and that magical kiss they had shared only the previous evening. And she found herself hoping and wishing for another and then another...

## 42

With the theme of *The Nutcracker* decided, Ethan knew that it would be all systems go to get everything up and ready for the first train ride on the first of December.

There was so much to do that he almost felt overwhelmed. But, thankfully, his skills and experience project planning in the past for work came to the fore. So he decided to view the Christmas train as a project for a customer, just trying to ignore the pressure and stress of making it perfect for his grandad.

The most important step as far as Ethan was concerned, after the train running properly of course, was setting up the decorations and theming. But he spent a very productive afternoon with Flora up at the farmhouse. Flora had been to art school and was great at picking out which decorations would work the best in each scene.

He was very grateful for her help, as well as his friends. Joe and Nico had already promised to help him lay the miles of cable for the lighting when it arrived in a couple of days.

Joe had also outdone himself by creating a website which meant that people could book their tickets online. They cobbled together some photographs of the steam train on its maiden journey, but they needed something more spectacular to whet people's appetite and get them to actually want to hand over money for the tickets.

'It needs something more visual,' said Joe, scrunching up his face in thought as they all looked at the website.

It was both eye-catching and easy to navigate. The problem was the lack of images of the train from anywhere other than the platform.

'I know! You need a drone.' Joe looked up at Ethan, who was standing next to him. 'Just imagine. A sunny day. The steam train trundling through the countryside. That would get people's imagination going.'

Ethan blew out a sigh. 'I guess, but where are we going to get a drone from? I'm already maxed out money wise sourcing all the decorations and lighting required.'

Joe broke into a smile. 'As it happens, I know a man who's just treated himself to one.'

'Who?' asked Ethan.

'Me,' Joe told him laughing. 'I told Harriet it was an early Christmas present to myself!'

'Well, a drone is for life, not just for Christmas,' conceded Ethan.

So, the following day, with Joe having practised a couple of times using it, Ethan and Bob took the train out for a run. It was a stunning day, the blue of the clear sky contrasting beautifully with the autumnal rainbow of colours that was lit across the landscape by the sun. The newly decorated steam engine looked magnificent in its shiny red paint too.

Whilst they drove the train, Bob told Ethan two important pieces of news.

'I heard from the Earl of Cranley,' he shouted, as they went past the old abandoned station. 'He's thrilled that it can be of some use.'

'That's great,' replied Ethan. 'Flora's already designed the scene, so it can be set up as soon as possible, which will be one more tick on the to-do list.'

After they had returned to Cranfield station and shut down the train, Bob announced an even more important item of news.

'Your grandad reckons they're going to let him come home after the weekend.'

Ethan was delighted. 'Dad, that's great news!' he said.

Bob nodded. 'It certainly is,' he replied, before climbing down the steps of the driver's cab.

There was more good news when they returned to the platform.

'We've got some amazing footage,' Joe told them as he rushed up. 'It looked even more dramatic this morning because it's slightly colder, so there was more steam thanks to the condensation. Here, I'll show you.'

Ethan thought it looked tremendous.

And he wasn't the only one. Libby joined them shortly afterwards as she came out of Platform 1 and agreed that the footage was incredible.

'There's just one problem,' she said to Ethan when it was just the two of them. 'We need some snow.'

'Sorry but my powers of persuasion aren't that good that I can change the weather,' Ethan replied, laughing.

'Can't we put down some fake stuff?' she asked. 'I think it would really make the whole thing come together. You know, that stuff out of a can?'

'We're going to need an awful lot of cans,' said Ethan, shaking his head. 'Besides, I honestly have no idea how to make snow.'

'I do!' said a familiar voice nearby.

Ethan inwardly groaned as they both turned around to come face to face with Dodgy Del.

'Del,' began Ethan.

But Dodgy Del was already holding up his hand. 'I know someone who knows someone,' he said, with a wink. 'Let me help out Uncle Eddie.'

'Like you did with the Halloween train?' asked Libby, scowling at him.

'That was an honest mistake,' said Dodgy Del quickly. 'So let me make amends. The stuff I've heard about will work wonders.'

'Will it?' Ethan sighed. 'I'm not so sure.'

Libby giggled and he smiled at her for a second before the air between them grew heavy.

Ethan knew that they were both thinking about the kiss. He had barely thought of anything else, his mind straying to Libby whenever he stopped thinking about the train for even a second.

'Now, let me show you what I can do,' carried on Dodgy Del, breaking their gaze as he came to stand next to them.

Libby said a quick goodbye and rushed off down the platform, leaving Ethan breathing in the soft whisper of her perfume after she had gone.

## 43

Libby placed the last of the boxes of all her cooking items into the large understairs cupboard at home. It was a bit of a tight squeeze, but she just about managed to get everything in.

'My word,' her dad gasped, nodding thoughtfully as he stared inside the cupboard now full from top to bottom. 'Who knew it took all this to make such delicious chocolate,' he said with a bewildered smile.

She hesitated before she brought out a small packet from her handbag, feeling nervous, all of a sudden.

'What's this?' asked her dad, as she placed the packet in his hands.

'Well, you said you'd never tasted my chocolate,' she told him. 'So I've got some samples for you to try. If you'd like.'

'Of course,' he replied, smiling broadly. 'Let's sit down, shall we?'

As they sat down at the kitchen table, Libby thought how much things had changed. He could now manage the washing and housekeeping at his own pace. He had even let her show him how to do online shopping for the supermarket, which had been delivered that morning. They were such small changes in the scheme of things and yet it had transformed him. He was a little more talkative and after so many years their relationship finally felt more balanced too.

He looked at the first truffle carefully before placing it in his mouth. She waited nervously for his assessment, having decided to start off with one of the plain flavours.

Finally, he gave her a delighted smile. 'They're delicious, Elizabeth,' he told her, reaching out to take her hand to give it a squeeze. 'Absolutely tremendous. You've got a real talent there.'

'You really like them?' she asked, desperate for his approval.

'Of course,' he replied. 'You know, they taste just like your mother's did.'

She nodded. 'I know. That's what I was aiming for.'

'Do you mind if I try another?' he asked.

'I think you'll like the coconut one too,' she told him, handing him over another truffle.

Libby was happy that he was enjoying them. But what pleased her even more was that they remained at the kitchen table for a long while, as her dad wanted to know more about the chocolate-making process and what it involved.

Later on, after dinner, they talked some more about *The Nutcracker* as he had found the transcript online and was editing the story to fit in with the Christmas train run time. She told him how pleased she was that he had agreed to narrate the story.

He nodded. 'I always love stories in the way that you can learn from them. In fact, I always loved everything to do with teaching. It felt like I was helping people. Giving them a step up.'

'You could still do that in some way,' she told him.

'Funny you should say that,' he replied. 'Because I have an idea to run past you.'

Libby couldn't think what on earth her dad was going to suggest so waited for him to speak.

'After my conversation with Eddie, I realised just how isolated I felt after my stroke,' said her dad. 'Of course, living out here in the countryside doesn't help as there aren't any stroke clubs or anything of that nature. But I was thinking that perhaps I could create one instead.'

Libby looked at him. 'You want to start a stroke club?' she said, amazed.

Her dad nodded. 'And even if there's only myself and Eddie there, at least I can pass on my knowledge and experience to one other person. Although it's so common, I'd be surprised if there weren't more people in the area who had suffered the same affliction.'

'Oh, Dad,' said Libby, getting up to rush around the table to give him a hug. 'I think it's a great idea!'

He patted her on the back with his good hand. 'Thank you, my dear. I was hoping you'd approve.'

Libby was feeling a little emotional as she sat back down at the table. It was such a turnaround for her dad to even mention talking to strangers. He had hidden himself away for so long that it really felt as if his depression had finally cleared.

'Although I must confess to feeling a little nervous,' said her dad.

'Nonsense,' replied Libby. 'You'll be amazing. And knowing you, you'll research everything and have so much to pass on to people.'

'Yes, what not to do, in my case,' said her dad, with a frown as he looked up at her. 'You've grown into a fine young woman, Elizabeth. I'm sorry I haven't said so before now.'

She shrugged her shoulders. 'It doesn't matter,' she muttered.

'You're just like your mother,' he told her with a soft smile.

'She had to learn to take a compliment as well.' He paused before carrying on. 'I hope you find a love as great as your mother and I had. It was special. She was my best friend. Maybe there's someone out there too that's your other half. The matching part.'

She briefly thought of Ethan, who knew her better than anyone else and yet there was still a gulf between them, even after their kiss.

'It's hard to get through life without a guide map sometimes,' Libby told her dad with a shrug.

He looked at her with a smile. 'Surely my clever daughter doesn't need one,' he said.

'Not so clever if I can't get another job,' she told him, biting her lip. She had already received another couple of rejection emails from airline companies, although in truth she didn't actually want to work as a flight attendant again, despite it being the only real job she had ever had. 'Now that I've finished that big order for the hotel, I'm at a loss as to what to do next.'

'Why work for someone else when you have everything you need already under our stairs?' asked her dad. 'You have a real gift, my dear,' he told her. 'So why not use it? Why not take a bit of time to see if you can make your hobby into something more permanent.'

Libby nodded thoughtfully. 'I did get that amazing feedback from the hotel and they offered to type up a glowing review that I could use any time.' She bit her lip. 'But do you really think I can pull it off?' she asked.

'I think you can pull off anything, my dear daughter.' He smiled at her. 'I think it's time for us both to be a little brave, Elizabeth.'

'You first,' she muttered, still feeling nervous.

'How about together?' he said, raising his mug of tea at her.

'Together,' she replied, before breaking into a wide smile.

'Cranfield had better watch out! There's no telling what we can pull off if we both put our minds to it!'

'That's the spirit,' said her dad.

She loved that she could see a sparkle in his eyes for the first time in many years and could feel herself also coming alive with the possibilities for their future plans.

Best of all, she felt herself growing even more closer to him day by day.

**44**

---

'Here we are, Grandad,' said Ethan, as he helped Eddie up the front path to the cottage.

Eddie nodded and smiled as he carefully stepped over the threshold into the small cottage that he shared with his son Bob. He looked around at the small front room before he went over to sit down in his high-back armchair with a satisfied nod.

'Here you go, Dad,' said Bob, coming out of the kitchen with a mug. 'Thought you might need a cup of tea after all the excitement this morning.'

Eddie had been discharged from the hospital earlier that day and Ryan and Ethan had gone to pick him up. The good news was that he was mobile once more. Taking his time, he could dress himself slowly, as well as manage a little walk each day. However, the doctor had advised that he would continue to be very tired for some considerable time, but that was entirely normal.

Eddie looked at the cup of tea that had just been placed next to him and nodded. 'It's good to be home,' he said.

'Good to have you home,' said Bob, sitting down on the other armchair. 'And you'll be glad to have some home cooking, I reckon. Maggie's popped round with a delicious cake for later.'

'And I've left a lasagne in the fridge for you both,' added Ryan.

'Thanks, lad,' said Eddie, nodding.

'You'll be glad to know that I haven't cooked anything for you,' added Ethan, with a grin.

'Which is another blessing for a speedy recovery,' said Bob, with a wink.

'But I've got some great plans for the Christmas train and the preparations are going well,' said Ethan.

'Good, good,' murmured Eddie, in a sleepy tone.

Ethan could see that he was starting to fall asleep and so he and Ryan quietly left the room.

'It's to be expected,' said Bob, giving them both a hug. 'And now that he's home, he'll rest better. Nobody can sleep properly in a hospital with all those alarms going off at all hours.'

'Of course,' said Ethan.

He was disappointed not to have had the opportunity to show his grandad what they had planned for the Christmas train, but perhaps Eddie didn't need to know everything down to the last detail. Ethan just needed to ensure that it was a great show and he felt the heavy weight of responsibility even more keenly.

'And how's our Christmas train coming along?' asked Bob. 'I'm afraid I'm going to have to keep an eye on your grandad for a while, so I won't be able to help as much as I'd like.'

'That's more important than the train,' said Ethan. 'Anyway, it's all in hand.'

'I'll text you later, Dad, to see how it's gone with Grandad today,' added Ryan. 'And to let you know what time to put the lasagne on.'

Then they both left.

Ethan exchanged a look with his brother once the front door had closed behind them.

'You heard what they said at the hospital,' said Ryan, as they walked down Railway Lane towards the station. 'He'll pick up again energy-wise soon, I'm sure.'

Ethan nodded.

'And is it all in hand?' asked Ryan.

Ethan grimaced. 'Just as soon as I find another six hours in the day, it'll be fine,' he told him.

It turned out that Joe's drone shots worked really well once they were uploaded onto the new website.

'Too well,' said Ethan, with a grimace as he leant against the doorframe of the kitchen in Platform 1 a while later, with a much-needed coffee in his hand.

'How can generating publicity be a bad thing?' asked Ryan, stirring the tomato sauce base for his pizzas on the hob.

'Because we're getting plenty of bookings,' Ethan told him.

Ryan looked confused. 'Yeah, I'm still not with you, bro,' he replied. 'Don't you need passengers to make it a success?'

'Yes, but it just adds to the pressure for it to be perfect,' Ethan told him. 'Let's not forget the disaster of the Halloween train.'

Ryan blew out a sigh. 'Not sure any of us will ever forget that train. Talk about giving us nightmares.' He looked at Ethan. 'Listen, don't put yourself under too much pressure.'

'Too late for that,' said Ethan, still looking at the steam engine website. The bookings were clocking up by the hour, it felt.

Not only was the website showing off the train to its best advantage, his dad had gone to the Cranbridge News office and all the local news and radio was flooded with excitement regarding the Christmas train. There was no going back now.

Ryan was still watching him with concern. 'What's going on inside that tiny brain of yours?' he asked.

Ethan blew out a sigh. 'I just don't want to let anyone down,' he told him.

'Grandad's home and on the mend,' replied Ryan. 'I think the thought of the Christmas train is getting him through each day, to be honest.'

That didn't help Ethan's nerves. But it wasn't just his grandad that concerned him. 'I don't want to let dad down again either,' he finally blurted out.

'Again?' asked Ryan, looking non-plussed.

Ethan hesitated. They never spoke about things like this. Anything serious, certainly not their parents' fake marriage. But being at home in Cranfield for all this time had brought everything to the forefront of his mind.

'I've just always felt like I let him down by not telling him about Mum,' muttered Ethan.

Ryan switched off the hob and wiped his hands on a nearby dishcloth. 'Yeah. I know,' he finally said, blowing out a long sigh.

'So what if I stuff up another train run?' carried on Ethan. 'I can't break his heart all over again.'

'You won't!' said Ryan, running a hand through his hair. 'After all, you're the one who's keeping his dream alive. Me?' He shrugged his shoulders. 'I just spruced up the station a bit.'

'You did more than that,' Ethan told him. 'It's a great business and means that the station didn't have to be sold. It's a family home forever now.'

'Yeah, yeah.' Ryan sighed again. 'But the trains? That was always your thing with Dad and Grandad.'

'Only because I'm rubbish at cooking.'

They both exchanged a small smile.

'Listen,' began Ryan. 'We both felt as if we needed to make amends for what happened in our childhood. We were young and stupid back then. We didn't know better.'

'You were more stupid,' said Ethan, with a small smile before he saw the look in his brother's eyes. 'Sorry. Serious tone. Got it.'

'You're punishing yourself for something that wasn't our fault,' carried on Ryan. 'You're being too hard on yourself. You need to forgive yourself and move on. They were the grown-ups, not us. But all the guilt somehow fell on our shoulders and that wasn't right.' He hesitated before carrying on. 'I've talked to Katy a lot about this.'

For a moment, Ethan wished that he too had someone that he could share that kind of thing with and realised that he did with Libby.

Ryan carried on. 'But Mum and Dad are both happy now. Be thankful for that. And maybe you'll start to be happy too. If I can move on, and Mum, and Dad too, then surely you can as well?'

Ethan knew that his brother was right.

'I'll try my best.' Ethan took a moment before carrying on. 'And in that spirit, I'm going to need some kind of snacks to serve on the train or beforehand. And I was thinking of course that you would be the perfect person. Superb chef. Gifted. Flavours of food like you wouldn't believe...'

'Listen, I'd love to help you out, bro, for Dad and Grandad as well as you,' said Ryan. 'But I'm swamped here. You know, with my full-time coffee shop and pizzeria. Now Katy's got a grand new idea for Christmas dinners too.'

'I know, but we need this to make it the best Christmas train ever,' Ethan told him, before pulling out the ultimate guilt card. 'And Grandad needs this.'

'That's pure bribery,' said Ryan, before his shoulders sagged. 'Fine. I'll see what I can do.'

'See? This is why you're my favourite brother,' said Ethan.

'If I wasn't your only brother, I'd be more flattered,' muttered Ryan. 'Get out of here.'

Ethan just managed to duck out of the doorway before the tea towel whistled past his head.

## 45

'I think it's a great idea about your dad doing the narration,' Harriet told Libby as she fixed a silver hair clip decorated with snowflakes into her long hair.

'He recorded it yesterday and he and Maggie have chosen the right length of musical interludes as well,' said Libby before looking at herself in the mirror and nodding. 'That's lovely,' she said, admiring the half-up, half-down hairstyle that they had decided on for the wedding.

'And you didn't need to apologise about needing us here tonight,' said Flora, zipping up the back of Katy's purple jump-suit. 'It's your wedding.'

Katy turned around and looked at her reflection. 'These are lovely,' she said. 'The perfect shade of lavender.'

'Of course,' said Harriet, beaming. 'Right, let's have a look at you all.'

Libby lined up along with Flora and Katy in front of the bride-to-be.

'My three bridesmaids,' said Harriet, looking tearful. 'You all look so beautiful.'

'Team bride looking awesome,' agreed Libby.

'So our outfits are sorted,' said Katy, going across to draw a tick on the worryingly large notepad that she had brought with her.

Harriet's work at the lavender spa was full time and she had begun to panic as to the sheer amount of administration involved in organising a wedding. Thankfully, despite Katy's work also being full time that hadn't stopped her offering to be Harriet's wedding co-ordinator.

'Shoes?' asked Katy, running her pen down the long list.

'On their way,' replied Harriet.

'Ring bearer?' said Katy, looking over at Paddington the dog who was sprawled on the floor nearby.

'His purple bow tie has arrived and he's booked into the dog groomers the day before,' Harriet told her.

'So the church is booked, invites sent out and I just need you and Joe to finalise the menu for the food you want for the meal,' said Katy.

Harriet frowned. 'We still don't want Ryan cooking on our wedding day though,' she said. 'After all, he's one of the best men.'

Libby rolled his eyes. 'He said he wants to cook for you both!' she said.

Katy nodded. 'She's right. He's a chef and his present to you will be loads of delicious Italian food.' She carefully slipped the snowflake clip out of her dark hair and placed it back in its box. 'I promise you that he won't spend the whole time in the kitchen. He says most of it can be prepared the day before.'

'Okay,' replied Harriet. 'Well, at least we know the food will be delicious.'

'It's going to be wonderful,' Flora told her. 'You wanted a simple wedding reception with just your favourite family and friends and good food. So you'll have the perfect day for you both.'

'I want to show you all the decorations that I've ordered for the reception in the station,' said Harriet.

She picked up her phone and they oohed and aahed at the dainty snowflakes and pale silver bunting and candles that she had bought.

'Of course, the wedding is easy compared to the long list of decorations that arrived this morning for the Christmas train,' said Flora. 'Thank goodness the campsite is shut, otherwise I'd never have time to help Ethan set everything up.'

'With help from your glamorous assistant – me,' added Libby, with a grin.

'Well, I can handle the ideas you had for the station,' said Katy, with a nod. 'That just needs to be full-on Christmas, so a massive tree, lots of holly and wreaths and twinkly lights absolutely everywhere.'

'Sounds perfect,' said Libby. 'And with time marching on too, it's a good job I'm around to help.'

'Still no sign of a job?' asked Katy.

Libby shook her head. 'No but...'

As her voice trailed off, her three friends looked at her expectantly.

'But...?' prompted Flora.

'Well, Dad and I were talking and he thinks that I should try to make a business out of the chocolate-making full-time,' she said. 'But that's crazy, isn't it?'

'Of course not!' Harriet told her. 'And your dad would never suggest something if he didn't think it would work. He's far too sensible for that.'

'I guess,' replied Libby. 'But how would I even go about starting from scratch?'

'Website,' said Katy, nodding thoughtfully. 'Getting the word out will definitely help. But the feedback from the hotel for your boxes of chocolates has already got loads of people interested and asking for more details. Anyway, this all works out perfectly for my master plan!'

Libby, Flora and Harriet tried and failed to stifle their groans.

'Here she goes again,' murmured Flora.

Katy's business ideas had caused all of them extra work over the past year, but they had to concede that they normally turned out for the best.

'How about a stall at the station when the Christmas train is up and running?' said Katy, with a large smile. 'The footfall from all those passengers will really up your chance of paying customers. Then the word of mouth spreads.'

Libby nodded. 'That sounds like a great idea,' she said. 'But it'll have to wait until the Christmas train is ready. That has to take priority. For Eddie's sake.'

They all agreed.

She certainly couldn't wait to start up her chocolate making once more. But that would mean probably using Ethan's kitchen again.

He was still her other half, she thought. The part of her that went missing whenever he went away. It would happen again in the new year, of course. But the fact that they were growing closer once more gave her hope that maybe they might just be friends at last.

Despite her wanting to be so much more.

## 46

It was nearing the end of November and Libby had spent nearly every minute of every day working on the preparations for the Christmas train.

Despite the hard work, it almost felt like a holiday after all the long hours working on the airlines and then the rush of the huge order for the boxes of chocolates. The hotel had paid her the large sum owed and so any financial pressure had eased temporarily, giving her time to breathe and even plan how she would move her chocolate business forward in the future.

She had enjoyed spending more time with her friends as they all helped set up the decorated scenes along the railway track, along with decorating the station as well. It was almost ready, although some people's help was more of a hindrance.

'This is going to make it all perfect,' declared Dodgy Del, who had returned with a worryingly large snow machine.

'Del,' warned Flora, putting her hands on her hips. 'We've literally just finished decorating this enormous tree,' she reminded him, gesturing at the huge Christmas tree they had placed halfway down the platform. 'Don't you dare go near it!'

'Yeah, but it's Christmas,' said Del, flicking a few switches and connecting up a hosepipe to a nearby outside tap. 'You've gotta have snow at Christmas.'

Libby groaned and went to stand in front of the huge pile of fake wrapped presents that they were about to place under the tree. 'I spent hours wrapping these,' she began. 'If you so much as ruin one box...'

But her words were drowned out by the enormous hum of the snow machine as it sprang into life.

Libby and Flora automatically huddled together in preparation for the oncoming snowstorm. But, to their relief, it never came. Instead, the large funnel at the top of the machine merely spat out a few snowflakes and lumps of what appeared to be grey snow which disappeared as soon as they reached the ground.

They watched on for a few more minutes until, thankfully, Ethan and Ryan marched out of Platform 1 and turned the machine off.

'That's quite enough of that,' said Ryan, glaring at his cousin. 'I can't hear myself think in my kitchen.'

Del looked down at the now damp ground in front of him. 'Can't think why it hasn't worked,' he said, with a frown. 'My mate said it would make the whole place look like Santa's grotto.'

'More grotty than grotto,' murmured Flora.

She and Libby exchanged looks of relief as Del disconnected the machine. 'I'll be back,' he promised.

'That's okay,' said Libby quickly. 'Thanks for trying anyway.'

'I can get a much bigger one, I'm sure,' carried on Del.

Libby shook her head even more violently. 'No worries, Del!' she said, almost shouting to make sure that he got the point. 'We can certainly manage without.'

They all sighed as he packed up the machine and left.

'Thank goodness for that,' said Ryan. 'So, I've got a spare half an hour, what's left to do?'

'Actually I think that's it,' said Ethan, looking up the platform.

Libby followed his gaze. The platform was now tastefully decorated with huge swags of fresh holly and pine branches, along with many fairy lights and red bows, lanterns full of large, thick candles and holly wreaths on every door and window.

She then looked back at the enormous Christmas tree, decorated from top to toe and surrounded by brightly coloured boxes. There was one particularly large present, as tall as she was, which had been placed on the other side of the tree for everyone to see the nutcracker doll inside.

'Hey, it's your dad,' said Flora, before greeting Philip as he walked out of Platform 1.

Libby looked around and smiled. 'Hi, Dad,' she said. 'How did your first stroke meeting go?' she asked.

Philip smiled. 'It was delightful,' he replied. 'I was so glad to see Eddie there, as well as a few other people in the community who could do with a hand.'

'He was determined to make it,' said Ethan.

'I'm so glad it worked out all right,' Libby told her dad. 'I'm sure it'll be a huge help for everyone.'

She was so pleased to see the change in her dad for the past couple of weeks. He was so much more positive and even had a spring in his step these days.

'Talking of help,' began Philip. 'It helps to have a purpose, a goal, so to speak. I've been doing a bit of research and apparently hobbies can be very relaxing, as well as taking one's mind off a current problem and thus aiding recovery.'

'What did you have in mind?' asked Libby.

'Well, they also say that being active helps, so I was hoping to combine the two. Do you remember when your mother used to paint pine cones in the wintertime?'

Libby nodded. 'Oh yes, lots of glitter too.'

'Well, I thought perhaps myself and my fellow members of the stroke club could head out next week for a small walk and collect some.' He gave her a sheepish grin. 'Then if you could perhaps show me how to decorate one, we could give that a go.'

Libby was delighted at the idea. 'How about we go out for a small walk of our own this afternoon and find one?' she suggested.

'It's a date,' he replied, smiling.

Libby couldn't remember the last time they had gone out for a walk together and couldn't stop herself from smiling at the thought. 'By the way, apparently they've uploaded your narration and music already for the dress rehearsal run.'

He nodded. 'I hope the timings are correct,' he said.

'It'll be just fine,' she told him. 'Flora said she and Grams listened to it last night and they said they were all ready for Christmas there and then! She said your storytelling technique is just as good as she remembers from school.'

Her dad smiled. 'Just like the pine cones, a bit of extra glitter to the magic always helps.'

'Yes, it does,' she told him, reaching up to give him a kiss on his cheek.

As he walked over to talk to Flora, Libby found Ethan in front of her.

'He looks pleased with himself,' he said.

She nodded. 'It's like he's had a new start. Talking of which,' she began. 'I was wondering whether, well, you see...'

She felt a little embarrassed and Ethan looked at her with raised eyebrows. 'What?' he asked.

'Everyone seems to think that I should set up my own chocolate-making business,' she carried on, her words rushed in her haste to get them out. 'And I figure, why not, as nobody seems to want me as a flight attendant any more. In any case, do I even want to be a flight attendant? Even Dad is encouraging me to do this, so it must be the right course, don't you think? Because he's never been so positive about anything I've ever done before.'

When she paused to take a breath, Ethan took her by the shoulders.

'Libs,' he said. 'It's me. Just ask the bloomin' question.'

Her shoulders sagged under his hands. 'Can I use your kitchen again?' she asked in a small tone.

'Did you even need to ask?' he said. 'Of course you can.'

She was delighted. 'Thank you!' she said. 'I mean, I won't have much time to get going with so much to do for the Christmas train, but maybe once that's up and running in December I could use your kitchen?'

'I said yes, didn't I?' he told her.

She felt relieved that not only did she have the kitchen at her disposal again but even better, she would be spending more time with Ethan.

'I can't wait to tell Dad,' she said, still smiling. 'He's been nagging me for days about this.'

'Well, he's normally right about almost everything,' said Ethan. 'Unlike my cousin, that is. We can't let him loose around here with a snow cannon, can we?'

'Well, he's been wrong so many times, surely he's due a break and he might actually bring something that works for once?' she said. 'Put it down to the magic of Christmas.'

As Ethan smiled down at her, Libby's heart skipped a beat. Standing there with the fairy lights all around them, she wondered whether there might just be a little bit of magic in the air after all.

## 47

Ethan took a deep breath. 'Well, there's no going back now,' he said, looking at his brother nervously.

'I think this calls for a speech, don't you?' Ryan told him.

Ethan nodded and went to stand in front of the group who were standing outside Platform 1. It was early evening and the only lights were coming from inside the coffee shop. But even in the dim light, he could see the excited faces of his family and friends. None were watching him with more expectation than his grandad. Eddie was sitting on one of the benches, looking up and down the platform at the train in front of him, as if seeing a long-lost friend for the first time in ages. He was still struggling with the weariness after his stroke but each day he was feeling a little stronger and more like his old self, he had told Ethan.

'I just wanted to say, on behalf of my dad, my grandad and myself, a huge thank you to you all for all your hard work to make this happen,' Ethan began. 'Tomorrow night is the very first run of the Christmas train, but tonight is just for you, our way of paying you back for all the many hours that you've volunteered to get everything ready. And we'd thought it had better be tonight as hopefully we'll be too busy to celebrate with all the hundreds of paying passengers over the next few weeks! As you know, the money raised from the Christmas train will go towards helping out a local charity.'

A small cheer went up, but Ethan knew that everyone was keeping their fingers crossed for the success of the train – none so more than him.

He headed over to the main circuit switch, which would be hidden once the passengers were around. But for tonight, he could make the grand gesture.

'Grandad, could you do the honours?' he said, pulling the long lead over to where Eddie sat.

'Shall we have a countdown?' asked Bob.

Everyone nodded enthusiastically and so they all began to shout.

'Three, two, one... Go!'

Eddie moved the switch in his hand and suddenly they were in the darkness no more. The whole station was illuminated with thousands of fairy lights, from the eaves above the platform, to the enormous tree and around every lamppost and fence. It looked amazing.

Applause broke out as everyone clapped and cheered at the scene in front of them. Then everyone turned expectantly to face the train.

Ethan walked over and climbed into the driver's cab, which now had a large wreath tied on either side.

'Everyone ready for another countdown?' he shouted out of the opening, holding a switch in his hand.

Once more, his family and friends called out, 'Three, two, one... Go!'

This time, it was the train that was illuminated in multi-coloured lights and yet more oohs and aahs rung out as Ethan climbed back down. He had tested the lighting a couple of times but had never seen properly in the darkness as he could do now.

He felt quite emotional as he looked along the engine to the carriages beyond, whose full length was dotted with thousands of lights. It looked magical.

With a deep breath, he went to stand in front of his grandad. 'Will it do?' he asked, feeling nervous.

Eddie smiled and nodded. 'Aye, lad. It'll do,' he said, with a smile.

But Ethan knew that it was the actual train ride that his grandad was waiting for, as was everyone else, so they brought out the special steps that Nico had built and placed them next to one of the carriage doors.

Eddie was helped up into the carriage, along with Harriet, Katy and Ryan. Ethan was also pleased to see Philip boarding the carriage, with Libby close behind him.

He thought back to the kiss they had shared. He still couldn't get it out of his head, but he had to for now, he reminded himself, because he had a train full of extremely important passengers to take on a special journey.

Once Grams, Flora and Nico had also boarded the carriage and everyone was safely indoors, Joe came along to join Ethan and Bob in the driver's cab.

'Everyone's all set,' he told them, as Ethan checked the oil and water gauges one last time.

Then he nodded at Joe to flick a different switch and suddenly the music of Tchaikovsky's *Nutcracker* rang out over the speaker above them.

Joe's phone lit up with a text from Harriet. 'Yup, it's playing in the carriage as well,' he told.

Ethan looked at his dad. 'Then let the Christmas train begin!' he said.

Bob nodded before turning to pull the chain and the toot-toot of the whistle rang out. Then Ethan pulled down the lever and the train began to move.

Although they were concentrating on the track, Ethan could also appreciate the wonder that both the music, story and lighting could create in the darkness.

Philip's narration was just enough to whet people's appetite and describe what was about to happen before the train went past the scene with the music playing.

Ethan hoped that Libby enjoyed her longed-for 'shazam' when he watched the lights flicker and create the magic as the Nutcracker doll came to life. He thought of her as well as they went past the battle scene, with its red firecracker effects creating the explosions that she had described.

In between the storytelling, the wonderful music created the right atmosphere and wonder required as the steam engine carried on in the darkness, its thousands of lights causing yet more magic.

They slowed the train as they travelled past the old aban-doned station, now transformed into The Kingdom of the Sweets, shining out in the darkness with its brightly coloured lollipops and candy canes, alongside wrapped candy and even a massive oversized chocolate bar.

All too soon it was time to slow the train down to a halt and begin the return journey, but Ethan was grateful that everything had run smoothly so far. He wasn't sure the thrill of driving the train would ever lessen for him and despite the stress of getting the train ready in time for its inaugural Christmas run, he finally felt at peace.

He just hoped his grandad felt the same way.

When they arrived back at Cranfield station, everyone rushed out of the carriages to tell them how wonderful it had been.

There were hugs, tears and laughter as everyone congratulated each other on a job well done.

Ethan even received a hug from Libby, although she had just given one to his dad as well. They locked eyes as she stepped away. The dark pink blush spreading across her cheeks told him that she hadn't forgotten about their kiss either.

She stepped aside and Ethan came face to face with Philip.

'Thank you for the wonderful narration,' Ethan told him. 'The storytelling was spot on.'

'Glad you enjoyed listening to it as much as I enjoyed telling it,' replied Philip, shaking his hand. 'I thought the whole light show was absolutely marvellous.'

Then it was time for the most important review of all.

His grandad slowly made his way down the platform from where he had been staring up at the train, still lit up in its Christmas lights.

Ethan suddenly felt nervous. What if it hadn't been all that his grandad had dreamt of? What if he had failed in his quest to help his grandad achieve his dream?

But as Eddie turned to look at his grandson with tears in his eyes, Ethan's shoulders sank back down in relief.

'You did it,' Eddie told him, as Ethan went forward to hug him briefly.

As Ethan stepped back, he said, 'No, Grandad. We did it.'

Eddie smiled. 'It's everything I dreamt of and more. Well done, lad. Bloody well done.'

Finally, Ethan could join in with everyone's else's smiles. 'Bring on the passengers!' he announced to another hearty cheer.

## 48

After the successful trial run of the Christmas train, there was nothing more for Libby to do. Which left her free to finally return to her chocolate making and, in truth, she was not only excited about that but also about being back in Ethan's company once more.

'I hope this still is okay,' she said to him, turning up at the old school the following morning with a large box in her hands and a car full of her equipment. 'I know you're busy getting ready for the grand opening tonight.'

'It's fine,' replied Ethan, taking the box from her.

'Thank goodness for that,' she told him. 'Can I start bringing the rest of my stuff in now because we can barely move in our place?'

'Sure,' he told her.

Once everything was back inside, it took her the rest of the morning to set everything up so that it was ready to use. She glanced around the clean and tidy kitchen and tried not to grimace with guilt over how she had filled it with heavy smoke the last time she had prepared her chocolate in there.

It was almost lunchtime when she was finally finished.

Ethan was sitting at the new breakfast bar, studying what looked like an extremely technical plan on his laptop.

'Hey,' she said, peering over his shoulder. 'What's that?'

'It's the plan of the circuit breakers and timer switches for the lighting,' he told her. 'Fingers crossed it all works.'

'It worked fine last night,' she reminded him.

He blew out a sigh. 'Yeah, I know.'

'What's the matter?' she asked.

'It just means so much to Grandad,' Ethan told her. 'He's got this other big dream about seeing the train on Christmas Eve in the snow! How am I going to manage that?'

'Well, if Dodgy Del can't, then nobody can,' she joked, before getting serious once more. 'Eddie loved the train. He told me so last night. You've done it. You've achieved his dream.'

'Yeah. I guess.' He looked up at her suddenly with clear blue eyes. 'And what's your dream?'

She gave a start. 'Me?' Libby shrugged her shoulders. 'I guess to have my own chocolate shop. A place of my own to sell whatever I like. Talking of which, I've got something to show you.'

Feeling rather proud, she led him over to reveal her newest idea. She had seen the chocolate moulds online and hadn't been able to stop herself from buying them. She had tested them out at home the previous evening.

'Ta da!' she said, with a flourish as she brought out the box of ready-made shapes.

'It's a chocolate train!' exclaimed Ethan, picking it up. 'Wow.'

He turned the chocolate over in his hands, looking down at in wonder.

'Isn't it great?' she said. 'I've got little carriages too,' she carried on, reaching over to show him the empty moulds.

'This is amazing, Libs,' he told her. 'You're going to sell loads.'

'I hope so,' she replied. 'I mean, there isn't that much room in Platform 1, but even if I just sell one train, I'll be happy.'

Ethan frowned. 'So how are you going to make a profit or sell as many chocolates as you need to?' he asked.

'I'll be fine,' she told him briskly, even though it had been a worry at the back of her mind. 'Anyway, I'm making chocolate again. That's all that matters.'

He looked around at the kitchen. 'I guess all this is a far cry from your heady nights away with the airline crew,' he said.

She shook her head. 'Actually, I used to be what they call a "slam clicker" on layovers.'

'A what?' he asked.

'It means I used to shut my hotel door, clicked the lock and didn't see my fellow crew members until we showed up to fly again the following day,' she told him. 'Layovers were my time for myself. I used to read up on chocolate or explore the local food scene.' She looked up at him. 'What about you? I heard you led a pretty wild nightlife whilst you were away all those years.'

'It meant nothing to me,' he told her. 'It was all so frivolous and fake.' He paused before carrying on, 'Unlike you, Mrs Connolly. You were the real deal.'

She took a sharp intake of breath. 'So any near Mrs since then?' she quipped, trying to keep the atmosphere light.

He smiled. 'Many,' he replied. 'But nobody else came close to making me hear wedding bells.'

She raised a sardonic eyebrow. 'Don't you mean hearing a synthetic organ in an Elvis chapel?' she said, with a grin.

'Actually I found it very romantic,' he said.

She laughed. 'We were both drunk!'

But Ethan wasn't laughing. 'I wasn't that drunk,' he told her, shaking his head.

He took a step forward until their bodies were almost touching.

'Ethan,' she whispered, staring up at the intensity in his eyes.

He didn't need to tell her what he was thinking. She knew exactly what he wanted. And she wanted it too.

She couldn't stop herself from reaching up to draw him closer to her. Her hands automatically crept around his shoulders and up to his head to draw his down to hers.

She heard him groan briefly before dropping his lips onto hers and then she was lost in time. Everything stood still and it was just them. She was back in his arms at last. Back where she had always wanted to be.

She felt his hands on her back, pulling her against him so that there was no space between them at all. It felt so right, as his kiss deepened. She felt whole again, as if the other half of her that had been missing for so long was finally complete once more.

At some point, in a daze, she felt him pull back slightly.

'Libby,' he whispered before stepping away from her and running a hand through his hair. 'I'm sorry. I shouldn't have done that.'

'Why not?' she blurted out.

'Because this doesn't end well for us,' he told her. 'Because no relationship of mine ends in a happy ever after, however much I care for you. It's all fake and lies.'

'You think that kiss was fake?' she asked, hurt and confused. 'Did it feel fake to you?'

'No,' he replied. 'And it never did. But...'

Libby stood still, holding her breath and waiting for him to pull her close once more. She silently willed him to trust her and not the cynicism that his mum had shown him throughout his childhood.

But instead, he turned his back on her, pulling out his phone. 'I've got quite a bit to do before the first train run later,' he said. 'I'll see you on the platform tonight?'

She nodded, even though he was halfway across the lounge by now.

He was running away again, she thought, thinking back to when he had told her about his mum's cheating.

As she watched him leave, she wondered whether he was right. Perhaps it had been a mistake for them both to kiss. So why did she want nothing more than to run back into his arms?

## 49

Libby had enjoyed the Christmas train ride with her dad immensely. Hearing him narrate the story over the speakers had been the icing on the cake, as far as she was concerned. But the rest was so magical, so incredible, that she couldn't wait to have just a little more magic that evening when she had volunteered to help out at the station with the very first run for paying passengers.

She had spent a relaxed afternoon at home taking delivery of new ingredients, as well as researching new flavours and methods. Her fingers were itching to try out adding a scattering of Harriet's lavender petals to the outside of some plain truffles as a way of starting to experiment with flowers for a summer range of chocolates.

'I need to keep ahead of the trends,' she told her dad, when he expressed surprise that she hadn't stayed at the old school to use the kitchen.

But the truth was that she was avoiding Ethan. The kiss a few hours ago had shaken her up and it was hard to concentrate on anything else. It had felt so right and yet he had walked away.

Perhaps it really wasn't meant to be after all, she thought, regardless of how much her heart yearned for him.

Libby arrived early to help Katy switch everything on at Platform 1 and get prepared for what was being promised as a sold-out event.

Once darkness had fallen, the lights went back on at the station and the whole platform was lit up like a Christmas grotto.

Libby was especially thrilled to see the local television news station turn up with their cameras, which would be a great promotion for the remaining dates on the calendar.

'Just wish I'd got that snow sorted,' muttered Del, who had brought his mum along to ride the train.

'It looks great anyway,' Libby told him. 'It doesn't need it.'

Del's face begged to differ and Libby was hoping that she had done enough to dissuade him from bothering about the fake snow any longer.

Thankfully, all the other passengers were delighted with the Christmas train and the decorations at the station. Their faces, both young and old, lit up in wonder at both the station but especially the train. Libby saw Ethan in the distance chatting to everyone but she stayed away from him, hovering near the station entrance instead to help with any late arrivals.

Everyone was taking photographs and videos, especially when Bob gave the whistle a pull to indicate that everyone should start boarding.

Libby also made sure that she took some photos on her phone as the train began to move. She watched until it disappeared into the darkness, only a dimly lit blur in the far distance.

'We've got about an hour,' said Katy, after checking that nobody had left anything behind on the station. 'I've got to get going.'

'You have?' Libby was surprised. 'Why? What are you doing?'

'Just this and that,' muttered Katy, avoiding eye contact. 'Why don't you go and see Ryan? Stay inside in the warm?'

Libby frowned, under the distinct impression that her friend was hiding something. But she headed inside anyway and chatted with Ryan whilst he prepared for a busy pizza takeout service.

An hour later, they heard the familiar sound of the steam engine pulling into the station and headed outside. There was an air of excitement as the passengers began to disembark the train. Everyone was wearing cheerful expressions as they climbed down from the train.

'That was wonderful,' everyone kept telling Libby.

'Magical,' was another popular description.

'I loved the story,' said someone else.

Most of all, everyone was promising that they would be back to enjoy it again before Christmas.

'It sounds like you've got a hit on your hands,' Libby told Bob as they met on the platform after everyone had left.

She glanced up at Ethan as he climbed out of the driver's cab, but he didn't say anything.

'Isn't it great?' asked Bob, beaming with joy. 'It was a huge success! I can't wait to tell dad all about it.'

'Absolutely,' replied Katy, coming to join them. 'Come on. You must be desperate for your dinner. I've got tea all ready for you and Eddie.'

'Where have you been?' asked Libby.

'Ask him,' said Katy, nodding towards Ethan as he stood nearby. 'It was his big idea.'

They wished the others goodnight and then suddenly it was just Libby and Ethan left alone on the platform.

'What's all the secrecy with Katy?' asked Libby.

He cleared his throat, looking quite nervous. 'She's been

doing me a favour, actually. Well, you were talking about setting up your own shop and I figured now is the best time, what with all the footfall from the passengers, so there you go.'

Libby followed his gaze to where a gazebo had been placed nearby. She hadn't spotted it before, she realised. As they walked towards it, she realised that it had been decorated with Christmas swags and holly wreaths, in keeping with the rest of the platform.

Ethan went behind the table and fiddled with something on the floor. Suddenly, the whole gazebo was lit up with fairy lights.

'It's amazing,' she told him, hardly believing that she finally had her own stall where she could sell her very own chocolate.

'Well, it's all down to Katy, really,' said Ethan, with a shrug. 'I just suggested it.'

'And did the wiring so that I've got lights,' she said.

'And a heater too,' he muttered. 'You know, it gets cold out here.'

'Why?' she asked softly.

He groaned, finally making eye contact. 'You know why, Libs. You're my oldest friend.'

She baulked at the word friend. His kisses had told her that she was so much more to him and yet she knew that was what he was telling himself as he tried to deal with his relationship demons.

Perhaps it would be enough to be just friends, she tried to tell herself. She knew that she wanted so much more from him but if he couldn't give her all of his heart, then perhaps it was better that they stay as friends. Because she would rather have him in her life as a friend than not at all.

'Well, thank you,' she told him.

'You're welcome.'

There was another short silence and then they both spoke at once.

'Well, I should probably...' said Libby.

'I should get back home...' began Ethan.

They exchanged a smile, but neither of them carried on talking, so they made their silent way back down the platform, with only the whisper of the wind in the trees making any noise.

## 50

The next few weeks spun past in a whirl, it seemed to Ethan. Like everything, the best things always seemed to rush by too fast.

The Christmas train was a huge success. The local television news on the first night had brought so much publicity that they had had to put on a train nearly every night to keep up with demand.

His dad and grandad were thrilled and, even better, Eddie seemed to thrive along with the Christmas train. He had more of a spring in his step with each day and had begun to take a daily walk with Philip to Cranbridge and back. He was even planning to join them in the driver's cab for the Christmas Eve run.

Ethan knew how important that particular night, the very last night, of the Christmas train was to his grandad. It was the anniversary of the proposal to his late wife. The culmination of his grandad's long-held dream. Ethan was keeping everything crossed that his grandad would be well enough for that journey.

The train was bringing much prosperity to Cranfield and Ethan was glad that everyone was benefitting. Platform 1 had had a huge bump in customers, thanks to the train passengers discovering both the cosy coffee shop and their delicious pizzas.

Harriet had never been busier in her lavender spa and had set up a stall selling her lavender products alongside Libby's.

Libby's temporary chocolate shop was also a success. She could barely keep up with the demand for her chocolate trains and so was using his kitchen every day, working to create even more of her delicious chocolate. His home now smelled of cocoa, sweet and welcoming, hitting him in the senses whenever he headed through the front door. But it wasn't chocolate he was craving. It was Libby.

Her friends had given her an apron as a gift which said Kiss The Cook on the front. He was shocked by how much he wanted to do that exact thing. But he continued to hold back, deliberately keeping their conversations light and the length of the kitchen between them at all times.

It was better this way, he told himself, no matter how he longed to kiss her again and again.

His mother's words that love would bring him no joy still weighed heavy on him. She had repeated the sentiment over and over and he had seen first hand how miserable both his parents had been in the marriage, despite declaring that they loved each other. Love would never have a place in his heart, he told himself.

But despite his feelings, he still couldn't keep away from Libby. So on the morning of Christmas Eve, he found himself offering to walk along to Platform 1 with her for an early coffee.

'I've got so much to do today, making sure I've got enough stock for tonight,' Libby told him as they went down Railway Lane. 'Did I tell you that I've got an order for ten boxes of truffles for a New Year's party! I can't believe how quickly business has taken off.'

Her blue eyes shone with the thrill of the success of her business and he found himself temporarily mesmerised until he almost walked into a lamppost.

'Well, take the business whilst you can,' said Ethan, dodging the lamppost at the last minute. 'Tonight is the last of the Christmas train runs.'

'Can you believe it's gone so quickly?' asked Libby.

Ethan shook his head.

'But you're staying on until the wedding at the end of January?' she asked.

Ethan nodded. 'Everyone seems so keen that the train keeps running that we'll have a service each weekend, as so many people have requested it.'

'That's great,' replied Libby. 'Then you'll be onto Valentine's and then Easter too. I don't know how I'm going to keep up with demand!'

But Ethan had realised that he wouldn't be there for those times. He had already agreed another work contract and would be heading abroad after Harriet and Joe's wedding.

He felt sad, having missed out on so many family occasions by being away so often. But he knew that it was his choice to leave, although this time it felt harder and less appealing than before.

In the meantime, he had to make sure that the Christmas Eve train was the biggest and best of them all.

Running through his to-do list, he followed Libby down the small passage between the main station and Harriet's lavender spa. However, he almost bumped into her when she stopped abruptly in front of him when they reached the station platform.

Looking around, he could immediately see why. Whereas the remainder of Cranfield was coated in a frost after a cold winter's night, the station appeared to be foot deep in snow!

'What the...?' Ethan's voice trailed off as he stared around before he caught sight of an enormous industrial-sized snow machine. Then he roared, 'Del!'

Libby burst into shocked laughter. 'I don't believe it,' she said, giggling.

'I do!' snapped Ethan. 'I'll kill him!'

'Why?' she said, still laughing. 'It looks wonderful!'

'Yes, but he's covered the railway tracks!' Ethan told her, pointing down to where the snow had spilled over onto the line. 'It's going to take me all day to clear this so we can actually move the train later!'

'Walking in a winter wonderland,' she hummed, still smiling broadly as she picked up a handful of snow and threw it in his face.

Before she could shower him in more snow, he grabbed both her hands and drew her to him. There were snowflakes in her hair, her cheeks were bright pink in the cold and her eyes had never been more blue. If the snow didn't take his breath away, her beauty at that moment did. And he bent forward to break every promise to himself that he would make sure they stayed as just friends. Because nothing was going to stop him from kissing her at that moment.

It was just as sweet as it had ever been and it took every strength of his will to pull away from her.

'Why can't you move on?' she whispered, hanging onto the lapels of his coat and not letting go. 'Your mum has. So has your dad with Maggie.'

'I don't know. I just can't,' he blurted out.

At that moment, they were interrupted by Ryan and Katy coming out to ooh and aah at the fake snow fall on the station.

Ethan took the opportunity to walk away from Libby, whilst he still could. Even though it felt so right to be kissing her.

Even if he only felt complete when he was holding her in his arms.

The snow on Cranfield station might have been a Christmas miracle, but Ethan knew that they didn't really exist in real life. Not for him anyway.

## 51

Libby could still feel Ethan's lips on hers as he walked away from her on the snowy platform. She knew he cared for her. She knew it, deep in her heart. And yet she couldn't seem to break through the protective shell that he had built around himself.

So she busied herself with another manic day trying to keep up with demand for her chocolate. She was absolutely thrilled with the success that the chocolate shop had brought her. Each evening, the passengers would gather around her stall, buying hot chocolate as well as her truffles. But the chocolate trains were her bestseller.

After readying the stall, she picked up a couple of coffees and took them back to her cottage as a treat for her and her dad. He was also enjoying a sort-of success as the stroke club had become a bi-weekly meeting due to its popularity. He was so much happier in himself and Libby was pleased by how much closer they had become.

'I got us both a mince pie for later,' she told him when she headed into the kitchen.

'Well, what a treat,' her dad replied, his eyes lighting up as she took the pastries out of the takeout bag.

Libby hesitated before she spoke again. 'There was one other extra treat I had for you.'

Her dad raised his eyebrows in question. 'Oh yes?' he asked.

Libby nodded and headed over to one of the kitchen cupboards. She pulled out a box and placed it on the table. Her dad looked down and smiled at the Christmas ribbon that she had tied on the top.

'More chocolates?' he asked, sitting down at the table.

Libby sat down next to him. 'Actually, they're a special flavour,' she told him.

He pulled on the ribbon and then lifted up the lid and took an appreciative breath. 'Smells as wonderful as always.'

Libby bit her lip, feeling a little nervous, as she watched him pop one of the truffles in his mouth.

After he had finished eating, he looked at her with wide eyes.

'It's chocolate ginger,' she told him. 'Mum's favourite.'

He nodded. 'Yes,' he said, his voice croaky with emotion. 'It was.'

Then they were both hugging and sharing their tears.

'I miss her,' Libby murmured into her dad's shoulder.

'Me too, my darling girl,' he replied.

Libby leant back, wiping her wet cheeks. 'But she'd be getting cross at us crying at Christmas, wouldn't she?' she said.

Her dad gave her a teary smile. 'Absolutely,' he replied, nodding. But he took her hand in his good one and gave it a squeeze. 'Well, we'd better have that coffee. We've both got a busy day ahead for the train run tonight.'

Her dad had volunteered to help out for the Christmas Eve run. Normally, Eddie would take people's tickets as they came onto the platform, check them and then return them as souvenirs. But Ethan had planned an extra-special surprise for his grandad. Earlier that afternoon, he had delivered a present to Eddie, with instructions for it to be used that evening.

Just before the passengers began to arrive, all their friends and family gathered on the platform for the special arrival.

Finally, Bob came through the doors from Platform 1 and turned around to smile at his father as he walked out.

Eddie came out slowly, but with an extremely proud look on his face. He was wearing a brand new stationmaster's uniform, an exact replica of the one that had been worn when the steam train had originally run. Everyone clapped and cheered as he took off his cap and doffed it to them all, smiling all the while.

His smile faltered as he looked around the station in wonder. Dodgy Del's fake snow had lasted the day and so Eddie's dream of seeing the steam engine in the snow had come true. He looked at Ethan with teary eyes and they both stepped forward at the same time to embrace.

'It's perfect,' Libby heard him say to Ethan. 'Just like I had imagined.'

Eddie spent the rest of the time before the train set off mingling with the passengers, sharing train trivia with those who asked. Libby thought what a tonic the train had been for him. He was not quite as mobile as he had once been, but he was much better and would keep improving. Perhaps he would never be quite the same, but he had a quality of life as did her own dad now and she was pleased for them both.

Eddie rode the train that evening, going up and down the corridor, revelling in the attention and even having his photograph taken.

As the train drew into the station one last time all dressed in its festive finery, everyone clapped and cheered.

Libby hugged and applauded along with everyone else once

the passengers had finally gone home to wait for Father Christmas's arrival. She watched with tears in her eyes as Eddie walked up to Ethan with tears of his own streaming down his face.

'You did it, lad,' said Eddie.

Ethan smiled, his face almost black with the soot and dust from the engine, but his blue eyes shone out.

'I'm so proud of you,' she heard Eddie carry on. 'And your grandmother would have been too.'

Then they hugged and everyone cheered once more.

'I have a further announcement,' shouted Bob, checking the piece of paper that Ryan had just handed him. 'As you know, the profits made from the Christmas train were all going to a local charity. And I'm thrilled to announce that we've decided to donate the money to our local stroke club.'

Libby and her dad exchanged delighted smiles.

'How wonderful,' said Philip, looking amazed. 'And how generous. Thank you. I shall ensure that it benefits as many people as we can muster.'

'Champagne inside to celebrate!' announced Ryan and everyone began to head inside.

Libby found she was holding herself back, anxious to wait for Ethan. He was using a cloth to wipe his face and had unzipped his blue overalls so that he was wearing just his jumper and a pair of jeans.

'Well, that was a great success,' she said.

He nodded. 'It was,' he replied, stepping away from her.

'Ethan,' she said to his back. 'Please look at me.'

She watched as he sighed before he finally turned around.

'Don't do this,' he told her, shaking his head. 'I'm no good for you. You deserve the best and I can't be that person you want me to be. After all that stuff with Mum, I can't believe in love.'

'I know,' she replied.

And she did. She knew all this because she knew him so well. She knew that he still had to leave, that he couldn't stay in Cranfield forever. That he couldn't love her the way that she wanted him to. And yet, she couldn't go on like this either.

'I still have to leave at the end of January,' he said.

'Then we'd better not waste any more time,' she told him, reaching out to take his hand in hers. 'Don't think about anything. Just kiss me again.'

She had wondered whether he would pull away from her again, but as soon as her hand touched his, he groaned and pulled her to him.

'Libby,' he whispered, before he dropped his head down to kiss her.

And then there was nothing but him.

## 52

It was the best of times and the worst of times, thought Ethan.

'No chocolate tastes as sweet as you,' he would tell Libby each day in his kitchen, kissing her bare neck where she had her hair scraped back into a messy bun revealing that soft, pale skin underneath.

'Stop distracting me,' she would reply. But she never seemed able to stop herself from turning around and kissing him back.

And those kisses never seemed to be enough for him to quell the need for more from her. But he had to make do during the busy hours servicing and running the train throughout January until he could be alone with her once more.

All he wanted to do was slow time down, to make the nights even longer, but they whizzed past in a blur with just a whisper of the memory of holding Libby in his arms in the darkness.

Each morning before dawn, she would creep out of the old school and back to her cottage before her dad would know that she was gone.

It was a secret love. But perhaps not so secret.

His brother cornered him one day with a knowing look.

'Must say, I'm glad that you two have finally got together,' said Ryan. 'It's only been, what, almost thirty years?'

Ethan looked at him. 'How did you know?' he couldn't help but ask.

'Because you look happy, bro,' Ryan told him, clapping a hand on his shoulder. 'Have you told her how you feel?'

Ethan gulped and shrugged his shoulders in response.

Ryan looked a little worried at his brother's expression. 'Maybe her psychic powers aren't as strong as you think they should be.'

'Maybe everyone should mind their own business,' Ethan told him before walking away.

But he wasn't so quick that he noticed the sad shake of his brother's head.

Surely Ryan of all people understood? Ethan couldn't love anyone like that. It was too dangerous to open his heart up to the hurt that would surely happen when the relationship inevitably failed. Because love never lasted, did it? His mum had shown him what happened when the love stopped. That was when the real pain began for everyone and he just couldn't do that to Libby.

And yet, despite his confused feelings, he rushed back to her each and every night, sweeping Libby into his arms as soon as he saw her and holding her tight, so tight, so that she could never leave him.

It was getting so bad that, only hours after she had crept home in the wee small hours of the morning, he would meet her at the front gate on her way for an early coffee at Platform 1.

'Aren't you sleeping?' he asked her, desperate to reach for her hand but stopping himself as they nodded at a couple of dog walkers heading past.

'Not especially,' she replied, a smile playing on her lips. 'At this rate, I'll need extra make-up for Harriet's wedding because I look so haggard.'

One glance at her face confirmed to Ethan that she was still the most beautiful woman he had ever seen.

He felt himself growing closer and closer to her. One night they even finally spoke about Las Vegas.

'I knew deep down that I wanted to marry you that night,' he told her.

She stared up at him. 'You did? Why? You've always been against marriage.'

'Why?' repeated Ethan before laughing. 'For someone awfully bright, you're remarkably stupid sometimes.'

'Hey!' she said, giving him a playful push with her hand.

But he didn't move. Instead, he pulled her closer to him once more, letting his kisses replace the three words that he could never say.

One morning, as the end of January grew nearer, Ryan looked at him. 'Do you really have to leave after the wedding? It's clear how much you care for her,' he said.

Ethan sighed and shook his head. 'Don't go there,' he replied.

'Why not?' said Ryan. 'It's been as plain as day for years. I can't remember a time when it wasn't you and Libby.'

Ethan went to walk away, but his brother blocked his path. 'You're telling me that she doesn't make each day better? That you can't wait to see her? That she's your other half? That she completes you?'

Ethan gulped. 'It won't work.'

'I love you, bro, but don't do this,' Ryan told him. 'Don't be the world's biggest idiot. If you let her go this time, that will be it. Forever. And that's a long time to regret not having the love of your life in your actual life.'

Ethan sighed and then looked at his brother. 'Since when did you get so wise?' he asked.

'I was always wise,' said Ryan, with a grin. 'You were just too dumb to notice.'

As they hugged, Ethan thought how grateful he was that he was closer than ever to Ryan. That he enjoyed having real friends in the village. Being close to his family and his roots.

And Libby, always Libby.

He had wondered over the years about getting the marriage annulled. Although he wasn't sure he wanted to move on from being married to her.

And right at that moment, he would marry her all over again in a heartbeat.

Ethan shook his head. But he still needed to leave, didn't he? After the wedding, he would move on once more. That way he wouldn't get hurt and, more importantly, neither would she. Leaving was the only safe option for the both of them.

But this time the thought didn't give him any sense of relief. It merely highlighted how much he would be giving up.

## 53

Two days before Harriet and Joe's wedding and Libby couldn't believe that it was beginning to snow outside.

She stood by the kitchen window in the old school and looked outside at the falling snow, deep in thought.

It had been an incredible few weeks where all her dreams had finally become true. Thanks to Joe helping create a new website, her chocolate was selling in high numbers and she had a business that she both enjoyed and was proud of.

Her relationship with her dad had never been better and it was a joy to be so close to him, closer than she had ever been. He too was looking so much happier these days. The stroke club was now meeting twice a week and new people were joining them all the time. Her dad was coming back to life and even volunteering at church. She was thrilled to see the positive change in him.

And yet, the biggest dream of all had been the change in her relationship with Ethan. Finally, after so many years of denying herself the dream she had always secretly had, she had given in to temptation. And it had never felt so right.

Her inner cynic was in a battle for her heart with its new

loved-up spirit. She had even looked at one of Harriet's wedding magazines the other day and had given a little sigh at the hope that she and Ethan might have their own special day.

She had been wrong all along about love and romance. Her friends had been right. She loved being in love, being in someone's arms. Nothing had ever felt so right or so good as when she was with Ethan.

She knew that he was still planning to leave after the wedding and had told herself that it would be fine. She understood. The pain of his parents' failed marriage still haunted him. But with every passing day, she was falling more and more in love with him. She had never told him. She knew it would break the magic and their relationship was so fragile, so special, that she couldn't bear to change things in any way.

And yet it was getting harder not to tell him how she really felt.

If only he would stay. But she knew that she wasn't enough to make that happen and it was stopping her heart from being completely full.

'Hey, it's snowing,' she heard Ethan say as his arms suddenly wrapped around her.

'I know,' she replied, leaning back against him as they watched. 'So much for my planned walk this afternoon. I might as well carry on working.' She turned around to look up at him. 'After all, what else is there to do on a snowy winter's day?'

His eyes gleamed with promise as he drew her close. Her heart thumped in her chest. She would never be able to resist him.

Pretty soon, she forgot all about the chocolate.

But later on in the afternoon, as she tidied up the kitchen, she knew that she wouldn't be making any chocolate for a couple of days. The next day was the eve of the wedding and then there was the big day itself.

And then Ethan would leave and she felt a dull pain deep inside. He had promised to leave her the keys to the front door so that she could come and go as she pleased. But Libby knew that it wasn't enough. That he had the keys to her heart as well.

So when he kissed her a while later, she found herself saying, 'I'm going to miss you when you leave.'

He groaned. 'Me too. Libs—'

She shook her head. 'Don't do it, Ethan,' she said. 'Don't leave.'

She felt his whole body stiffen under her hands. 'I've got to,' he replied. 'You know I do. I can't fall in love. Not with anyone.'

'But that's rubbish,' she told him, reaching up to take his face in her hands. 'You love lots of people. You love your dad. Your grandad. Your brother. Why can't you love me?'

'Because it won't last,' he replied, shaking his face away from her touch. 'It never does.'

'I'm not your mother,' she reminded him.

'I know,' he said. 'And I care about you, you know I do. You're my best friend and I don't want to lose you.'

'I don't want to lose you either,' she told him. But already she knew that it was time to face up to the truth that she had been hiding from for the past few months. Ever since he had moved into the school, in fact. 'But the truth is that I love you,' she told him. 'I love you with every breath in my body. And I always will.'

Ethan sucked in a deep breath as if in shock.

Libby knew that she had to be the strong one. 'But I can't be in a relationship that's so one-sided. I can't be with someone who doesn't feel strong enough to stay and be with me. I've tried so hard not so say how much I love you, but I can't lie. Not to you.' She tried to smile, even though her heart was breaking. 'You're my best friend too so at the very least we have to be honest with each other. I deserve to be with someone who loves me as much as I love them. And if you don't want that commitment, then I understand. I really do. But if you care for me as much as you say you do, then you have to let me go now. After all these years, I think I deserve that, don't you?'

He was still for a long while and for a moment she thought he was going to step forward and take her in his arms once more, to finally tell her what she longed to hear.

But in the end, he merely nodded and dropped his arms down to his side.

She felt a chill run through her. He had made his choice and it wasn't her.

'Okay,' she told him in a shaky voice. 'Well, thank you for listening to me.'

She knew that she had to walk away from him whilst she was strong enough to. But it was the hardest thing she had ever had to face and she only held back the tears until she had walked out of the old school.

## 54

'After Dodgy Del's snowy surprise at the station on Christmas Eve, I can't believe it's actually snowed for real on my wedding day a month later!' said Harriet, with a groan.

Libby shook her head. 'It doesn't matter,' she told her. 'It's your big day and not even the weather can spoil it.'

'How can it?' said Flora, going over to the window. 'It looks magical out there!'

It had begun to snow the day before and now, on the actual wedding day, it was still snowing. The whole area was coated in six inches of snow and chaos had ensued as to the wedding preparation.

The plan had always been for most people to walk to the tiny church in Cranbridge as Harriet wanted to go past her lavender fields, which were such a strong link to her late beloved aunt and uncle. But that was going to be impossible in deep snow with a long gown as well as the return journey to the station for the reception.

Consequently, rides had been hurriedly organised and guests

were being ferried over to the church with only half an hour to go.

'Ryan says the roads are getting worse,' said Katy, looking at her phone and grimacing. 'You know, this is why I used to live in a city!' But she was smiling as she went over to fix a stray red hair of Harriet's under her veil.

'You look beautiful,' said Flora.

Harriet was wearing a long gown of white silk and lace and looked every inch the beautiful bride.

Harriet blushed. 'Well, I didn't want anything fancy,' she told them.

'Simple, elegant and exquisite,' said Katy, with an approving nod.

Libby had to agree. Harriet looked wonderful and for the first time in two days, she found that she was smiling.

It had been a wretched couple of days ever since she had walked away from Ethan. Was it possible to miss someone that much? To lose one's oldest friend and still survive? Because she ached inside at not seeing him every day. Her skin yearned for his touch. Her mouth wanted to be kissed over and over by him. But none of that would ever happen again.

She knew she had been right to walk away. That perhaps one day, a long time in the future, she would get over him. But at the moment, she was so heartbroken that she felt that she was only functioning on autopilot just to get through each day.

Her dad had not questioned when she had arrived back home with a car full of her cooking equipment the previous day, after she had gone into the old school when she knew Ethan wouldn't be there. But she found that he had been making her more cups of tea and giving her hand a squeeze more often than he had ever done before.

All she needed to do was get through the wedding day, she

reminded herself. Ethan would be on the first plane out of there soon after and then she could relax, maybe even heal.

But she knew that her heart would never mend. It had always been Ethan for as long as she could remember. For all of her life, he had been her first and forever love. She just wasn't his.

'Do you love him?'

For a moment, Libby thought she had spoken out loud and then she realised that it was Harriet's voice she had heard. She looked over to see her three best friends watching her with worried looks.

She took in a shaky breath before nodding, finally able to admit the truth to them.

'Then you have to tell him,' said Flora, with an impatient shake of her head.

Libby gave them a sad smile. 'I have,' she told them.

The truth was that he just didn't feel the same way.

Her friends exchanged looks and then rushed forward as one unit to embrace her in a hug. For a second, she let them comfort her. And then she stepped away.

'Right, come on, bridal party, this is supposed to be a happy day,' she told them, despite her broken heart.

'Shall we have another glass of champagne?' said Katy, grabbing the nearby bottle and glasses.

'Absolutely,' agreed Libby.

Once they all had a glass of champagne, Katy did the toast.

'Here's to love,' she said, with a smile. 'Love for a soon-to-be married couple, love between neighbours and families, and love between friends. Best friends.'

'To love,' they all said in unison, clinking their glasses before taking a sip of the delicious drink.

'But unless love comes with a snowplough, we'd better get a wriggle on,' said Flora and they all nodded their agreement.

A few moments later, Harriet was carefully ensconced in the back of Ryan's Range Rover, along with Paddington the dog and Flora.

Ethan had been waiting in his car. Libby knew that she would have to cope with seeing him that day and it was fine. Perfectly fine, she tried to tell herself.

Except he suddenly leapt out of the driving seat and rushed over. 'I've forgotten the rings!' he told them, hurrying away through the snow in his suit towards the school.

Libby rolled her eyes. 'You'd all better get going,' she told them. 'I can check that he's got them.'

'Are you sure?' asked Katy, with worried eyes from the passenger seat. 'I could wait for him instead?'

'You're already in there,' Libby told her. 'Don't crease your jumpsuit by getting in and out. It's fine. We'll be right behind you. Harriet's the important one! See you there!'

And with a wave, she watched as they carefully drove away.

She shivered, but it wasn't the cold winter air that made her feel that way. It was being in close proximity to Ethan once more.

But she could get through the toughest of days. Because it was Harriet's wedding day so it was the happiest of days as well, despite her broken heart.

## 55

Ethan couldn't believe he could have been so stupid as to forget the wedding rings. The only reason he could think of was that he hadn't slept properly the last couple of nights. Ever since Libby had walked away from him, in fact.

He knew that it was all his fault that he no longer saw her. His fault that his arms ached without her in them. That he missed her with every fibre of his being. And yet he still held back. He just had to get through today and then he would be leaving. At least then he could begin to move on with his life without Libby, he tried to remind himself. But the thought gave him no joy.

As he marched into the bedroom, his phone rang with a text from his mum. He quickly read the message. Her latest romance was coming apart at the seams. Ethan wasn't surprised. She had always bored within a short time of each relationship. Nothing new there.

The next text he received from her confirmed what he had already suspected. That she was already moving on to someone else. It was the same old attitude. She was always looking for the next big thing.

Lucky her, thought Ethan. There would never be anyone better for him than Libby. He had everything he had ever wanted with her, she was his best friend, his other half. Why on earth would he move on with someone else?

Ethan stopped abruptly in the middle of his bedroom as the realisation washed over him. He wasn't like his mum at all. In any way, in fact.

Everything she had told him had been wrong and it had been the biggest mistake of his life to believe her. Love was something to cherish, not fear. He couldn't deny that the past few weeks with Libby had brought him the joy that his mum had always told him wouldn't come. And that relationship, that joy, had changed him. Forever.

He now knew why he had married Libby all those years ago. Why he had rushed inside to save her from a smoke-filled house. Why he had set her up a chocolate stall. Why he would give her everything in the world and more, if he could.

She was the one. She was the love of his life. She always had been.

With that thought, he could feel the anger and frustrations of his youth finally slipping away. He could make peace with himself and move on at last. Ryan had been right. The happy moments did outweigh the bad stuff after all. He'd just been too blinkered to see it.

And that left Libby. It had always been Libby. No one else would ever come close.

But he would have to talk to her later, he reminded himself. There was a very important wedding waiting to happen first.

Ethan opened up the drawer in his bedside table where there were two ring boxes. In a rush, he grabbed both and put them in his jacket pocket, intending to quickly identify the correct ones before he went into church.

He rushed out of the school to find that only Libby was stood by his car. She looked beautiful, standing there in the snow, the purple jumpsuit showing off her long legs and incredible figure. She could still take his breath away, each and every time he saw her.

'The others have gone,' she told him, hugging her arms around her, obviously cold. She was only wearing a short fluffy white cape across her shoulders.

He unlocked the car and she immediately got inside.

He quickly got inside the driver's seat. But when he turned the key in the ignition, the engine didn't fire up.

'Try it again,' said Libby, wiggling in her seat both from tension as well as cold.

But the battery appeared to be flat.

'Where's your car?' he asked, turning to her in what felt like real panic now. There was a bride and groom at church waiting for their wedding rings and the ceremony was about to start at any moment!

'At the church,' she told him. 'So many people needed extra lifts this morning.'

They looked at each aghast.

'What do we do?' he asked.

'Have you got any spare wellies?' she asked.

Minutes later, she was pulling on his green wellington boots over the trousers of her jumpsuit, quickly followed by his black puffa jacket. It looked enormous on her, but he had thought it would be warmer than the anorak that he put on. He was now wearing his spare wellington boots and they were both striding down the platform as quickly as they could, despite the deep snow.

'We're never going to make it on time,' said Libby, with a

groan as they reached the bridge, clutching her silver high heels in one hand. 'We should have asked for Ryan to come back.'

'No time,' said Ethan, taking her by the hand and pulling her up and over the bridge with him.

The steps were icy underneath his feet, but still they rushed down the other side. They were only a couple of steps from the bottom when Libby slipped in her haste and fell into the snow.

Ethan hurried towards her.

'Are you okay?' he asked, bending down to check on her as she was sprawled in the snow. As he did so, both ring boxes fell out of his jacket pocket into a deep snowdrift beside them.

'I'm fine,' she told him. 'Just a bit soggy.' She turned her head. 'What was that falling out of your pocket?'

'Oh God! The rings!' said Ethan, diving his hand into the cold snow to feel around for them.

Libby gasped and followed suit, feeling around with her fingers. After a few moments, she brought out a box. 'It's okay. I've found them,' she said, with a relieved smile.

But one glance at the lid of the box and the all too familiar gold writing on it, Ethan shook his head. 'Not those,' he said, carrying on feeling around in the snow until he finally connected with the other box. 'Thank goodness. I've found them.'

He looked down at the smaller box in his hand and sighed with relief before looking over to Libby. But unknown to him, she had lifted the lid on the box she was holding and was now staring down at the inside of the lid, which he knew read Las Vegas Wedding Chapel.

After waking up the morning after their wedding and finding Libby's ring on the bedside cabinet, Ethan had slipped off his own ring and placed them both back inside the box. But he had always kept the ring box close by, wherever he had gone in the world. It was a cherished reminder of that one perfect night.

Libby looked up at him with tears in her blue eyes.

'They're our wedding rings,' she whispered.

He nodded, his eyes drawn to the two gold bands nestled in the velvet. 'Yes, they are,' he said, his voice hoarse.

And, to his horror, Libby began to cry.

## 56

'Don't cry, Libs,' she heard Ethan say. 'I hate it when you cry.'

But Libby found that she couldn't stop. The shock of seeing their wedding rings, the very idea that he had kept them, was just too overwhelming for her to comprehend.

'Please,' he said, pulling her up next to him and drawing her against him.

She leant against his chest, relishing the strength and warmth of him, but knowing that she must pull away from him eventually.

'You kept them,' she whispered, only able to focus on the rings.

'I couldn't throw them away,' he said, sounding shocked that she would think he would do so.

'Why not?' she said, against his chest.

'Because I love you.'

She went still. For a moment, she thought that she had misheard him. Then, when she stepped back to look up into his face, she realised that he she hadn't. He really had said those words.

'What?' she said, wiping the tears from her face.

'It's always been you, Libs,' he told her. 'I've loved you since as long as I can remember. Growing up, every single day. And then I lost you at the prom and found you in Vegas. And I wanted you forever. That was why I married you. And would marry you again if you'd have me.' He took her face in his hands. 'I'm not leaving. I'll never leave you again. I want to see you every day, be with you every day. I never thought I would miss anyone so much as I've missed you these past two days. All those years I promised myself that I wouldn't fall for you. That I couldn't possibly love you. But that was before I lost you. Now I realise how empty my life has been without you. It's you, Libs. You're the love of my life.'

The silence stretched out as she tried to take in what he was telling her.

In the end, she blurted out, 'You're such an idiot!'

He burst out laughing before he looked serious once more. 'Yes, I am,' he told her, nodding. 'But please tell me you still feel the same way. That you haven't changed your mind.'

She rolled her eyes. 'Of course it's you. There's never been anyone else anywhere near close to driving me crazy like you do. I love you. Body and soul. So very much. And I will go on loving you forever and a day. If you leave now, you'll be taking my other half with me.'

He shook his head. 'I'm afraid you're stuck with me forever.'

'Good,' she told him, as she pulled his head down to hers. 'That sounds like the most sensible thing you've said all week.'

Any tiny doubts were dispelled when his lips touched hers. It was a kiss of true love, forever love. She could feel how much it meant to them both and they were both smiling when they finally drew apart.

'I love you,' he told her, in a stunned voice, staring down at her. 'You took the best bit of me when you left me in Las Vegas.

But now I want to celebrate all the wedding anniversaries with you. I want this to be it. Forever.' She felt him take the box from her fingers and open it once more. 'One day very soon, we're going to take these and slip them on each other's fingers in front of our friends and families. Because when we marry each other again, I want to do it properly. Okay?'

She nodded. 'Yes, please.'

Then they kissed once more.

'Mr Connolly,' she murmured.

'Mrs Connolly,' he whispered back. 'My forever bride.'

'Bride!' Libby gasped in horror. 'Oh my days! The wedding!'

She pulled up her now sodden trouser bottoms away from her wellington boots and began to run with Ethan alongside her towards Cranbridge.

As they reached the church, everyone was already inside and so there was just room for them to slip in at the back. Ethan managed to get the correct ring box forwarded on to the groom and finally they could relax and enjoy the wedding ceremony.

Harriet stood at the altar, holding hands with Joe, with Paddington the dog alongside them.

'Dearly beloved,' began the vicar.

Standing at the back of the tiny, crowded church, Libby felt Ethan's hand slip into hers. And as Harriet and Joe said their vows at the altar, they squeezed each other's hand in silent renewal of their own wedding vows.

And this time she knew it would be forever.

## 57

Libby didn't think she'd ever seen a happier newly-wed couple as Harriet and Joe.

She watched as Harriet beamed from ear to ear as she sipped her champagne and hung on to Joe with her other hand, staring around as if she couldn't quite believe that it was her wedding day.

Libby had to admit that Katy had outdone herself with the decorations for the wedding reception in Platform 1, with Flora's artistic help, of course. In the early evening, it looked magical, with fairy lights twinkling from every corner of the waiting room and sprigs of lavender dipped in silver glitter glistening from crystal vases on every table.

Relaxed conversation and laughter floated all around her as their friends and family enjoyed the happy atmosphere. The drinks were flowing and everyone had enjoyed Ryan's delicious Italian cuisine. Libby thought it had been one of the best meals that she had ever eaten.

In fact, the ambience was so relaxed that nobody minded too much when Paddington the dog helped himself to a large chunk of the amazing wedding cake that Maggie had made, which was thankfully only Victoria sponge. He was now hiding in semi-disgrace under one of the tables, but his golden tail was thumping along to the soft music playing over the speakers.

Libby found her eyes searching out Ethan's across the crowded room, laughing at something that Nico had just said. She sighed with contentment, still reeling from Ethan's declaration of love. Had that really happened? Had he really, finally, told her that he loved her and that they were together for all time? The smile that she could feel on her face confirmed that he most definitely had.

'Well, look at you, Libby Jacobs, smiling and happy at a wedding,' said Flora as she came up to give Libby a nudge with her elbow.

'I know,' added Katy, as she joined them. 'It's like she's changed into a whole different person. Evil twin swap, do you think?'

'Overdosed on too much cocoa, I reckon,' replied Flora. 'Is there such a thing as too much chocolate?'

'Possibly, but what a way to go,' said Harriet, coming to join them.

'Can't I just enjoy my best friend's wedding?' Libby told them, laughing as she drew them into a group hug.

'Miss Cynical, can't stand romance, hit it with a shovel and bury it in the back garden Jacobs?' Katy laughed.

'Yeah, her enjoying a wedding?' added Flora. 'Sounds fishy to me.'

Libby rolled her eyes but was smiling as they all giggled with their arms around each other.

'Only one thing can make a person smile like that,' said Harriet, glancing at her wedding ring before looking back at Libby. 'Love.'

They all looked at her expectantly and Libby couldn't help but throw her hands up in the air in resignation.

'Fine! You win!' she told them. 'I love Ethan Connolly and he loves me!'

She was suddenly aware that she must have said it far too loudly as the room came to an abrupt halt as everyone looked over to her group of friends.

'Now you've done it,' murmured Flora, even though she was smiling.

But Libby found that she didn't care. There were only two people in the room whose reactions she cared about.

She found the first as she looked around, saw her dad seated nearby and knew from his expression that he had definitely heard her declaration of love. He nodded his head as they locked eyes before smiling warmly and raising the champagne glass in his hand at her.

Libby sighed with relief. It was his blessing and she was grateful for his love and support.

She was about to look around for Ethan but found she didn't need to as he suddenly materialised next to her.

'Weren't we just going to pretend to be really good friends for now?' he asked her, with a grin.

She took his hand and pulled him close to her. 'How about friends that kiss?' she told him.

In the soft light, she saw his eyes gleam as he stepped forward to take her in his arms. His head dropped down to hers and their kiss was just as sweet as all the others that had come before.

Except this time it appeared to come with a round of applause and whooping, she realised as they drew apart.

But she couldn't stop smiling as he took her hand. 'Shall we take this private exchange outside for a moment?' he asked.

'Absolutely,' she told him as he led her away. 'Back in five minutes!' she announced.

They walked outside hand in hand and onto the platform. Shivering at the sudden blast of snowy cold air, she was grateful when he enveloped her into his jacket, wrapping around them both.

'I can't believe you kissed me in front of everyone,' she told him, running her hands around to his back.

'You were the one who declared our love to the world,' he reminded her.

'But they might have mistaken that for something else,' she said. 'Your act of kissing me was the deal-breaker.'

'So I've got, what, thirty seconds until you break a marble slab over my head?' he asked, bending down so that their foreheads touched.

'It didn't work the first time, did it?' she replied, with a soft smile.

'So what now?' he asked.

'Shut up and kiss me,' she said.

Seconds later, Ethan did exactly as he was told.

## 58

Ethan looked up at his grandad, who was wearing his stationmaster's uniform with a proud look on his face as they stood next to the steam engine.

'All set?' Ethan asked.

Eddie nodded. 'Yup. All set.'

As the cameras whirred and clicked around them, Ethan looked past the train and along the railway line to where it disappeared off in the distance.

Daffodils were nodding their bright yellow heads in the gentle breeze alongside the track. Spring had arrived and brought with it blue skies and bursts of colour everywhere, from the violet crocuses to the fresh green growth as new shoots appeared on every hedgerow and tree.

Ethan felt as if he were coming back to life as well, after so many years hiding away from his friends and family.

His eyes slid to the old school, which he had finally been able to finish renovating with the train rides taking a break during the coldest winter months. Since she had moved in, Libby had transformed the place so that it felt more cosy, with her additional touches, such as photographs and candles, as well as the constant aroma of her chocolate making wafting from the busy kitchen.

Of course, the train was likely to be equally busy very soon. Ethan had also spent the winter making great plans for the busy spring and summer season ahead. They had even approached local schools, inviting them to come along so that the children could learn about the history of steam engines. Perhaps there would be another budding engineer amongst them?

The train rides would happen at the weekends, apart from during the school holidays, when they would put on an extra few dates. It had been Philip who had suggested themed weekends, so they'd already had made plans for a special cream tea run where all the passengers would be provided by a delicious picnic prepared by his brother.

Ryan had complained about the extra work, of course, but Ethan knew that his brother was pleased that they were becoming closer with each passing week. Ethan was pleased too. He finally felt as if he could let go of the past and face a future filled with happiness and love as they made new memories in his home village.

In two years, Cranfield had been transformed. It was now a winter tourist destination, thanks to the success of the Christmas train. The long summer days would be equally busy with the glamping campsite and lavender fields. And Platform 1 would provide any refreshments desired. Pride had been rekindled in their village. And in the villagers too.

Ethan caught eyes with his dad who gave him a wink and a smile from a short distance away, as he stood hand in hand with Maggie. Ethan was glad to see his dad in a healthy relationship based on friendship and respect. Most of all, he was grateful that his dad was happy at last.

At the sound of familiar laughter, Ethan spun around and smiled as he watched Libby joke with her dad and Eddie.

Both men had also formed a bond as they continued to recover from their strokes. Philip's stroke club had become a fixed date in the diaries for many stroke survivors in the area. In addition, he had begun to concentrate his love of reading on researching an ever-increasing amount of steam engine information to provide to future passengers.

Eddie had been thrilled to have yet another steam train enthusiast join him and Bob. He would never quite be as agile or quick as he had been before the stroke, but he had recovered enough to take pride of place alongside Ethan and Bob in the driver's cab when needed.

Libby glanced over at Ethan and her face lit up into a warm smile. Ethan immediately felt the warmth and love that she gave him every day.

They had never confessed about their actual marriage to anyone. That was their secret to keep. But everyone else seemed very enthused about their whirlwind engagement soon after Harriet and Joe's wedding day.

'It only took thirty years for you two to get together,' Ryan had said, rolling his eyes.

But he had looked emotional when Ethan had asked him to be his best man.

'Maybe you can repay me the favour next year,' he murmured.

Ethan had been delighted for his brother.

Ryan had also been a mine of information when Ethan had told him that he wanted to build Libby a proper shop within the grounds of the old school. That was a secret plan to reveal in the upcoming weeks.

Ethan finally believed in love, true love. His mother had been wrong and he had been mistaken to believe her.

The past wouldn't repeat itself, that much he knew. The love between him and Libby was stronger than anything he had ever known and whatever life threw at them, they would face it together.

Because love did exist, between families and friends, as well as for him and Libby. It was true and good and he was happier than he had ever been because of it. He was back home at last, where he belonged, alongside Libby.

\* \* \*

Libby reached over to give her dad a peck on the cheek. 'You're not overdoing it, are you?' she warned him. 'It's been a busy day already.'

'Of course not,' he replied, with a warm smile. 'Eddie and I were just saying that we're both ready for a cup of tea and a slice of delicious cake.'

'Too right,' added Eddie.

Libby smiled at them both. It warmed her heart to see her dad having close friends again. He had flourished in the past few months and she was as proud of him for the success of the stroke club as she knew he was.

He would often pop in to see Eddie at home or head to the train workshop to chat to him and Bob. In addition, meeting strangers at the stroke club seemed to have helped him overcome his shyness and she was glad to find him so much more enthusiastic about facing new people and situations.

In fact, it had been his idea to prompt her to move in with Ethan at the old school.

She had rebelled against the idea until he had finally been able to persuade her that he was happy with the idea.

'It's the natural order of things,' he had told her. 'And you're literally a minute's walk away!'

Libby had agreed, knowing that it was the right thing to do for her and Ethan but it had also appeared to have helped her dad as well. Philip was more independent these days, organising his own supermarket deliveries and even heading to Platform 1 for coffee a couple of times a week.

She was equally thrilled to see how much he enjoyed the chocolate that she made for him. He was always willing to try out new flavours and boast about what a success his daughter was.

Even Libby was surprised at how busy her chocolate-making business continued to be. She had expected a slump in orders after the success running up to Christmas, but instead it had gone from strength to strength. Valentine's Day had been one of her best weeks ever profit-wise and her Easter eggs were proving to be equally as popular. She had plans to start making tins of upmarket hot chocolate, as well as introducing different flavours of truffles to coincide with each new season.

But even she was allowed a day off, especially when it was such a special celebration as that day.

Ethan walked up to her and smiled as he held out his hand. He looked so handsome in his suit and she couldn't help but be amazed once more that they would spend their lives together.

They both headed to the front of the train and, ever the gentleman, he let her climb the steps of the driver's cab first and she was grateful that she had chosen a knee-length dress.

Once they were both inside, Ethan wrapped his arm around her.

'Mrs Connolly,' he murmured, pulling her close to him and kissing her.

'Mr Connolly,' she replied when they finally drew apart.

She had never known such happiness and she knew it was because she had everything she wanted in Ethan. He was her best friend, her soulmate, the love of her life. She trusted him with both her heart and the life they were going to make together in the years and decades ahead.

With the cameras clicking and whirring once more, Libby and Ethan leaned out of the window to wave back to their family and friends to give them all the perfect photograph.

And as they went to kiss each other once more, the Just Married sign on the front of the train fluttered in the gentle breeze of a warm spring wedding day.

# ACKNOWLEDGEMENTS

A huge thank you to my wonderful editor Caroline Ridding for always knowing exactly what each of my stories needs to make it better and for her endless enthusiasm.

Thank you to everyone at Boldwood Books for all their hard work on this book, especially Nia Beynon and Claire Fenby for all their marketing skills behind the scenes and Jade Craddock for her tremendous editing skills once more.

I would also like to thank my lovely fellow Team Boldwood authors for their good cheer and support which makes working with them all such a joy.

Thank you to all my friends for their encouragement and support, especially Jo Botelle, who is always an inspiration where chocolate is concerned.

Thanks to my wonderful family, especially Gill, Simon, Louise, Ross, Lee, Cara and Sian.

A huge thank you to my husband Dave for letting me drag him to a fabulous cream tea on the BlueBell Railway for research purposes. How he suffers for my work! As always, this book could never have been written without your love and support.

Finally, a heartfelt thank you to all the readers out there who have been so amazing in their enthusiasm for the Railway Lane series. I have taken huge comfort and pleasure in the feedback from readers who have found it a lovely place to escape to during the tougher times in life. So, dear reader, this book is for you.

Alison x

# ABOUT THE AUTHOR

**Alison Sherlock** is the author of the bestselling *Willow Tree Hall* books. Alison enjoyed reading and writing stories from an early age and gave up office life to follow her dream. Her series for Boldwood is set in a fictional Cotswold village.

Sign up to Alison Sherlock's mailing list for news, competitions and updates on future books.

Follow Alison on social media:

facebook.com/alison.sherlock.73

x.com/AlisonSherlock

# ALSO BY ALISON SHERLOCK

**The Riverside Lane Series**

The Village Shop for Lonely Hearts

The Village of Lost and Found

The Village Inn of Secret Dreams

The Village of Happy Ever Afters

**The Railway Lane Series**

Heading Home to Lavender Cottage

New Beginnings on Railway Lane

Sunrise over Strawberry Hill Farm

Winter Magic on Railway Lane

WHERE ALL YOUR ROMANCE
DREAMS COME TRUE!

THE HOME OF BESTSELLING
ROMANCE AND WOMEN'S
FICTION

 WARNING:
MAY CONTAIN SPICE

SIGN UP TO OUR
NEWSLETTER

https://bit.ly/Lovenotesnews

# Boldw∞d

Boldwood Books is an award-winning fiction publishing company seeking out the best stories from around the world.

**Find out more at www.boldwoodbooks.com**

Join our reader community for brilliant books, competitions and offers!

Follow us
@BoldwoodBooks
@TheBoldBookClub

Sign up to our weekly deals newsletter

https://bit.ly/BoldwoodBNewsletter

Printed in Great Britain
by Amazon